FREE FROM SIN

Karen Ann Hopkins

© 2022 Karen Ann Hopkins
All rights reserved.

ISBN: 9798799900489 (paperback)

Books by Karen Ann Hopkins

Serenity's Plain Secrets
in reading order
LAMB TO THE SLAUGHTER
WHISPERS FROM THE DEAD
SECRETS IN THE GRAVE
HIDDEN IN PLAIN SIGHT
PAPER ROSES
FORBIDDEN WAYS (a romantic companion novel)
EVIL IN MY TOWN
UNHOLY GROUND
SWEET REGRETS (a romantic companion novel)
BLOODY TIES
THE WIDOW
WICKED LEGACY
BLOOD ROCK
THE OFFERING
SERENITY

Wings of War
in reading order
EMBERS
GAIA
TEMPEST
ETERNITY

The Temptation Novels
in reading order
TEMPTATION
BELONGING
FOREVER
DECEPTION
JOURNEY (coming in 2022)

Willow Creek (in partnership with HarperCollins/ One More Chapter)
The Fortuna Coin

The Possum Gap Novels
FREE FROM SIN
DARK HOLLOW ROAD (coming in 2022)

For anyone who's ever lived in the mountains, you know. You've seen the rundown trailer parks, junk cars, and trash alongside the road. You've witnessed poverty and driven through dying towns. But you've also seen misty tenacles of fog fading to reveal a rugged mountaintop or had your breath taken away by the beauty of a hillside dotted with dainty white dogwood booms and perky pink redbuds. You've spied deer, fox, and an occasionally black bear through lush, green foliage. Icy cold creek water has touched your toes and you've tasted the gritty sweetness of wild black berries on your tongue. A bobcat's shriek has stopped your heart and the chirpy call of a whip-poor-will has calmed your nerves. The mountains are a mixed bag for sure—but a place you know you'll never forget.

—Karen Ann Hopkins

ACKNOWLEDGMENTS

Many thanks to Heather, Caroline, and Katie for editing and proofreading this installment, and Ricbre and Danny for beta reading.

Appreciation to Melissa of The Illustrated Cover Design Services for the lovely cover!

EbookPbook provided the formatting of this book.

1

CHARLIE

Possum Gap, Kentucky

The horse's black fur felt warm and slick beneath my fingertips. I glanced both ways. No one was paying attention, so I leaned in closer and inhaled deeply. The horse smelled nice too. It was a sweet mixture of grass, sunshine, and a little bit of dust thrown in.

"Do ya like horses?"

The voice crept up from behind, making me jump sideways. I looked up. A young woman—perhaps ten years older than me—smiled back. She was slim, and judging from her tanned arms and face she spent a lot of hours outside. A few strands of her blonde hair escaped the white cap she wore, and she reached up with her free hand to tuck them in. Her other hand grasped a chubby baby girl. They both wore teal-colored polyester dresses, white aprons that matched the white caps on their heads, and black tennis shoes.

The woman smiled in a friendly way, and I realized she wasn't angry that I had been petting her horse. I took a long breath as I glanced down at my naked toes, suddenly aware that my feet were dirty. I'd outgrown my shoes, and the pink flip flops were all that fit anymore. Slowly lifting my gaze and hoping the Amish woman hadn't noticed my gross toes, I found my voice.

"I'm not sure." I shrugged, shifting my face to catch the breeze. The sun was so bright it hurt my eyes. I didn't like sweating either. "I never touched one before."

The woman's eyes flared. "You've never petted a horse before?" The baby began to wriggle in her arms, and the woman expertly shifted the weight to her other arm while she continued to stare at me.

I shook my head, growing uncomfortable under the woman's intense gaze. "I grew up in the city. There weren't any horses there."

"What city?"

Why was this stranger so persistent? I glanced over my shoulder and, seeing that we were still alone, I exhaled, feeling a little better. There were other people around, but they were ignoring us. A steady stream of people, both Amish and non-Amish, went in and out of the market. The sun glared off the metal roof, blinding me when I tilted my head. I turned back to the bright-eyed woman.

"Cincinnati," I said quietly. The large horse made a deep rumbling sound when another horse walked too close, pulling a similar buggy as the one attached to it. I stepped sideways.

The woman's hand came forward. "Don't worry. Goliath is a saint. He's well-trained and wouldn't even hurt a pesky fly. He's just flirting with the mare that passed by."

"Goliath? Like the giant in the Bible story?" I made no move to step closer. The woman might mean well, but she couldn't guarantee that the large animal wouldn't accidentally stomp me. There were no guarantees in life.

Her smile deepened. "Why, yes. That's the one." She rested her hand on Goliath's neck. "Except this Goliath is good, not bad." She flicked her wrist. "Come on, you can pet him again."

I liked talking to this woman. Her mellow voice and doelike eyes soothed my thumping heart. Slowly, I stepped back up to the black horse. This time, when I touched his fur, I wasn't as tense as before. "I almost went to a horse race once, but then—" I snapped my mouth shut. I wasn't supposed to talk about it, and even if I was, this lady wouldn't want to hear about me.

My mouth went dry and I licked my cracked lips. It stung to do so. I wished I had some water.

Our eyes met, and she brushed by me to open the small door on the side of the buggy. The woman set the baby down on the floorboard and reached for something. When she pulled her hand back out, I was amazed to see her holding a plastic water bottle. She must have read my mind.

"You look thirsty."

I didn't argue when she handed me the bottle. My nana had often said I was stubborn, but not dumb. I could still hear her sharp voice and cackling laughter in my mind.

"Thanks," I muttered, hurrying to pull the cap off then taking a long swig.

The cool liquid brought my empty stomach to life. When it gurgled loudly, I saw the corner of the woman's mouth raise just before her upper body disappeared back inside the buggy. This time, she emerged with something wrapped in her hand.

"Do you like apple or cherry fried pies?"

My mouth watered. Either would suit me just fine. I worked

hard to keep my expression bland. The woman didn't need to know I hadn't eaten anything since the night before, and I was starving. "Oh, are you giving one away?" I asked casually.

Her stare intensified, and I could tell by the way her jaw sagged that she was deliberating what to do. Experiencing a thrilling little rush in my chest, I dropped my gaze, unable to maintain eye contact any longer, but then I saw my feet again. Busying myself by pulling my faded blue jeans back up over my hips, I started to think the Amish woman had just been teasing me about a pie.

She went back into the buggy without another word. When she turned around, she handed me two wrapped pies. "I know it's difficult to choose. They're both delicious."

I swallowed the hard lump down my tight throat. My eyes stung. I quickly rubbed them with the back of my hand.

The woman thrust the pies at me. "Go on, take them." She lowered her voice. "It's okay, really. I have a box full. I'm delivering them to the ball game this afternoon. The teenagers can spare a couple." She pressed the pies into my hand. "How old are you anyway?"

It was a rude question, but since she'd given me the pies, I quickly answered. "Eighteen last month."

"You look younger." Her tone was unreadable. She cocked her head. "Do you live around here? I can't recall seeing you at the market before."

I thought up a lie and began to tell it to her when I saw her eyes growing large, and her mouth gape open widely. I spun around, but it was too late.

A hand grabbed my shoulder, squeezed it hard, then jerked me backward. The precious pies dropped out of my hands.

"What the hell are you doing, Charlie? I told you to stay in the fucking car."

Dillon's voice cut through the air like a punch after my quiet conversation with the Amish woman. I slapped my hands to my ears. "I'm sorry, Dillon. I wanted to pet the horse, that's all. We hardly talked. I promise."

I tried to keep my footing as Dillon yanked me toward the car, but I stumbled. His tight grip was the only thing that kept me from falling. The scene blurred through my tears. I saw the pies lying in the grass, and a sharp pang of regret twisted my empty stomach. Oh, how I wished I had taken one bite before Dillon ruined everything.

I didn't even know the nice woman's name, and yet she lurched after me, shouting, "Let go of her, you brute!"

"This ain't your fucking business," Dillon retorted, not even giving the woman the courtesy of looking at her.

Her hand closed around mine, and our eyes met. Through the tears, I saw the panic in her brown eyes. He swatted her hand away without looking up as he threw open the Malibu's door before shoving me inside. The heat inside the car was unbearable when the door slammed shut. Hungry, exhausted, and hot, I slumped in the passenger seat, staring straight ahead. I couldn't look out the window because I'd see the woman standing there, her mouth hanging open and her cap askew. I didn't mean to waste her pies, and Dillon shouldn't have said that filthy word to her. I wanted to sink down deeper and disappear in the seat.

Dillon hurled a few more obscenities before he jumped in and started the engine. I caught a glimpse of Goliath shying back when the Malibu peeled away, tearing up the grass right where I'd dropped the pies.

My stomach growled again, but Dillon didn't hear it. He was too busy shouting about how stupid I was and that he couldn't take me anywhere. I folded my hands on my lap and closed my eyes. There was no way Dillon would feed me now. It would be the next morning at the earliest before he'd give me something to eat.

Dillon's rant sounded faraway. I brought my fingers to my nose and sniffed. *Sunshine and grass.* I found the scent comforting, and in that moment, I decided that I liked horses very much.

2

LUCINDA

The drive home seemed longer than usual. I kept Goliath in a steady trot down Willow Springs Road, only slowing the buggy to turn into the gravel driveway. Josh was the first one out of the house. My oldest child had turned ten years old a few days earlier, and he was already acting like a little man, mimicking his da in most ways.

"Did you buy some bubblegum?" He jogged down the front porch steps.

I put on the brake and reached for Phoebe. She was the youngest of my brood and had the same easy temperament as Josh. With arms outstretched and eyes wide, she waited for me to scoop her up and step out of the buggy. The windows were too small to catch much of the breeze, and the interior had been uncomfortably warm. Sweat made the place between my breasts sticky, and without looking, I knew my dress was stained beneath the arms. I hated the hot months.

Phoebe's bottom rested on my hip while I pulled a small bag out of the purse I had looped over my shoulder. I held it up in front of Josh and his face beamed. He made a grab for it, but I snatched it back. Luckily, I was still several inches taller than the boy. In a year or two, that wouldn't be the case, and silly games like this one would be impossible.

"Now, now. Don't you think you ought to unhitch Goliath for your mamma?" With my free hand, I tugged out the grocery bags, setting them onto the grass.

His face and shoulders sagged. "Ya, suppose so."

"Get to it quick, then. Your stash is safe with me until you finish."

"Thank you, Ma." Josh took hold of Goliath's reins and turned around.

"Brush him off well. He worked hard in the heat today," I instructed in a firm voice.

I was satisfied when Josh's hand went up, acknowledging that he'd heard me. Like his da, he fancied himself a horse trainer and would take the job seriously. If it wasn't ninety degrees, the poor lad would have gone about it with a smile on his face. I shifted Phoebe's weight to pick up the bags and groaned a little when her sticky arms closed around my neck, nearly choking me.

"Ack, girl. You're growing too fast. I won't be able to carry you much longer." I paused, looking Phoebe in the eye. "Then what are you going to do?"

Phoebe's already wide eyes grew larger. She pursed her plump lips, looking like she might cry. "Da Da."

"Oh, so that's your answer, is it? Ha. That will only work if Da's home, which he isn't during the day," I muttered to the baby as I slowly climbed the steps. "Sarah!" I shouted, knowing she'd be able to hear me through the open windows. Where could that dreamy child be?

"Coming," Sarah answered from inside. Sounding like what I'd imagine the noise a charging buffalo would make, she barreled down the stairs.

The door flung open, and she met me on the top step. She didn't have her cap on, and most of her hair was loose from her bun. Her dress wasn't much tidier. Stains and dust from the morning chores still clung to it. Sarah caught me looking at her appearance, and her mouth scrunched. Being a witty child, she grasped Phoebe, relieving me of the load. The sudden lightness was wonderful, temporarily giving Sarah a reprieve from a scolding that would come soon enough. How the child, only eight and half my size could even carry Phoebe was beyond me. She wobbled a bit, planted her bare feet firmly beneath her, and took one careful step at a time into the house. I followed closely on her heels. When she stopped to take a breath, I bumped into her back.

"Sarah, move your feet. I have to put the ice cream into the freezer before it melts." I assumed the hot drive home had already softened it thoroughly.

"Ice cream?" Sarah managed to step out of the way. "Why aren't you making it?"

Now the child sounded like her da. I snorted loudly. "Someday, when you have a house to clean and several children to feed, you'll realize that in order to make it through the day, you must cut a few corners." I dropped the bags onto the kitchen table and quickly fished out the bucket and crossed the room to stuff it into the crowded freezer." With that done, I exhaled. "The Lord gave us markets for a reason, Sarah."

I placed my hands on my hips and turned to my oldest daughter. She still struggled to hold onto Phoebe, who made chirping sounds like she knew her safety was compromised in the skinny arms of her sister. "Why don't you take Phoebe's dress off and see if she'll take a nap before dinner."

Sarah nodded instead of speaking. Just maneuvering through the family room with her full arms took all her attention. The side of my mouth rose at the sight of Sarah struggling with Phoebe. Someday, the sisters would be fast friends and enjoy each other's company. But for now, it was a lopsided relationship.

Not hearing a peep from the girls prompted me to empty the bags quickly. I might be able to start supper before Phoebe awoke, which would be a pleasant change. As I gathered the butter, bread, and pork chops onto the table, thoughts of the young woman at the market filled my head. The poor thing was dirty and hungry. I blew out a hard breath when I recalled the way the man had yanked her like he was jerking clothes off a line as a rainstorm approached.

The room had darkened while I worked, and I snapped my head up. "Shew!" I hurried to the window above the sink and looked out. The yellow gingham curtains snapped in the growing wind. Dark clouds had indeed gathered to the west. I caught a whiff of rain in the air. Here, I thought I was a step ahead of the chores, and I'd completely forgotten about the laundry. With super speed, I sliced the apples and seasoned the chops inside the casserole dish. The potatoes would have to wait. Sliding the dish into the oven, I set the temperature and timer, then ran out the screen door.

The air that struck my face took my breath away and sent tingles racing along my arms. A jagged flash of lightning within the gray clouds caught my eye, making me run faster. "Ach, first it's too hot and muggy to breathe, then a storm rolls in, threatening to drench me," I muttered the words to myself, tugging

FREE FROM SIN

the clothes off the line and tossing them into the laundry basket. I usually took the time to fold them first, but the first raindrop striking my nose put an end to my routine.

I managed to squash all the clothes into the single basket and tuck it under my arm before I made a run for the porch. Goliath's head poked out the window opening from his stall in the stable. I was relieved that Josh had the sense to leave the horse inside until the storm passed over.

I made it halfway across the yard when the sky opened up, and the deluge came. I stiffened under the cold, pelting rain, mindful not to complain about it. The sweat was being washed away, and the garden, crops, and hayfield were getting a much-needed watering. I'd say a prayer of thanks once I'd dried off.

The roar of an engine turned my head. James must have quit early due to the rain. His driver's dually truck had no problem making it over the suddenly formed trenches of rushing water in the now rutted driveway. The truck stopped in front of the porch, and James jumped out. If his desire to seek cover had been high, he didn't show it by his clenched jaw. James made a beeline to intersect me. The pouring rain turned the farm into a water-drenched, hazy green world. Barely visible to me, James grabbed the basket, and side by side, we sprinted for the porch.

As Mr. Benson pulled away, his brake lights were like bright red beacons in the gray, wet gloom while it bounced down the driveway. At the top of the steps and finally, out of the deluge, Sarah poked her head out the doorway.

"Close the windows!" I shouted at her.

Sarah dashed back inside. James set the basket down on a rocking chair and faced me while I wiped my eyes with wet hands.

"I bet you were complaining about the heat, weren't you, Mrs. Coblentz?" He gestured beyond the porch where rain poured out of the sky in straight sheets. "Now this…" The corner of his lips trembled, then rose playfully.

I rolled my eyes. James knew me too well. I swatted his chest, and he caught my hand in the air. He barked out a laugh before his mouth came down on mine. Our kiss was a combination of frantic passion and comfort. We'd been married for eleven years and weren't school kids anymore, and yet every time my husband touched me, something close to newness stirred in my belly. I loved the sensation and ignored the wet chill making me shiver, clutching James like it was our very first kiss all over again.

He was the one who broke our embrace. "Later, Mrs. Coblentz. We'll continue this when darkness falls and the children are tucked in their beds."

The promise caused my stomach to flutter with joy. I dropped my hands to my sides and waited for him to pick up the basket. When he draped his arm around my shoulder, I sighed and pressed into his side. I was indeed a lucky woman.

"May I be excused?" Josh half rose, pausing on the balls of his feet.

"Did you get your chores done, son?" James asked as he dragged his hand through his thick, brown hair.

We were the same age, although most of the time, I felt like my husband's elder. The mischievous spark of childhood had never abandoned him. His gleaming eyes fixated on Josh. I could tell by the twitch of his lips that he worked hard to keep from grinning.

"Yes, sir. Since the rain has stopped, I'd like to ride the new horse around the yard for a bit."

James cupped his chin with his hand, pretending to mull the request over. Before he opened his mouth, I was sure he'd say yes. "All right." Josh bolted from the chair and had made it halfway to the door when James added, "As long as you close up the chicken coop first."

Josh nodded vigorously and went out the door before either of us could think up anything else for him to do. Sarah huffed and folded her arms around her chest tightly. "Not fair. I have to clean the kitchen while Josh only has to shut the chicken door. I want to ride my pony, but it will be dark by the time"—she unclutched her arms long enough to gesture widely with them—"this mess is cleaned up."

I dipped my head and hid my smile behind my hand. Sarah was a saucy little thing. Her disgruntled tone didn't sound like it came from an eight-year-old. When I'd managed to contain my mirth, I turned to James. "What do you think? Should Sarah slave away in the kitchen until dark, or do we allow her a night off? Only after she takes the muck bucket out to feed the potbelly pigs, which, if I remember correctly, are supposed to be her pets anyway."

Sarah's gaze darted to her father as she hovered over her seat, bouncing lightly in place. "Oh, please, please. I'll feed Miss Piggy and Petunia right away!"

James rubbed his jaw, taking just as much effort to act the part of the conflicted man as he had with Josh. Of course, it was all for show. Sarah knew it too. That's why she could hardly contain herself. "I guess so—"

Sarah leaped out of her chair and into James' lap. Her hug was brief. "Oh, thank you!" Then she was gone as fast as Josh.

Phoebe squealed from her highchair, waving her arms wildly. She wanted to go too. "Sorry, baby girl. You can't run with the big kids yet."

"Soon, she will be. They grow up in the blink of an eye." James sat back in the chair with a slack face. He had a thoughtful spirit that leaned toward melancholy when talking about certain subjects—like change. James despised change.

I rested my hand on his shoulder, and he reached up to cover it with his own. "Ah, James, don't get yourself worked up. That one over there"—I raised my chin at Phoebe—"is only thirteen months old. We have many years to go before the house empties out."

"Especially if we add a couple more to the brood."

I dropped my head back. "Ack, we've discussed this before. Three is enough for me and you. I don't want my uterus falling out like poor Aunt Rebecca after she bore twelve."

"Twelve? That's too many for me. Maybe one more to make an even number?" His mouth slanted into a small grin.

The mischief on James' face told me he teased, but deep down, I knew his heart. We were both nineteen when we married, and now we were thirty. By community standards, we had another decade or more to grow our family. I wouldn't rule it out, but I'd witnessed how the other women, even Ma, had worn themselves out at an early age with so many children. I had been careful to avoid the same fate, and since James was an even-tempered man who wanted nothing more than to please me, he'd gone along with it. We'd even used the Englisher's birth control methods at times, although neither one of us would ever tell a soul.

I softened my voice. "Let Phoebe be our baby for a while longer. We can discuss another when she's old enough to ride a pony by herself." James smiled broadly. By his bright expression, he liked the suggestion. It wasn't my intention to ruin his day, but I couldn't keep my thoughts in any longer. Since Phoebe seemed content to play with the remnants of her food and the other children were outside, we could speak frankly. "There was some trouble at the market today."

James lost his smile. "Tell me about it."

Taking a deep breath, I plopped down on the chair that Josh had left. I wasn't sure where to begin. Folding my hands on my lap, I thought back to the girl from the market. Because her face had been thin, her greenish-brown eyes had looked huge, reminding me of a cartoon character in one of Sarah's books. The girl's long brown hair had been straight, dull, and a little greasy. The clothes she had on were worn and faded from too many washings. She'd been polite and inquisitive, and yet I got the impression she didn't get out much. Her awkwardness had made me pity her at first sight. When my mind drifted to her companion and how he'd treated her, the knot in my belly turned to fire, and I felt my face heat.

James reached over and squeezed my knee. "What's amiss?"

"I met a teenaged English girl—said she was eighteen. When I came out of the market, I found her standing next to Goliath. She touched his neck in such a tentative way, I guessed she'd never stroked a horse before." I noticed his eyes lift with interest, but I didn't become distracted from telling the story. "Her clothing was tattered and she was rail thin. I felt sorry for her. Inclined to have a conversation with her, I asked her a few questions, eventually offering water and a couple of fried pies." When James' brows arched, I quickly added, "Poor girl was thirsty and hungry."

"Was she alone?" James asked.

"That's the troubling part of the tale. A man who looked to be twice her age came up and ordered her inside a dented-up, old brown car. She didn't move fast enough for him, so he yanked her over the grass like he was pulling a sack of corn across the yard." I shook my head several times in quick succession at the horrible memory, and James' hand on my knee squeezed a little harder. "The girl dropped her pies, and her eyes were as wide as saucers. The look on her face was a mixture of fear and embarrassment."

When I paused for a breath, James said in a gentle voice, "What did you do, Lucinda?"

Ah, he knew me well. I breathed out a throaty sight. "It took a few seconds for the shock to wear off, but when it did, I tried to stop him from taking her." I glanced up under my lashes at James. His jaw was set, and his mouth pressed in a grim line. "I called out after him, but was ignored. Several people watched it happen, yet no one else intervened. The man drove away with her in a reckless manner, and then they were gone." I looked past James out the kitchen window. The sky was thick and gray. It wasn't raining anymore, but dusk had set in. I caught Sarah's giggle on the breeze and then Josh's voice. He was attempting to give her instructions about how to properly ride her pony. From the sound of it, the girl wasn't listening. I cocked my head and focused on James' face again. "I don't even know her name."

"Have you seen the girl or man before?"

"No. Never."

James released my knee and slumped in his seat. He looked as tired as I felt. "I'm sorry you had to witness that.

The outside world is full of wickedness. I'm afraid the girl you befriended is in a bad way."

"Can't we help her?" My question came out of my mouth with whooshing force.

James frowned back at me. "She's not a stray pup you found on the side of the road, sweetheart. If she's eighteen, she's old enough to choose her own path. You cannot rescue someone who doesn't want to be."

"Oh, I believe she does, James," I said firmly, ignoring the shuddering feeling in my chest.

"Ack. Even so, you don't have any information about her—where she lives, what her name is—you may never see her again. It is beyond us to help this person." I dropped my head and toyed with my fingers in my lap. I didn't want him to see the disappointment in my eyes. James leaned forward and softened his voice. "We will say a prayer for her tonight."

Yes, I would pray that the English stranger was saved from the cruel man, but I feared it would take a miracle to set her free. I'd seen the hopelessness in her large, sad eyes.

3

SADIE

"Why do you have to drop me off so early? My shift doesn't begin until noon."

I glanced over at Chloe. The sixteen-year-old scowled at me from behind a sunburned face and a lot of freckles. "You better start wearing sun protection. It's only your second day, and you're already peeling."

"You're just going to ignore my question?" Chloe's whiny voice made me grip the steering wheel harder.

I exhaled loudly. "Are we doing this again? I have to be at the department at ten o'clock. You can hang out under the pavilion and read a book for a couple of hours. It won't kill you."

She thudded her head back against the headrest. "You usually have Saturdays off."

Constantly repeating myself was getting old. Back in the day, my only child would be satisfied with my answers and move onto a new question. Not anymore. When I didn't give Chloe the answer she wanted, she'd pester me with the same one five more times, hoping for a different answer. It was exhausting.

FREE FROM SIN

I pressed the brakes to make the turn into Possum Gap's recreational park. The potted holes that riddled the gravel road were still filled with water from the heavy rain a few days before. Keeping the cruiser slow, I dodged the ruts the best I could. "I'm the sheriff. Unexpected things pop up all the time. You know that."

"Can't you get Buddy to take care of whatever it is? We can grab breakfast or something."

"You already had a bowl of cereal twenty minutes ago. You can't possibly be hungry," I argued.

Chloe moaned. "I just don't want to wait around for two hours." She swiveled in the passenger seat. "If I had my license, I could drive myself, and then you wouldn't have to chauffeur me around."

Ha. For the past two months, every conversation ended here. "You just turned sixteen. There's plenty of time. Besides, as you know, we don't have an extra vehicle for you to drive anyway."

"You won't let me drive because of Simone Porter," Chloe accused in a quivering, overly excited voice.

I parked beneath the huge oak tree that shaded the walkway leading to the community pool. The parking lot was already full, but I'd lucked out and turned in right behind a vehicle pulling away. Cutting off the engine, I shifted my gaze to Chloe, who looked in the opposite direction out the window.

"Hello, Sheriff Mills!" A lady I didn't recognize greeted me through the open window as she walked by.

I raised my hand and smiled back. "Perfect day for a swim." I tried to be polite when the last thing I wanted to do was to have small talk with a woman I couldn't remember.

"I wish you'd put on an act with me," Chloe muttered, still looking away.

I inhaled deeply. Being a single mom to an independent and stubborn almost-adult girl wasn't an easy task. My line of work made it even more difficult. Chloe was right about Simone Porter. Buddy and I had been the first responders to the accident scene. Simone had veered off the road and hit a tree at high speed. She'd been texting when she lost control of her car. I'd held the teen's hand while she'd taken her last breath, and I had watched firefighters lift her limp body out of the wreckage with the jaws of life. I had a right to be paranoid.

"Look, I get it. You want your license, a new car, and the glam job at the Dollar Store, but you're going to have to wait a few months. There's a lot on my plate right now at the department, and I don't have time to properly teach you how to drive." It wasn't a lie, but I still felt guilty saying it. I wasn't too old to remember what it was like to crave the freedom driving gave you.

"I never asked for a new car. Maybe Dad can teach me."

I wasn't sure if it was a question or statement. I was glad I wore large aviator sunglasses to hide my eyes when I rolled them. *Sure, Chloe, good luck with that.* It was nearly impossible to get my ex to spend time with his daughter, but Ted was suddenly going to be available for driving lessons and a father-of-the-year award? I'd bet against that working out. Of course, I couldn't speak my mind. I'd learned the hard way that it only hurt Chloe's feelings and made me the bad guy.

"That's a good idea." When Chloe sat up straighter and finally glanced my way, I quickly added, "You just had your birthday. I'm sure your dad will agree that waiting a couple of months isn't a big deal." It would be just my luck that Ted finally got his act together at the moment when I'd rather he didn't. Seeing the explosion of excitement on her face immediately disappear prompted me to say more. "Chloe, the type of deadly car accident that Simone had is rare, but it's much more likely to happen to young drivers. She got her license six months after she turned sixteen and only had it for three days when she hit that tree. We'll never know for sure if her age was a factor in the accident, but it certainly looks that way."

"Yeah, I get it, Mom. But a lot of other kids got their license right away and haven't had a wreck. You're manipulating data for your own agenda." Chloe pulled her tote bag off the floorboard and grasped the door handle.

"My agenda is to keep you safe. Trust me, it's not you I'm worried about. It's everyone else on the road." As I spoke, Chloe stepped out of the cruiser. I had to bend forward and speak louder. "Tanya will pick you up at five. There's leftover chicken in the fridge."

"Your chicken is more likely to kill me than a car," Chloe said as she walked sluggishly away from the cruiser.

I opened my mouth to defend my cooking but snapped it shut when a couple of middle-school-aged kids and their grandma walked by. Grunting, I started the engine and backed out of the space. I feared the next couple of parenting years would only get worse.

※

"You're awfully quiet," Buddy commented. He handed me the paperwork over the desk and sat back down.

We were alone. Possum Gap was a small town in southeastern Kentucky, bordered by the rough hills of the Appalachian

Mountains on one side and quaint farmland on the other. Because of our small population, a sheriff and four deputies were enough to police the entire jurisdiction. That didn't mean that the town was free of crime, though. We had our fair share of drug dealing, petty larcenies, and domestic violence. Lately, our office had been busier than usual, with four arrests that week after an out-of-control barfight. Ever since we lost the paper mill and the coal mine had shut down, the local bars were crowded with frustrated men who were now too poor to afford a drinking pastime. It was a recipe for calamity and one of the reasons I'd come into the office on a Saturday.

When I glanced out the window, I could see rocky, tree-covered hills in the distance. Although there were only a few puffy white clouds dotting the deep blue sky, I knew the weather forecast called for rain and possibly even storms later in the day. The limestone walls of the courthouse and its intricate clock tower stood out from the surrounding green landscape. I'd always thought it was too fancy for the likes of Possum Gap. Once upon a time, Possum Gap had been prosperous enough to warrant such a grand structure in the center of town. The courthouse teased at the prosperity of a long-gone era. It was a glaring reminder of how far we'd fallen.

Dropping my gaze to the stack of reports in front of me, I sifted through them, randomly pulled one out, and then looked up. "Chloe is driving me nuts. Her birthday was a few days ago, and she's already harassing me to start driving."

Buddy made a growling humming noise that made me lean back. When he spoke, my small office amplified his deep voice. "It's probably the hardest thing we have to do as parents—turning our kids loose with a car. My insurance went up two hundred dollars a month when Sam started driving." He shook his head. "A year later, it was Mike's turn, and I put my foot down and made him get a job to pay for the insurance hike with his own earnings. Money management is an important thing to teach a kid."

I pursed my lips and stared past my first deputy at the outdated striped wallpaper. Buddy was fifteen years my senior and could have been elected to the head position if he'd been more motivated. The burly man towered over everyone in town at six foot seven. His full head of snowy white hair with matching trim beard contrasted in a startling way with his tanned face and broad features. For as long as I could remember, Buddy had white hair. Someone had told me that not long after his brother drowned in the Puissant River, Buddy's hair turned snow colored. He was only fifteen at the time of the accident. I often thought that if you combined Clint Eastwood's and Santa's DNA, you'd come up with Buddy. At first glance, he was intimidating. Once you got to know him, you quickly found that Buddy was a great big softy who would give you the shirt off his back in a snowstorm. Buddy had no interest in leadership. Being a good soldier came naturally to him. He was loyal to a fault and had an opinion about everything.

"It's not about the cost. Chloe's not ready for that kind of responsibility yet. She's making progress, but she's still too immature."

Buddy chuckled, then took a gulp of his coffee. "It's usually the whole driving thing that straightens most kids out."

"That didn't work so well for Simone Porter." I didn't look up from the report in my hand.

"Aw, take it from someone who's raised two kids. If you shelter them too much, it'll backfire."

Buddy was right, but I wasn't ready to admit it out loud. I

needed a couple more months to accept that my little girl was almost grown-up and to wipe the horrible images of Simone's lifeless body from my mind.

Pulling a paper with handwritten notes out of the pile of reports, I glanced up. "What's this?"

Buddy visibly swallowed hard and smacked his lips. His sudden discomfort put me on high alert, making me sit up straighter. "There's the contact information for the K9 program and a trainer in Tennessee. He has the perfect dog for us—a Belgian Malinois. Affordable too."

I let out a whistling breath and slumped in the chair. "We've already gone over this, Buddy. The department funds won't allow for a K9 unit at this time—"

He interrupted with raised hands. "I get that, I do. Think about how often we have to run down someone on foot or the rise in drug use. Hell, sheriff, we had five overdoses last month. A K9 in the department will not only make our lives easier, but it will also protect our community."

I finished off my coffee and set the cup down. Buddy loved dogs, and he'd been bugging me for three years to let him partner with one. He looked at me with the wide-eyed expectation of an oversized kid on Christmas morning. Chloe was already mad at me, and it wasn't even noon. I hated adding Buddy to the list. I set the paper with the K9 information aside. "Look, I can't make any promises. I'm willing to mention it to the mayor, but you know how difficult Gretchen can be."

His huge smile nearly cracked his face in two. "She's an advocate for the animal shelter. I'm sure she'll be all in."

I snorted. "I like dogs as well. That's not the issue. Hiring a K9 has benefits, for sure. But we also must consider the overall cost and liability. We operate on a shoestring budget as it is."

"Seems the only changes we have around here are negative, like the drugs and poverty. It's about time Possum Gap had something positive happen."

I dropped my head and smiled. If a dog could solve all of Possum Gap's problems, I would have fit the cost into the budget a long time ago. A particular memo caught my eye, and I focused on it. "A sex trafficking ring involving minors was broken up in a nearby county last night," I read out loud, then lifted my gaze. "Did you know about this?"

"Gary called it in first thing this morning. Up until now, the only publicity Russell County received was for its best pie contest at the local fair. Hard to believe a prostitution ring can operate out of a country-town like that."

"Not really. Think about the meth labs and moonshine operations that exist for years in the wooded hills without anyone the wiser. The countryside is the best place to get away with criminal activity. Homesteads are well-hidden, and people mind their own business. Isolation creates nefarious opportunities." I set the memo down. "It used to be that only the big states like California, New York, Texas, and Florida had sex slavery to worry about. Now, the trade has spread into less populated states like Kentucky. It makes perfect sense. The lack of good-paying jobs has made our town ripe for drugs and burglary. Why not prostitution?"

Buddy scratched his head. "I hope you're wrong, sheriff. That's the last thing we need."

Just then, Darcy Beaumont stepped into my office, holding two cups of fresh coffee. I inhaled the light, earthy scent of the warm brew in the air and smiled at her. She'd straightened her black, kinky curls and instead of her usual blue jeans, casual top, and cowboy boots, she had on a floral sundress and heeled shoes. A decade younger than me, she'd come into the department one day and talked her way right into the secretary-bookkeeping position without any prior experience. Darcy's sunny disposition and witty mind made her the perfect candidate for the demanding job. It also hadn't hurt her chances that her older sister, Tanya, was my best friend.

She set down the cups in front of us and pulled up the empty chair. "Did you all hear about all that craziness over in Russell County?"

"We were just discussing it." I eyed her smooth, dark skin. She was even wearing eye makeup. I couldn't hold in my curiosity any longer. "What are you all gussied up for?"

Darcy's mouth curved, and her eyes twinkled. "Raymond is fixin' to take me out for lunch." She made a show of looking at her watch. "He'll be here any minute now."

"Raymond, the new coroner—that Raymond?" I glanced between Buddy and Darcy. He gave me a quick nod. Why was I always the last to know?

"Oh, Sadie, he's a sweet man. We bumped into each other at the library last week. And you know what? That man likes to read as much as I do. A book reading man is a rare commodity around here. I thought I better scoop him up in a hurry." Darcy's mouth quivered as she tried to stop it from breaking into a full smile.

Our previous coroner, Johnny Clifton, owned the local funeral home and died at the beginning of summer. He worked straight up to the day a sudden heart attack took him out at the age of eighty-four. Since none of his children followed in their father's mortician's footsteps, the Clifton family—and founders of our little town—were as interested in finding just the right person to take over Johnny's business as the mayor and I were in hiring a new coroner. Natural deaths counted for most of Possum Gap's deceased, but with the rise of drug ODs and the occasional backwoods clan killing, we didn't want to rely on the surrounding counties for resources. Raymond Russo had interviewed for the job by Zoom from New Jersey. He was fresh out of mortician school and willing to pick up and move across the country to the hills of Kentucky. I thought it odd, but we didn't have a lot of candidates applying for the job. The Clifton family thought they'd struck gold with their new funeral director and mortician, so my queasy gut about the guy didn't come into play during the hiring process.

Only one month living in Possum Gap, and he had asked out one of my favorite people, adding to my paranoia. I had to be careful how I handled my reservations with Darcy, though. She'd been searching for her Prince Charming for nearly her entire twenty-five years. Her greatest downfall in the search was staying in Possum Gap. Most of the guys here were either married, rednecks, drunks, or all three. I could understand her enthusiasm about the Yankee transplant.

I squashed the first things that came to mind and tried to be diplomatic. "I guess a lunch date is a good way to get to know someone without too much pressure."

Darcy crossed her arms, frowned deeply, and made a growling noise in her throat. "You don't approve? Why?"

She was perceptive, another positive job attribute. My shoulders sagged when I decided to be real with her. "Russo hasn't been here long, and what do we really know about him?"

I sank back in my chair when her eyes shot skyward. "I feel sorry for any boy who comes to court Chloe. You'll be sure to give him hell, won't you?"

I took a deep breath. Boys were probably the next hurdle. I worked hard to convince myself this wasn't about my daughter for a change. "Don't you think it's strange that he'd want to move to a broken, backwater town like Possum Gap from the hustle and bustle of New Jersey?"

"You're the one who hired the man!" Darcy's voice rose a pitch, and as if she was suddenly aware that she had gotten overly excited, she shook her head lightly and scrunched her mouth, looking sheepish. "If it makes you feel better, I asked him the same question."

I didn't lose the serious tone. "What did he say?"

"Just that he wanted some fresh air and new experiences. Believe it or not, the city isn't all it's cracked up to be."

I caught Buddy's warning look out of the corner of my eye. Darcy was a grown woman and could date whoever she wanted. Russo had done a good job so far. He was polite, dependable, and smart. I probably was overreacting and worrying about nothing at all.

"You look great. If your goal is to make an impression, I'm sure you'll succeed." I tried for an apologetic smile and held my breath to see if it worked.

Darcy's features relaxed. "Girl, you know I don't like dressing up. I certainly hope he appreciates it."

"Oh, he will, Darcy." Buddy cocked his head at me. "Unlike Sadie, I like Russo. Anyone who can keep a smile on his face while he cuts up bodies has my full respect."

The handheld radio on my belt buzzed, and I picked it up.

"Domestic situation at the end of Old Hollow Road. Shots fired. Unknown man on the ground in the front yard. Ambulance is en route," a crackled voice came through the speaker.

Buddy and I rose at the same time.

"Should I cancel my lunch plans?" Darcy asked, jumping up right behind us.

"No, you go have fun. We'll take care of this." I grabbed the fresh cup of coffee and followed Buddy's hulking frame into the hallway at a fast clip.

All thoughts about Chloe driving and Darcy's date with the new guy in town flew straight out the window. I was used to telling myself tumult was relative—something worse always popped up. I hated being right all the time.

4

CHARLIE

A shard of sunlight shone through a gap in the curtains. Sticky sweat covered me. I turned my head away from the man who was zipping up his pants and pulling his shirt back on. If someone asked me what he looked like, I wouldn't be able to say because I had no idea. I'd kept my eyes tightly shut the entire time. That's what I always did—pretend I was dead and hope the jerk didn't speak to me. Usually, they didn't, but sometimes I'd get a talker who wouldn't shut up. It was the worst when they asked me nosy questions, trying to be my friend. I'd rather get it over with as quickly as possible, and chitchat slowed down the process.

This guy went out the door without a single word, which suited me fine. I scrambled into a sitting position on the bed and reached for the cigarettes Dillon had left there that morning. My fingers used to shake when I lit up. Not anymore. Taking a long drag, I leaned back on the pillows, not bothering to cover my nakedness with the nasty sheet. It was so damn hot. Smoking settled my nerves. I'd smoke one first and then take a shower. The water would be ice cold since the heater hadn't worked since the day we'd arrived at the single-wide trailer two weeks ago. Very little breeze or fresh air stirred through the small window. The blind was broken in several places, the plastic strips sticking out all over the place. Still, if I craned my neck, I could see the wall of greenery at the edge of the forest behind the trailer. With little else to do, I often found myself searching through the broken shards of the blinds and daydreaming about bears or worse, mountain lions stalking the shade beneath the tall trees. Deer grazed the unkempt backyard during the day, and raccoons with their shiny yellow eyes knocked over the trash cans every single night. Dillon had shot at the masked bandits several times while they raided the trash but had missed. It made me smile when anyone or anything gave him a hard time, and the coons certainly kept him in an agitated state. In that way, the little rascals were my allies. One night, Dillon's aim would be true, and I prepared myself every morning to discover a gory scene beyond the window.

My gaze drifted from the yellow-stained walls to the lopsided dresser in the corner. This joint was worse than the last one. Exhaling, I watched the smoke settle in the thick, humid air. My insides returned to feeling numb as I searched my memories for the encounter from a few days earlier. Rubbing my fingertips softly together, I could almost feel Goliath's silky fur. The sour, moldy smell of the trailer kept his sweet smell at bay. A vision of the Amish woman and her chubby baby formed at the foot of the bed. Her dress had been frumpy, but the teal color was pretty. She had a fresh, clean face and bright eyes. The usual questions about how old I was or where I came from hadn't bothered me coming from her. More than anything, I would have liked to talk with her longer. My mouth watered when I thought about the fried pies that ended up in the grass. Such a waste.

The door opened a few inches, and I jerked the sheet up to my hips. Seeing that it was just Christen, I didn't bother covering my breasts. We were both girls, after all. My body wasn't my own anymore. The way Christen averted her eyes caused my face to heat, a feeling I hadn't experienced in a while. Her discomfort with my nudity made me tug the sheet up higher. When I was covered, our eyes met.

"Dillon says I have to do the next guy," Christen whispered.

She still wore the jogging suit pants and t-shirt she had on when Dillon brought her to the trailer. Her eyes were bloodshot and watery, and she kept rubbing them. It had only been a couple days, and Christen had spent most of the time high on the dope Dillon gave her. She was a year younger than me, but since she had round hips and large breasts, she could have passed for several years older. When Dillon stopped feeding her, she'd lose the extra pounds and resemble a boy like I did.

Soon, Dillon would give her some more dope, and she'd be out of it again. That would be the best time to introduce her to her new life. Just like me, it was her own fault she ended up here. We'd both wanted something that Dillon provided. For her, it was drugs and maybe a crush; my wish was freedom. At the time, I didn't realize that Dillon was a hell of a lot worse than my stepdad.

Still, a tiny part of me remembered what it was like the first few times Dillon had pimped me out. I guessed deep down, I'd known that he wasn't a nice person, but desperation ruled my actions back then. That was two years ago, but it seemed like a lifetime. I couldn't even remember what Mom looked like. She probably wouldn't recognize me either. I'd learned that dwelling on the past didn't help the present. And arguing with Dillon would give you a busted lip and no food for a day. Christen hadn't learned all that yet.

"It's not a big deal. You've been fucking Dillon on the hour. What's the difference?" I kept my voice low. I didn't want him to barge in and ruin my smoking time.

Christen wrinkled her nose. "You're kidding, right? Dillon might be in his thirties, but he's still good looking." She glanced over her shoulder as if she thought someone might have snuck up on her. "How do you do it? The guy that just came out of here was gross."

I took another drag of the cigarette and blew the smoke right into Christen's face. Damnit. That's why I didn't open my eyes. I wouldn't know what they looked like, so I wouldn't remember them. Christen's big mouth had given me a hint about the man that I didn't ask for. As far as Dillon was concerned, all I saw was a scowling man with a plain face, some cheap tattoos, and a receding hairline. That hadn't always been the case, but it sure was now.

I leaned forward, and through stupid tears that came out of nowhere, I gave her some advice. "Do what Dillon tells you to do. Don't argue with him or think that because he fucked you, he likes you. Cause he doesn't. You're working for him now. If you don't watch yourself and get with the program, you'll end up without any precious dope and sporting a black eye. The men who come here don't give a shit about your face, neither does Dillon."

Her eyes bulged, and she swayed back as if I'd pushed her. "Don't say things like that. I'll walk out of here before he pulls anything like that with me."

I barked out a laugh louder than intended. "I'd like to see you try. You don't have any more of a chance escaping Dillon than I do."

Her gaping mouth caused a twinge of guilt to drill a hole in my belly. But I wasn't her friend or her babysitter. No point in hiding the truth, I convinced myself.

Christen slid off the bed and slammed the door behind her.

I put out the cigarette and dropped it into the tray beside the bed. A few more minutes passed, and the still, hot air made me sleepy. I laid back and closed my eyes. Dillon would be pissed if I took a nap, but I was so tired. The heavy sensation in my head was too much to fight. I'd learned that the best way to rid myself of the constricted hunger in my belly was to sleep. I welcomed the darkness when it came.

I woke to the sound of loud voices and a thud against the wall. My mind still groggy, I sat up and listened. Nothing. Sunlight spilled through the curtain gap, but the strip of light had moved several inches. I'd slept longer than I'd planned. Throwing my legs over the side of the bed, I grabbed my jeans and t-shirt off the floor. My limbs were stiff from lying in bed so long.

Another shout made me pause with one arm through a sleeve. It had been a man's voice, but not Dillon's. *What is going on?* Hurrying, I wiggled into the shirt. Standing up abruptly caused the blood to rush to my head. Dizziness made me wobble. I blinked at the spots in my vision when Christen came running through the door. Dillon was right behind her.

Her wild eyes locked on mine as Dillon caught her shoulder and jerked her back into the hallway.

"Fucking bitch, get back in there!"

They struggled in the doorway while I stood frozen in place. Dillon's size was average, like everything else about him, but he was still a lot stronger than Christen. It took less than a minute for him to get control of her by locking his arms around her stomach and heaving her backward. As suddenly as they burst in, they were gone. My muscles came alive, and I padded over to the door on bare feet and shut it. Leaning against the wall, I let out a long breath. "Stupid girl," I muttered.

There were more shouts and another thud. My heart pounded in my chest. If Christen kept on fighting, Dillon might send the man in here. I sucked in a breath, not for me, but for her. Dillon would beat her to a pulp if that happened.

Pop! Pop! Pop! Pop! Gunshots boomed outside the door. I immediately dropped to the floor and crawled to the bed. It was two mattresses stacked on top of each other, so I couldn't hide beneath them and this room didn't have a closet like the other one. *Pop! Pop! Pop!*

Why was someone shooting? My thoughts went blank when two final shots went off. A dribble of sounds reached my ears. Muffled crying, then a moment later, the roar of an engine. The silence that followed was even worse. Gripping my knees to my chin, I didn't move. The pounding of my heart was so loud I was sure someone could hear it from the next room. I struggled not to take a breath. Whatever was going on, I didn't want any attention on me. Softly, I rocked in place, waiting to hear another gunshot or some more shouting. It remained quiet.

A few more minutes passed. I hadn't left my spot next to the bed. Lifting my head, I strained to hear signs of movement or voices—*anything*. I didn't know how long I remained frozen. It might have been a few minutes or an hour. I felt lightheaded from the shallow breaths I took, and it was hard to push the fog from my mind. Finally, my heart quivered and a burst of adrenaline shot through me, clearing my head. I had to get up.

Slowly, I rose, keeping my eyes on the door. Taking steadier, deeper breaths and trying to stop my hands from shaking, I stuck my leg into a pant leg, then the other. I bounced once, pulling the jeans over my boney hips and buttoning them.

Another noise reached my ears, wailing sirens from far away, gaining volume quickly. The cops were coming. "Shit!" I mumbled as I tiptoed across the floor and peeked out the doorway. I could see part of the kitchen table. A case of beer still sat there, and the empty pizza box I'd seen that morning had fallen to the floor. Dragging in a deeper breath to give me strength to move my legs, I stepped sideways, passing several gunshot holes in the wall until I reached the other bedroom. The door was flung wide open. Holding my breath, I looked around the corner. A man lay face down on the floor. It wasn't Dillon. There was a puddle of blood seeping out from beneath him and another swath of the stuff on the yellow-stained mattress. Backing away, I bumped into the wall.

I hesitated, then took a long breath. "Dillon?"

No one answered. Lengthening my strides, I crossed the hallway into the family room. My senses came alive. The smell of gun smoke hovered in the stale air. A wooden chair had been turned over, and there was a plastic bag on the dirty tan-colored carpet. It was full of brownish-sugary powder—heroin.

Next to the bag was another body. This one was face up. His glassy eyes stared blankly at the ceiling. I didn't notice his injuries, only the mop of bright red hair fanning out around his head before I looked out the front door that was thrown wide open. Beyond the stoop was a third man. He was bearded and shirtless. His bulging stomach faced skyward. I didn't recognize either man. Dillon was nowhere to be seen. The junky car he drove was still parked in the gravel space beside the road.

The sirens grew louder, echoing inside my ears. I caught a glimpse of flashing lights at the place where the main road turned onto the long dirt driveway that led to the trailer.

I have to get out of here.

The desire to escape filled my head with such force that I turned on my heel and sprinted back through the trailer until I reached the room I'd hid in. Grabbing the pack of cigarettes and lighter off the nightstand, I stuffed them into my pocket. Looking over my shoulder, I paused. If I talked to the police, maybe they would help me.

No, there were three dead people and a bag of drugs about to be discovered. They wouldn't believe me. I stared out the doorway, hearing the roar of the police car in front of the trailer.

If they found me, they'd put me in jail. My past would eventually catch up with me, but not today.

I jerked the blinds aside and pushed out the screen with my hands. Voices were not far behind when I thrust my legs through the opening and dropped down several feet to the clump of pricker bushes below. Spiky branches poked my arms as I stumbled forward, then caught myself with my hands in the grass before I went completely down.

Blood trickled out of the stinging cuts on my arms.

Barefoot, I sprang forward, not looking back or stopping until I reached the forest behind the trailer.

I welcomed the cool shadows beneath the trees and ignored the jabs to the bottom of my feet and ran like my life depended on it, knowing full well that it did.

5

SADIE

The pale torso of the man's body stood out against the grass from the roadway. Buddy parked behind a four-door, dented Malibu and we exited the cruiser with our guns drawn. The ambulance parked on the road and with a simple raised hand gesture, the EMTs remained in the vehicle.

Sun glared down on the scene of the crime with jolting clarity. My heart raced at seeing the body, but my mind remained steady as I surveyed the overgrown grass and the rotted wooden steps leading up to the rusty trailer. The front door was open. Other than birds chirping, all was eerily silent. Buddy took the lead, jogging straight to the steps. For such a giant, he was spry on his feet. I paused next to the body. The white male had two gunshot holes in his bare, barrel-shaped chest. He quickly died where he had been shot. I didn't know him personally but recognized his puffy red face as a regular of the Spur Saloon on West Main Street. The twenty-something-year-old man was a heavy drinker who laughed a lot. In death, he wasn't smiling. I thought his name was Billy.

I moved on, sidestepping the body, glancing down each side of the trailer. My gut told me the scene wasn't active. Still, Buddy and I had to go slowly to be thorough. The shooter might be lurking around any corner.

Buddy pressed his back against the trailer's wall and shouted, "Police! We're coming in!"

He looked back at me, and I nodded. I talked into my handheld radio. "We have a deceased male in the front yard. Going into the trailer." When Buddy stepped aside, I saw the second body.

"Well, damn," Buddy muttered. He continued onward with his gun raised.

What had initially looked like a drug deal gone bad or a domestic issue suddenly turned into something more sinister. This man appeared to be close to the same age as the outside victim. He was face up and had been shot several times, twice in the stomach area and once in the neck. A bag of something that looked like heroin lay beside him.

I concentrated on breathing normally and tried to focus on the surroundings instead of envisioning what went down here less than thirty minutes ago. The smell of stale cigarettes and mold made me wrinkle my nose. Even without the fresh bloodstains the carpet was soiled and the walls were yellowed with grime and nicotine. The kitchen sink overflowed with cheap-looking dishes and a case of beer took up most of the small tabletop. There wasn't any proper household furniture—only wooden chairs spread out around the room. One had been knocked over.

"Second male victim in the front room of the trailer," I reported into the radio.

Buddy paused at the door opening into the hallway. "Clear," he said, turning right.

I glanced over my shoulder. I could see the waiting ambulance's flashing lights through the window. The inside of the trailer was dark compared to the bright light beyond the front door, and I had to blink several times to see better into the narrow hallway. Drawing in a deep breath, I went left. It wouldn't be good for both of us to be trapped at the end of a corridor. A few steps brought me to an open door. My heart rate spiked when I peeked inside. There was another man, face down on the floor in a pool of his own blood.

"We have another man down in a bedroom!" I shouted out to Buddy as I crossed the small, stuffy room.

Buddy burst in. "Good Lord, three murders?" His shock was evident in his raised voice. "The rest of the trailer is clear."

My gaze traveled over the third man's body. All the blood came from a large caliber gunshot to his back. I looked around. Other than a mattress in the corner of the room, it was empty. This wasn't a home. It was a place for criminal activity.

A slight breeze trickled in through the window. Using a gloved hand, I pushed aside the torn screen and looked outside. Below the window, several branches of a thorny rose bush were broken off. My gaze followed the depression in the tall grass straight into the woods behind the trailer. The brush under the trees was thick, and the hot, humid air felt like a steam bath outside. It wouldn't be an easy trail to follow.

I straightened back up and looked over at Buddy. "Someone fled the trailer through this window. I'm sure of it."

"Do you think it was the shooter?" Buddy crossed his arms. "There are peel marks where the driveway meets the road.

According to dispatch, the neighbor said after he heard the gunshots, he saw a red, older model pickup truck squealing tires away from the trailer. The guy didn't see anyone on foot."

The neighbor's doublewide was a half-mile away. Sure, a red truck making a commotion would be noticeable. Anything else would be near impossible to spot. "Is the neighbor still here?"

Buddy nodded. "Maybe someone left via the truck in a hurry, and another person went out the back window?"

It was a reasonable deduction. I stared at the stacked mattresses. The top one was stained, and sheets were waded up on the floor. A ceramic dish was the only thing that sat on the banged-up nightstand. Inside the dish were a couple of cigarette butts.

I gestured at the dish. "Bag these. We can get DNA off the cigarettes. Take the dirty cups out of the sink. We'll test them as well."

"On it." Buddy looked at his watch. "Russo is heading our way. He should be here any minute."

My eyes flicked from the mattresses to the window. "What do you suspect happened here?"

Buddy had been on the job longer than me, and he'd seen some crazy things in the backwoods, but it had been several years since we'd had multiple bodies at a single location. The last time was when four people died in a meth lab explosion. That trailer was similar to this one in a remote, wooded part of the county.

"I'm guessing it has to do with drugs. We'll wait for confirmation from the lab, but I'd bet money the contents of the bag found in the front room is poor quality heroin. If there had been a gal here, I would suspect a jilted lover or revenge scenario, but with three dead men, that doesn't make sense."

"I hate to say it, but the setup is similar to the Russell County sex ring bust-up."

"No one died there," Buddy pointed out.

"Several partially dressed, underage girls were found in a rundown trailer full of drugs and grown men. The main difference here is we have no women that we know of."

Buddy removed his hat, wiped the sweat from his brow, and grunted.

Standing in the hot room any longer bordered on torture, so when I heard Russo clear his throat and mutter a few unintelligible words in the next room, I went to meet him. Buddy stayed directly on my heels. I was sure he wanted out of the sticky, hot room as much as I did.

Raymond Russo was a few inches taller than my five-foot-seven inches, but he looked like a scrawny teenager standing next to Buddy. His dark brown hair was perfectly cut and styled, and he always wore khaki dress pants and a suit jacket. To say he was overdressed for Possum Gap was putting it mildly. I fought the urge to ask him how his date with Darcy went when I stepped up to him.

"Sheriff." He dipped his head. "It's good to see you." He stopped and tilted his head as something seemed to occur to him. "Well, it's inappropriate to use the word *good* under the circumstances."

I wasn't sure if Russo was being genuine or funny. He was a hard man to read sometimes. "Have you ever worked a case like this?" When he continued to look at me, waiting for more elaboration, I added, "Three murder victims in a remote location?" I didn't want to come right out and question his experience with multiple homicide scenes but I worried this investigation might overwhelm him.

"Ohhh," he said in an exaggerated way. "Yes. Well, I assisted on a grocery store shooting case with four dead." He pursed his lips as he thought. "Then there was the murder-suicide that took out a family of five." He offered a weak smile. "I could go on and on if you want but"—his gaze dropped to the dead guy on the floor—"there's so much work to do."

"Did you get a look at the body in the yard?" I asked. Buddy had confirmed that I was right. It was the same Billy Becker who used to spend all his free time at the Spur Saloon.

"I did." Russo slipped on his gloves. "Two gunshots to the heart were Billy's death sentence." He hadn't been in Possum Gap long enough to know Billy Becker. It was his style to talk in a familiar way about everyone. "The gunman"—he eyed me—"or woman had to be a sharpshooter."

I'd already made a mental note of the precise killing shots fired. The redheaded man's injuries were not the same. Either he'd been struck accidentally in the chaos or by a different shooter with less skill than the person who had taken out the other two men had shot him.

Russo snapped a dozen or more photos of the redhead in the living room before he set the camera down. "Buddy, give me a hand."

The victim's eyes were open and empty. Three dots beneath his left eye might have been freckles, or they could have been a tattoo signifying that he served time and was part of a gang. Since Buddy already had gloves on from gathering evidence, he reached for the victim in Russo's direction and rolled the body over.

Russo knelt beside the unidentified man and with a pencil pointed at the back, he spoke in a rambling, excited fashion. "This guy was shot in the back, unlike Billy where the gunshots hit their mark in the heart area." Using the end of the pencil, he lifted the blood-matted hair up. "You can see one bullet struck his neck, and the other two were widely spaced lower on his back. I think it's safe to assume that the shot to the neck killed him fairly quickly. The other wounds were lethal too but would have taken longer to get the job done."

I gave a brisk nod. I wasn't new to gunshot wounds.

Russo pointed toward the front door. "This fellow made a run for it but was shot from behind." He looked into the hallway. "His forward momentum carried him from the hallway into this room where he finally went down."

Interesting. "The last man is in the bedroom straight through there," I said. "He has a gunshot wound to his chest. Looks like he dropped where he was hit." I paused, walking to the edge of the hallway. "You believe this guy could have been shot in that room and made it out here on his own power?"

Russo rose quickly and went into the hallway, glanced around, then disappeared into the bedroom. He appeared again with wide eyes. "Oh, yes, it's possible." He directed his pencil at a dent in the paneled section of the wall. I leaned closer and sucked in a breath. "After being shot in the doorway of the bedroom, he slammed into this wall with his shoulder, came around the corner, and fell there."

"That makes sense," I agreed. Russo was either full of bullshit or brilliant. "What about the guy in the bedroom?" I dipped my head in the direction of the room.

Russo squeezed by me again to reach the last corpse. I followed his quick steps. He studied the body for some seconds, darted his eyes around the room, and then squatted to get a better look. This victim was older than the previous two. His thinning hair, lines around his eyes, and pot-belly physique made me guess his age to be late thirties or early forties. I didn't recognize him. His dead eyes were hooded, and his mouth was set in an uncomfortable grimace. At a glance, it appeared he'd been shot once in the chest.

Buddy spoke up. "Let me get this straight." He lifted a brow at Russo. "You think the guy in the front room shot this guy and then was shot himself?" We could just see the corner of the front room from our position in the bedroom doorway. "What about the guy in the yard? Who shot him?"

Russo gave Buddy a patient smile. "It's all conjecture at this point. Violence like this doesn't happen cleanly. I can say from a cursory glance around and the position of the two bodies that more than one person fired shots. The deceased men out there were in the process of fleeing when they were killed, and I'd wager a truckload of money the bag of heroin left behind was the catalyst to a friendly encounter turning into murder."

"If you're right, at least one person got away. Why didn't they take the dope?" I glanced between Buddy and Russo. The question was for either of them.

Buddy answered first. "Maybe they were in a hurry to get out of here and didn't have time?"

Russo's suggestion followed. "The person or persons most interested in the drugs were already dead or suffering life-threatening injuries?"

Both suggestions worked. The heat inside the trailer was becoming stifling, and if I took a deep breath, I was sure I would be able to smell the scent of congealing blood on the floor. The sight of blood didn't bother me, but the combination of the faint aroma of death mixed with the extreme heat and humidity, made me queasy. I swallowed down the thick acid in my throat and decided it was a good time to interview the neighbor. "Buddy, help Russo with this. I'll be outside."

I found the neighbor leaning against a blue pickup truck that had been patched together with a gray door and a black tailgate. The front plate had a snarling bear on it, and the rifle rack inside the cab was clearly visible from six feet away. Several guns were brazenly showcased on the rack. It was completely legal to carry hunting weapons in a vehicle this way in Kentucky, but considering there were three dead men not too far away, it was a tad unnerving. I was prepared for anything as I walked up to the small group clustered around the man with the short, black beard.

"John Dover?" The bearded man nodded. "May I speak with you for a moment or two?" John pursed his lips out and shrugged. When the small crowd, a mixture of men and women, probably extended family, stayed rooted in place, I raised my chin and said loudly, "Alone."

John's mouth curved into a lopsided grin. The man was around my age, tall, and wearing faded blue jeans and a black t-shirt that said *A BONFIRE IS BASICALLY JUST A REDNECK NIGHTCLUB*. His muscular biceps bulged out of it. Women who liked rugged, dangerous-looking men would have swooned over him. For the backwoods persona wafting off him, his dark hair was clean and the flash of his teeth confirmed that he had all of them. He took his sweet time eyeing me up and down before he made a shooing sound to the others.

I was glad to see them leave, although their slow movements and smirks illustrated how little respect they had for law enforcement. There was a corpse a stone's throw away and it didn't seem to faze any of them. It was quite disconcerting.

Officer Mendez guarded the yellow tape area, waiting for Russo to finish his job and the order to be given to load up the bodies. Even with three law officers and a savvy coroner on site, the number of people who showed up to gawk put me on edge. From where I stood beside John's truck, there was only one other residence within sight, and that was his doublewide. Where had the crowd even come from?

Once everyone was out of earshot, I stepped forward. "You called this in to 911?"

"That's right." John's southern drawl didn't surprise me.

Some people in this part of Kentucky spoke with a deep southern accent, while others clung to a tamer midwestern dialect. Having grown up in Possum Gap myself but having parents from Ohio, I fell into the latter group.

I paused, glancing up as a cloud blocked out the sun. Darker clouds were building to the west, and the fresh scent of rain permeated the air. We might get a shower by evening. I returned my attention to the wiry man who, despite our little conversation, I sensed was quite full of himself. John's shoulder-length hair was tied back in a ponytail, which wasn't uncommon for men around here. "Do you live alone?"

"Depends on my girlfriend's mood. Right now, she's pissed at me, so I'm fending for myself, so to speak."

"Were you alone when you heard the shots fired?" I pulled the small notebook out of my back pocket and began to write.

He nodded. "Trying to take a nap."

His manner was polite yet reserved. He wasn't the kind of eyewitness to volunteer information. I'd have to dig for it.

"Do you know the people who live here?" This was the million-dollar question.

He stared at me with a twitching mouth. "They just moved

in a couple of weeks ago. Waving was my only contact with any of them."

"Who owns the trailer?"

"Miss Fancy."

I knew her. The elderly woman owned a cluster of junk apartment buildings in town. She'd recently moved into the assisted living facility. Since she had no children, her niece, Jessica, collected the rent money from her various businesses. I jotted their names down. "Do you have names for anyone who lived here?"

"I just told you, my only contact with any of them was a friendly wave when they drove by." His expression was relaxed, like he wasn't in a hurry to leave.

"You keep saying them. How many people did you see coming and going?"

"Ahh…maybe fourteen or fifteen different cars."

My hand paused above the notebook. "Can you describe the vehicles and the occupants?"

Too quickly, he said, "Nope, can't recall. Some were cars, others were trucks. I never saw anyone's face either."

The pit of my stomach churned. He knew more than he was saying. I thrust my hand at the bulge Billy's body made under the blanket. "Do you know him?"

"Can't say that I do, sheriff." The friendly smile affixed to his mouth gave me heartburn.

I wasn't ready to give up yet. "You don't seem at all shaken by the fact a few of your neighbors were just gunned down."

John crossed his feet. "I keep to myself. I have my own arsenal handy in case anyone's stupid enough to trespass on my property. I sleep well at night."

I wasn't getting anything useful from John Dover. His

evasive attitude was exactly why bad things happened all the time in the country, and no one was the wiser. Rarely did the locals come to law enforcement for assistance, even when things got out of hand like in this instance.

"The woods out back. Do you know the closest road that comes in behind it?"

John's brows rose. I'd piqued his curiosity. "My oh my, do you think someone fled out the back of the trailer?"

I could be just as tight lipped. "Just wondering."

His smile deepened. "State Route 27, I think. The road that goes through the Amish settlement."

I wrote the word *Amish* and closed the notebook. "If you remember something that might be important, give me a call."

"Sure thing, sheriff." I turned to go, and he added, "Several families hunt those woods. It's dangerous to be strolling around back there. You know what I mean?"

I rounded on the man, stepping into his personal space. He swayed backward but held his ground. Keeping my voice level and low, I asked, "Is that a threat?"

"Just some advice, that's all." He cocked his head and smiled.

I wasn't sure if he had good intentions, but the advice was sound. I wasn't prepared for the softening of his eyes and the sudden tightening of my stomach. The tickling sensation surprised me. I'd been pretty much numb to feelings of attraction since my divorce nine years ago. I had Chloe. I had my job. My quicky teen marriage had soured me about men and romance in general, so the strange sensation in my gut surprised me. Sure, John Dover was an attractive man, but that was all he had going for him. His rebel persona and the Dover name were instant checks against him.

When I left John, the small crowd closed back in. I heard their hushed conversations and felt like I was in hostile territory. These people knew what went down in the trailer and probably had a good idea why there was a shootout today. The Dovers were well known in Possum Gap. Their clan was a large homesteading family that mostly lived in Jewelweed Hollow. The fact that John had picked to settle down in a location on the outskirts of clan land was intriguing. Family members tended to stay close, spending most of their time with blood kin. I suspected that although on decent terms with the other Dovers, he was an outcast of sorts.

The frustrating reality was that the locals wouldn't be much help. The only course of action was good, old-fashioned investigative work. These people were welcome to their secrets. That's the thing about secrets—they are always, eventually, revealed.

6

CHARLIE

Sunbeams fell through the canopy of leaves, dappling the ground and making the quiet forest seem happy. The earthy smells of pine needles and decaying leaves flooded my senses, distracting me from the constant jabs to my bloody feet. I didn't slow down to rest, and when I came to the edge of a trickling brook and the cold water sliced into my numerous cuts, I didn't cry out at the stinging pain. I gathered my muscles and leaped the rest of the distance, and kept on running.

I'm not sure how long I dashed between tree trunks and climbed over fallen limbs. It felt like hours. Without a full view of the sky, a cell phone, or a wristwatch, I was blind to the time and the direction. Fumbling along, I tried to stay in a straight line, but several times I looped back around and ended up next to the same jagged cliff or moss-covered boulder I'd passed before. Occasionally, I ended up on what might have been a deer path, but the narrow break in the foliage never lasted long. My lungs burned, and my muscles ached, but I didn't dare stop.

The dead bodies back in the trailer were the least of my problems. If Dillon had escaped, he'd come looking for me—and so would the police. My foot caught on an exposed root, tripping me. With flailing arms, I grabbed for tree branches but missed. The bumpy forest floor rose up, and I hit face first with a smacking thud.

I rolled over but once on the ground, exhaustion and having the wind knocked out of my lungs kept me from moving. Except for the heaving rise and fall of my chest as I gasped for air, I lay there motionless, staring up at the tiny bits of sky through the swaying branches. It took all of a minute before I caught a full breath. Every ounce of me sagged toward the ground. My limbs were numb and my feet throbbed.

Laying there, the forest above my head spun, and I had to close my eyes. I thought I might be dying. If that were the case, it was probably for the best. I wouldn't have to run or hide anymore. I'd be free of Dillon and strangers' sweaty palms groping my breasts and other places. The hunger would end. It wouldn't matter if I had nothing to wear that fit me or was clean. I'd have no feelings, except maybe peacefulness. That would be nice.

With my eyes closed, the spinning stopped and the fuzziness in my head disappeared. Silence pressed in all around, making me sleepy. If I wasn't dying, a nap wouldn't hurt. I must have come a long way. A hawk screeched somewhere overhead, and my eyes fluttered back open. I became aware of little aches and pains all over, then my empty stomach grumbled, reminding me I hadn't eaten anything for two days. When was the last time I'd felt good? I couldn't recall. I'd been with Dillon for two years, and none of that time could be described as anything close to nice. The memories from before my time with him were foggy and had been shrinking over time. As I often did, I tried to picture Mom's face, but as always, it was just a blur. My stepdad's twisted mouth was all I could see when I thought about him. Lucy had become just a name in my mind. As hard as I tried, I could not conjure up a clear image of my little sister. It was like she didn't even exist. They were all gone.

A tear burned a track down my cheek. I forced my hand to my face and rubbed vigorously. I was done crying. I had promised myself a long time ago that I wouldn't shed another tear for the past. Emotions made me weak. They made me hurt.

Clutching the side of my head, I muttered, "Stop it, Charlie." The breath caught in my dry throat as the discomfort grew in my mind. I saw bright red splotches everywhere. Raising my other hand, I squeezed my temples. "Stop remembering. Stop remembering," I whispered over and over until my voice gained volume, and the words didn't make sense anymore.

The pain in my head exploded. I rocked forward and screamed.

When I shut my mouth, a crow cawed in the trees. Far away, a rumbling sound reached my ears, causing my rocking to stop, and I lifted my head to listen. I held my breath until I was sure what made the noise. Slowly, I exhaled. The inside of my mouth was scratchy and raw, and my empty stomach pinched even more. Another glance upwards, and I realized the sun had disappeared. The sky was gray and flat. A gust lifted my damp hair from my sweaty neck. I blinked. The air felt cooler, and my heart pounded harder. A splatter of water struck my nose, then another.

I tried not to look at my feet but caught a glimpse and

cringed. They were caked with dried blood, and in the curve of my left foot, a deep tear gaped open. I ignored what I saw and pushed up on shaky legs. Oh, how it hurt to stand, but the rumbling sound and multiplying raindrops gave me a burst of energy. Limping forward, I aimed for the rumble. Trees bent in the increasing wind and the sky darkened. The clouds opened, and rain poured down. I wiped my eyes with wet hands but that didn't really help me see. I couldn't hear anything except the drumming of the rain as I continued in the same direction. Moments ago, I'd been burning up, and now cold wetness seeped into my broken skin. It felt like a million bee stings, but at least the blood and dirt was being washed away.

The rain came down harder, blurring my vision and changing the world into a hazy picture of brilliant greens and glistening browns. I dodged the sheets of pouring rain, my feet splashing with each stride. A dazzling claw of lightning brightened the forest. Immediately after the light blinked out, a clap of thunder roared, shaking the earth. My breathing became frantic, and my heart was beating so hard I could feel it banging in my chest. Soaked to the bone, it was difficult to move my sore legs, but I pushed on until I broke free of the forest. I stopped at the edge of a shallow ditch where water gushed through a culvert.

The rain lessened, revealing a road. I stepped behind a tree when a car passed and remained there until I was fairly certain no one had seen me. A cornfield stretched the length of the road on the other side. Thinking quickly, I made up my mind and looked each way. It was clear. Pumping my legs with renewed energy and ignoring the pain that shot through my hip, I sprinted across the road and didn't stop until the tall cornstalks provided me with cover. Slipping in the mud, I slowed my pace but pressed on. Corn leaves sliced into my arms like long paper cuts, but I kept going.

We had passed a cornfield on our way to the Amish market the other day. At the realization, hope sprang to life in my gut. I just had to reach the other side. I hadn't prayed in forever, but I took a chance and closed my eyes, moving my lips with the silent request.

When I opened them, the rain had become a steady drizzle. I folded my arms around my chest in an attempt to chase the cold away. It didn't work, but it kept my arms away from the razor-sharp leaves. The misty, low-hanging clouds and ever-darkening sky made me speed up. I didn't have much time.

At the end of the row, I saw green grass and picked up speed again. Reaching the edge of the cornfield was a relief, although I didn't want to be out in the open either. Surveying the hay field, I heard *clip-clops* on pavement and craned my neck to see. A horse, its coat shiny with droplets, pulled a buggy. It moved at a faster clip than I thought possible. I ducked into the corn when it passed by and listened. Frogs croaking and the saturated ground bubbling were the only things I heard. After deliberating which way to go, I made a random guess and stretched my legs.

I might have covered a mile of fast walking when I began to slow. My legs weakened, and I kept tripping. I couldn't go much further. I had skipped several red-sided barns, not finding what I was looking for. If my legs stopped working, I'd collapse outside. That wasn't something I wanted to risk.

Seeing another barn in the distance, I made up my mind. It would have to do. I cut across a cabbage field, my toes squishing into the mud the entire way. It was almost dark when I got close enough to see the two-story farmhouse next to the barn. A vegetable garden sat between the buildings. Behind the barn was a field where six horses and a pony grazed. Lights flickered from the windows of the house. I tried not to think about the dry warmth and food inside. With the little strength I had left, I climbed over the fence and made my way toward the sliding door on the back side of the barn. At first, I skirted the horses, but as the pain in my side grew, I ventured closer to them in order to reach the barn quicker.

A horse's whinny froze me in place. I searched the distance to the small herd. One horse stood a little apart. It was tall and black, and it saw me. The horse snorted and ambled forward. I swear my heart stopped beating as the giant animal came close. I finally found what I had been looking for.

He stopped a few feet away, and we stood looking at each other as the drizzle turned back into a steady rain. I had come so far. I wasn't going to let this beast scare me.

Besides, my prayers had been answered.

I raised a trembling hand, and the horse sniffed it. He greeted me with a stream of warm breath.

"Hello, Goliath. I found you."

7

CHARLIE

My eyes fluttered open to a rooster crowing. I stretched, shifting my stiff body. Hay poked into my back, but I couldn't motivate myself to stand up. I was so tired, and my eyes felt scratchy. The sneeze came fast and hard, causing me to curl up and brace my stomach with my hands. It was a fine time to find out I was allergic to hay. I sat up, muffling another sneeze with my hand. I hazarded a glance down at myself, and I frowned. Sleeping one night in a hay loft, maybe two, was doable. But I had to get cleaned up and find something to eat soon.

The rooster was at it again. I looked around. It was still dark between the slender gaps of the barn's wooden siding. The dumb bird woke up early. If I had the time to count them, I was sure there were a thousand bales stacked in the loft. Sniffing in the sweetness of leafy, green hay wouldn't have been so bad if it didn't make my eyes water. Beneath the loft were two rows of stalls that I assumed were for the horses. Stumbling into the barn the night before, I hadn't seen much.

FREE FROM SIN

Once I made it to the loft, I had collapsed onto the hay and fell right to sleep.

Something nudged my back, and I spun my upper body around. Yellow eyes stared back at me, and I blew out a breath of relief. "Just a cat," I muttered. The cat bumped its head into me again. "You're a bossy thing," I said, petting the orange fur. Its hind end rose with each stroke. "So, where can I get some food, kitty?" The cat purred loudly in response. I felt along her sides. "You're pretty plump. Someone must feed you."

The loft had brightened a little during my one-sided conversation with the cat. People would soon be awake. *I better get moving*, I told myself. I pushed up and felt my way alongside the stack of hay to the ladder. I swept the cat away with my foot when it insisted on weaving through my legs. "You're going to make me fall," I hissed, grasping the top of the ladder. I swung my leg around, sucking in a gasp when pain shot through it.

As quietly and carefully as I could, I descended to the first floor. When my foot touched the dirt, I exhaled softly. My eyes adjusted to the dull light, and I hurried to the nearest door; pausing to listen, I heard nothing except the rooster's persistent crowing. I turned the handle and peeked inside. There was a small window allowing enough light in for me to see the saddles and harnesses hung neatly on the wall. The orange cat shot around me, and I followed her. She jumped onto a ledge and buried her face in a bowl of dry cat food. I made a face and swallowed hard. My tight stomach growled, and my limbs were weak. I had to eat. If it was good enough for a cat, it wouldn't kill me.

Shooing the cat out of the way, I took a handful of the stuff. Without giving myself time to reconsider, I shoved the cat food into my mouth and chewed. The gritty texture made me gag. I managed to swallow it all down by taking care to hold my breath so that I wouldn't smell it. The cat chow wasn't as terrible as I expected, but when I took another bite, I couldn't keep from heaving. I bent over and threw up the half-chewed cat food and continued spitting until all the pieces were out of my mouth. Straightening, a wave of dizziness flooded my head. When it finally passed, the rooster crowed again.

A thought occurred to me, and I hurried out of the room, still feeling sick. I followed the rooster's call, exiting the barn through the gap where I'd entered the night before. The horses still grazed in the field. A dog barked in the distance. Damp air caressed my cheeks. It had stopped raining, but a heavy dew covered the grass, and it quickly saturated my feet and the cuffs of my jeans as I stalked alongside the barn. The sky turned to a hazy gray, and a sliver of sunshine appeared over the low hills. I sped up as birds began chirping.

The square shed with a pen attached was my destination. I thought I heard voices, but they weren't close, so I kept moving forward. When I went through the door, chickens squawked, fighting to get out of my way. Not wasting a moment, I reached into a nest box and felt around. Nothing. I tried the next one, and it was empty too. I didn't know anything about hens. Maybe they didn't lay eggs every day, or only at a certain time? When I stuck my hand into the next one, I felt feathers, then a sharp snap on the skin. "Ouch!" I snatched my hand back and peeked inside. An angry white hen stared back at me. Her feathers fluffed out, making her look huge as she threatened me with trilling noises. My stomach clenched, and I felt dizzy again. If I didn't eat something soon, I'd probably faint. And that would ruin everything.

Inhaling deeply, I got a lung full of dust and struggled to keep from coughing as I stuck my hand back into the box.

FREE FROM SIN

The hen attacked, but I didn't allow her jabs, flapping wings, or squawking to deter me. I searched until I found the warm egg. Carefully, I pulled it out and continued to the next box. After battling three hens, I'd collected four eggs. One of the places Dillon and I had stayed at the previous year had no electricity, and he'd made me eat raw eggs to keep my strength up. Those eggs had been store-bought, but I figured they were all pretty much the same. There wasn't any chewing involved in eating them, which would keep me from puking.

I cracked one egg on the edge of a nest box, and as efficiently as I could, tilted the shell into my mouth. I swallowed the slimy yolk whole and did the same with the next two eggs. Having a little something in my stomach felt good. I leaned against a roosting board, disrupting a dozing hen, and took a few breaths.

The voices I had heard a few moments before were louder, and my heart fluttered in my chest. Taking the last egg with me, I slipped out of the shed, shutting the door behind me. The one voice was a boy's, the other a girl's. Spotting a white cap between the paddock railings, I stretched into a jog.

I crept back into the hallway of the barn and had to duck into a stall when the front door rolled open. Holding my breath, I heard shuffling, then humming. When a shaggy, spotted dog flew around the corner and right into my face, I almost screamed. Its tail thumped against the wall as it licked my face. There was a whistle. The boy shouted out something in a language I didn't understand, and the dog raced out of the stall.

The boy continued to talk to the dog or himself, I couldn't tell which one, for several long minutes before silence fell inside the barn. I peeked over the stall door. The boy and dog were nowhere in sight. I wasted no time and made for the ladder. Holding the remaining egg carefully in my t-shirt, I shimmied up it, feeling more energetic than I had in days. My side and leg still hurt, and my feet throbbed with burning pain, but my stomach wasn't empty.

Now that the sun was up, enough light sliced into the loft through the windows that I easily navigated around the hay bales. I opened one of the windows, and felt a cool breeze on my face. Cracking the last egg, I slurped it down in one swallow. Eggs had a lot of protein. Four of them were a decent meal. I rested my arm on the windowsill and gazed out, surveying the farm.

I had a good view of the house. The porch swing caught my eye. Ferns hung from hooks, and pink and white petunias draped over the flower beds. I remembered their name because they were Mom's favorite. She used to say they were hard to kill, and that's why she liked them. I shook the memory away with a hard jerk and continued to scan the vast yard. There was a hitching rail and a swing set. The garden was huge. I could just make out a burst of red fruit on the bushy plants, and my heart stilled. Tonight, I would snag a few tomatoes for my dinner. The cornfield I'd trudged through the night before went on forever. Just beyond the corn was the road. A car sped by, then a horse and buggy appeared going much slower. It was strange to see them together. Hearing the *clip-clop, clip-clop* made me feel like I'd stepped back in time.

It was the clothesline that my gaze settled firmly on. At this early morning hour, it was already full of drying clothes. Blue, green, pink, and gray dresses flapped in the wind right alongside homemade-looking men's pants.

I glanced down at my t-shirt, jeans, and stained feet and then back at the dresses. I knew what I had to do, and it would be easier than I ever dreamed.

8

LUCINDA

Phoebe moved her wooden blocks around inside her playpen beneath the maple tree. The day had turned warm, and I was grateful for the shade the splendid tree provided. My hope was that the fresh air tired the child out so she'd take a long nap during the afternoon. I tugged James' pants off the line, and quickly folded and dropped them into the basket. The farm felt crisp and clean after the rainstorm. Dottie whined at my feet, and I paused from my work to pat her broad head.

"What's the matter, girl?"

I could have sworn she was trying to tell me something when she barked. My carefree thoughts from a moment before disappeared as I glanced sideways. Dottie had been acting strangely all morning, and she was a sensible dog.

Brushing off the ill feeling, I reached for a dress. As much as I enjoyed a pretty day, I hated doing the laundry. The only concession was how quickly it dried on a windy day like today. When I got to the last dress, I stopped and looked into the basket. "That's odd. I could have sworn I'd washed my favorite pink dress in this load," I mumbled.

"Mamma! Mamma! Come quick!" Sarah called out. I saw her waving her hands frantically next to the chicken coup.

I threw the last dress into the basket and ran to the barnyard. When I was a teen, I'd been the fastest girl in my class. These days, I moved slower, and I didn't find it as pleasant an activity as I used to.

I stopped when I was close enough for Sarah to hear me and bent over to catch my breath. "What's wrong?"

Sarah continued to pump her fists, motioning me to follow her. "Come on, come on!"

The urgency in her voice got me moving again. I went into the chicken coop right behind her. She stood to the side, pointing at the ground. I knelt and picked up an eggshell.

"Something got into the coop last night?" My skin bristled. We used to let our chickens free-range, but between the raccoons, foxes, and a hateful mink, we'd lost nearly our entire flock last summer. James had promised the new pen would keep our birds and their eggs safe. "Have you counted the chickens?"

"Ya. All sixteen of them are well, and the rooster too." Sarah's shrill voice made me pinch my eyes closed for an instant.

"Huh. Let's look for a break in the wire or a loose board. Whatever ate these eggs had to get in somehow."

We crawled over the packed dirt along the perimeter of the pen, pressing on the wire and knocking on boards. More than fifteen minutes later, I finally gave up. Crossing my arms, I turned to Sarah. "Are you sure the door was closed? Perhaps you forgot to shut it properly last night?"

My serious tone made her eyes grow large. "It was locked up tight, Ma. I promise."

"Hm. Maybe that's why Dottie has been acting strange today. She might know the critter stealing our eggs."

"At least the hens are all right," Sarah commented in a big girl way.

"For now. Most predators begin with the eggs and move onto the chickens. It's nature's way." Phoebe's cry reached my ears. *Oh, what a dreadful mother I am*, I thought, after forgetting all about the baby. "Latch the door, Sarah. We'll discuss it with your father tonight."

I hurried back to the tree and was still many yards away when Phoebe saw me coming. She stuck up her arms, pumping them impatiently. I wiped the dirt from my hands on the side of my brown dress and picked her up. "You hungry for your lunch, my girl?"

She grabbed the string from my cap and immediately twisted it around her hand in response. Phoebe was not happy I had made her wait.

"Hullo!"

I turned to look down the driveway. Martha Mast approached in her open buggy with her new gray gelding. The color of the horse had been a scandalous choice, but that's one of the reasons I enjoyed Martha's company. She didn't much care what the others thought. She was a widow, and the last of her four children had been married off at the beginning of summer. Martha had entered a stage of her life where her main goal was to take care of herself. If her renewed energy and rosy round cheeks were indicators, she was succeeding.

I hoisted the heavy baby onto my other hip. "I didn't expect you today."

"I have news, Lucinda. Important news." Martha engaged the buggy's brakes and jumped out. A moment later, she had the flashy horse tied to the hitching rail.

Martha was two inches taller than me and more muscular. She took Phoebe with an ease that I wish I possessed. "Good Lord, Lucinda. What have you been feeding this child?"

I chuckled at the exaggerated sound of my friend's voice. "Eh, nothing special. She's a hefty one."

Martha sat down on the first rocker she came to, and I took the swing. She made sure Phoebe was perched happily on her lap before she began talking. "There was a triple murder yesterday morning, just six miles away by way of a bird."

"Murder?" I repeated the word softly as my mind grasped the idea. "How horrible."

Martha nodded vigorously, shaking Phoebe with her movements. "Three men, all gunned down like in one of those Wild West stories my da used to read to me."

I knew nothing about the Wild West Martha talked about, but her words were troubling. "Have the police captured the shooter?"

Martha eyed me with raised brows. Her usually sharp blue eyes were extra focused. The lines around them crinkled. "From what Amos Yoder said—he heard it from his English driver—the authorities don't know who did the killing. Some are saying there were multiple shooters." Phoebe began to fuss, obviously uninterested in any further disruptions that kept her from her lunch. Martha made a funny face at Phoebe, then pulled a cookie out of her pocket, giving it to the baby. She saw the surprised look on my face and raised her free hand. "No worries. I baked it this morning."

I let out a sigh and pushed the swing back and forth without much thought to the movements. "Are we in danger?"

Martha pursed her lips. "Amos didn't think so. Then again, that man isn't the smartest peg in the congregation." She made a huffing sound. "We should be vigilant, Lucinda. Evil is everywhere. The word is that the murders were committed over drugs. I reckon a person involved in such a thing would flee to a faraway town."

I glanced at the mailbox. "The newspaper will be here any moment. Do you care to join us for lunch? Perhaps more information will be printed by the Englishers. I agree with you, we should stay informed. A person can't be too careful these days."

"No, they can't." Martha rose with Phoebe in her arms. "After a sandwich, we can discuss plans for the benefit quilt. Fannie Miller insists we do a star pattern, but I disagree. Don't you think the Celtic square would be pretty?"

Martha didn't stop talking when she opened the screen door and went straight into the kitchen. I paused at the door and looked over my shoulder. Sarah skipped toward the house, and Joshua emerged from the barn. My breaths came easier. The children were accounted for. My gaze found the chicken coop. It was almost as if whatever ate the eggs had opened the door and gone into the building on two legs.

The sun was high in a cloudless sky, and birds still sang cheerfully, yet goosebumps rose along my arms. I didn't like the way my heart raced. I told myself I was being silly, but I was never one to ignore my instincts. I closed my eyes and said a silent prayer to the Lord for protection over my family and community before going into the kitchen to prepare lunch.

9

SADIE

I gazed down the quiet, tree-lined road. The neighborhood was a cluttered blend of one-story homes and more ornate Victorians. Paint was peeling on some of the larger homes, giving them a rundown appearance, while others could have been featured on a magazine cover. The two-story brick house I parked in front of was one of the nicer residences. The neighbors had even mowed their lawn. Good for them. When I'd lived here, their mower had always been in the shop. The branches of the giant magnolia tree that spanned the front yard and hung over the edge of the road instantly shaded my car from the bright sunlight when I turned off the engine.

Oh, how I love this old tree, I thought. Only a couple of yellowed ropes still dangled where Chloe's swing used to be. The wooden seat rotted away long ago. As breath caught in my throat, melancholy settled into my bones. I'd probably spent a hundred hours pushing Chloe back and forth on that swing. I cracked a small smile when I remembered how she used to

FREE FROM SIN

cling to it for dear life when I'd send her higher and higher. But for all her squeals, when I'd ask her if she wanted to get down, she'd always shake her head and demand I push harder. I glanced sideways. Chloe faced the other way, purposely not looking at me. We hadn't spoken since I'd dropped her off at the pool the previous morning. The kid used to be so sweet—all hugs and kisses. Not anymore. Nowadays, she was as obstinate as a mule, and she was not thrilled about spending the week at her father's.

Sandra answered the door. The woman was everything I wasn't. Petite, blonde, perky. She managed the YMCA and always wore a skirt and heels, which struck me as odd since dressing more like an athlete would fit better at the sports complex. To each their own, I guessed. She wasn't as bad as a lot of the women in this town. Chloe was lucky Ted had picked her over his last girlfriend. That particular woman had a mean streak and six kids by three different men. She lived off her monthly government checks but had the funds to get a new tattoo on a monthly basis. Thankfully, for Chloe's sake, the relationship hadn't lasted long.

"Nasty business out in the hollow, I hear." Sandra oozed with pleasantries on the job. At home, she cut straight to the chase.

"Yep. It's going to keep me busy this week."

Chloe still hadn't turned around and Sandra noticed. Her brows arched, and she used her animated voice. "We're excited to have you, Chloe. There's a new movie coming out on Friday, and we can drive over to Upton to see it one day."

Chloe didn't say anything. Hiking her duffle bag higher on her shoulder, she brushed by Sandra straight into the house.

"Hey, come back here and answer Sandra!" I shouted after

69

my daughter. When she was younger, I would have given her an immediate dusting off for such insolence. Nowadays, I wasn't sure how to handle her rude behavior.

Sandra placed her hand on my arm, and I resisted the urge to shake it off. "She's at that age. We'll give her some space if that's what she wants." The corner of her mouth pinched. "Believe me, I work with young people all the time. Chloe's acting out because she's growing up, and all the changes are bugging her just as much as they're driving you crazy. We'll take good care of her. Don't you worry about a thing." She snorted and lowered her voice. "You and Buddy better focus on finding out what the hell happened in that trailer. If there's a lunatic on the loose, I won't sleep well."

Neither will I. "Thanks, Sandra. I appreciate you and Ted doing this on short notice. I'll check in with you tomorrow."

I had barely made it down the front steps when Ted called out, "Sadie, wait."

When I looked back, Sandra had disappeared into the house, and Ted was alone. He jogged down the steps. My ex was six feet tall, had a soccer player's wiry body, and his wavy brown hair was just the right amount of messy to make women turn their heads. As far as human beings went, he wasn't so bad. He loved fishing and UK basketball games. Ted had been my high school prom date. The night went too well, and we had Chloe nine months later. We married because we thought it was the right thing to do. We found out quickly that, other than sex and fishing, we had nothing in common and couldn't stand each other. When we were married, Ted drank too much and had a roving eye. Supposedly, he was reformed from both vices, but I didn't believe it.

I kept walking. "Thanks for keeping Chloe this week."

"Do you have a minute?" Ted touched my shoulder.

I stopped at the door of my cruiser, turned around, and forced an apologetic look on my tight face. "I'm late."

"It's about those killings." The words tumbled out of Ted's mouth like he wanted to get the conversation over with as quickly as possible.

I balled the car keys in my fist. "Go on."

"Do you have any idea who did it?" Ted's usually droopy brown eyes came alive. "This is serious."

I cocked my head as my cheeks warmed. The day had just begun, and my ex was already being annoying. If he wasn't taking Chloe for the week, I'd have a different response than the one that came out of my mouth. "Nothing for sure to report yet. We've sent samples to the lab. Talked to the Feds. They're too busy to bother with a backwoods shootout. They aren't interested in dead hillbillies." I opened the car door. "I'll be in touch with your office when I have something concrete, like always."

Ted took another step closer. "Billy Becker was into some shady stuff, Sadie. God only knows the kind of people he brought to our town."

His mention of Billy made me pivot towards him. "What do you know, Ted? Three men are dead, including Becker. That's how serious this is. If you know something, just spit it out," I demanded.

Ted ran his hand through his hair, looked away, and then back again. "I don't know anything for sure, just gossip I heard at The Saloon."

I swayed back until I pressed against the car's door. "Seriously, Ted. You're back at it again. How long have you been with Sandra—twelve, fourteen months?"

"It's not what you think. I get a drink after work to unwind, catch up on what's going on in town." Ted's gaze dropped to the pavement.

Yeah, right. That's what he used to say. For a man who survived law school and passed the bar, he was a dumb shit. None of that education amounted to a hill of beans. "Exactly what did the gossipers say?"

He glanced back at the house. When he was satisfied no one was listening, he lowered his voice anyway. "Billy was doing crack, but that's not the worst of it." His voice dropped another notch. "You know the prostitution ring that just got busted up in Russell County? I think something like that might be going on here."

"It was worse than a prostitution ring. Those underaged girls had been trafficked." My patience was getting thin. "Did Billy mention he was buying sex?"

"Something like that."

"You're a damn lawyer, and you can't even give me a straight answer? My God, Ted."

He shook his head briskly, and when he returned his gaze, his square jaw was set. "Look, there's a few prominent men in this town that might have made bad choices." When he saw my eyes flare, he quickly added, "Not me, of course. But I'm not going to spread rumors that might ruin someone's reputation and their marriage. I thought you should know what was going on. It might help your investigation. Please don't officially mention me—Chloe doesn't need to deal with that at school."

The fire in my stomach spread through my entire body. My neck muscles were so tight, they hurt. "You idiot," I hissed. "I'm going to find out what was going on in that trailer, and when I do, I'll make sure everything comes out. I don't care how far this shit goes up the food chain. No one is above the law." I jabbed my finger into his chest. "That includes you."

Ted backed away, and I got into the cruiser. As I pulled onto the road, I heard him say, "I'm only trying to help you, Sadie. Why do you have to turn everything into a fight?"

I had a hard time catching a calm breath the few miles it took to reach the department. I started out the day yesterday with three shot-up men at a rundown trailer on the end of a dirt road. A brief appraisal of the evidence suggested drugs. Now, my ex tells me that Billy Becker had ties to the sex trade, and prominent Possum Gap citizens had procured the services. I thudded my head back. What a nightmare.

"Do you have anything for me?" I asked Russo.

He looked the same as he had yesterday, dressed in khakis, a dress shirt, and jacket, with the same gleam in his eyes. Buddy held his cup of coffee close to his mouth. His expression was one of tired disgust.

"All the samples have been sent off to the state lab. I estimate getting reports back within ten days." I slumped in my chair, and he leaned forward, tapping his pencil on my desk. "Don't get depressed so fast, sheriff. I tested blood samples myself—of course, the findings wouldn't hold up in court, but they give us a bigger picture to work with faster." His smile was indulgent. "You said time was of the essence, correct?"

I flicked my hand in acknowledgment. Russo was proving to be more resourceful by the day. It was nice to strictly follow protocol, but when lives could be in danger, it wasn't always the best to play by the rules. I liked a man who understood that. "What kind of blood tests can you do that will help us unlock that trailer's secrets?"

Russo lifted a paper and wagged it in front of me. "The blood-stains in the first bedroom do not match the type of blood of the three vics." He looked at what he'd written down. "Bill Becker has A+ blood type. The guy in the front room, B+. Dead guy in the bedroom was O+. Which leaves us with the odd bloodstain on the bed, which didn't appear to belong to the deceased man lying ten feet away." He paused for effect. Buddy leaned forward with his elbows on his knees. I folded my arms on the desk. "Whoever bled on the bed had a blood type of AB-. It's very rare and places a fourth person at the scene."

I let his words sink in while I sipped my coffee. "Okay. That's good to know, but we suspected there was another shooter. The blood evidence supports that."

"Not so fast." His voice bounced with adrenaline. I wondered how much caffeine he'd already consumed that morning. "After we bagged the bodies, I went through the trash cans with Buddy. The one in the bathroom had a feminine wrapper in it—"

"For a tampon?" I interrupted and he nodded. Our new coroner was extremely thorough.

"The stains on the mattresses look like seminal fluid. That won't be confirmed until the lab results come back." His smile deepened. "I have my limitations."

What he said confirmed Ted's *gossip*. I glanced between the two men. I always spoke freely to Buddy; Russo wasn't part of my inner circle. He was an outsider who I wasn't sure I could trust. My gaze settled on the swarthy-looking man. He might not have earned my faith yet, but we were supposed to be on the same team. Russo wanted to solve the case as much as I did, that I was sure of. I drew in a breath and followed my gut.

"Ted."—I eyed Russo—"The DA, came to me with some interesting information about Billy Becker." Buddy perked up. Russo's small, knowing smile, and slight tilt to his head told me he already suspected what I was about to say. "He was involved in a sex-for-hire arrangement."

Buddy snorted. "Prostitution?"

"Maybe even trafficking." I faced Russo. "If there were women in that trailer, where did they go?"

"I'm wondering that as well. As far as the autopsies are concerned, Billy and the man in the bedroom were shot with a semi-automatic rifle, probably an AR-15. The redhead was taken out with a handgun—a 9MM to be exact. We'll have to wait for the forensics to come back to be sure, but it's safe to say two guns were used to kill three people. Since no guns were found at the scene, the person who sped away must have taken them with him—or her." He shrugged. "Since we suspect prostitution, it's plausible a woman could have fired a weapon and been the one to escape in the truck."

"Once we positively identify the other two dead men, we'll have a better idea if we're dealing with a drug deal or a paid hookup gone bad," I said.

"Might be both," Buddy spoke up.

I leaned back and looked out the window. The branches of the elm tree scratched on the glass from the strong breeze. I tried to imagine the crime scene, picturing the position of each body and even placing a woman on the mattress. Three bodies, four blood types, and two different guns. The trailer was a forensics mess. All those things were on my mind, but something else nagged strongly at me.

I looked back at Buddy, then Russo. "John Dover described a vehicle, but he couldn't or *wouldn't* say anything about who was in the truck. We put out an APB on it and haven't had any hits. No one else saw it."

Russo's mouth twitched. "What are you getting at?"

My gaze shifted to Buddy. "Run John's name in the system, and all of his closest relatives. Our entire

investigation hinges on his eyewitness account. I want to be sure he's not playing us."

Darcy walked in without knocking. The pinched look on her face made her look flustered. "We have an ID on the dead guy in the bedroom." All eyes were on Darcy. "Randall Birdie from Wilkins County."

10

CHARLIE

The kids had been in and out of the barn all day long, and when the husband arrived home, he fussed around in the tack room for over an hour. My stomach had started growling again around dusk. Now that it was dark outside, I pushed away from a bale and brushed off the hay sticking to the pink dress as I walked to the window. My feet still hurt, and I hated moving at all. The full moon shone brightly, lighting the barnyard. I spotted the orange cat prowling the fence line. The wind had died down to a soft breeze that stirred the leaves on the tree next to the house ever so slightly. I searched for a sign of the friendly dog. It must be in the house with the family. That dog had almost been my undoing. Leaning against the window frame, I glanced down at the plain dress. It did nothing to flatter a girl's figure, but it was a lightweight, comfortable material that kept my legs cool. I was glad to be out of the stained, tight-fitting jeans.

After my stomach rumbled again, I made up my mind. Shards of moonlight came through the gaps in the boards and lit my way down the ladder and across the empty hallway. A horse nickered from the dark, nearly giving me a heart attack. I didn't realize it was in the barn. Seeing that it was brown and not nearly as tall as Goliath, I continued by the stall.

Once outside, I was amazed at how bright the moonlight was. I could see so well it seemed like artificial lights lit up the barnyard. The cat appeared next to my foot, but I didn't slow down to give her a stroke. Lifting the latch, I slipped inside the chicken coop. This time, I was careful to stay pressed back against the wall so I wouldn't disturb the birds. If they squawked, the dog might hear and begin barking. At this late hour, most of the birds were sleepily perched on boards so it was easy to feel inside the boxes for eggs. By the time I reached the last box, my hands were still empty. Clutching the ridge of the box, I rocked back. "Dammit," I muttered. The hens hadn't laid any new eggs after the kids collected them earlier in the day. It meant I would have to wake up extra early to check the boxes before the Amish family woke up.

A scraping noise made me spin around and then the door flung wide open. Bright light flashed into my face. Shielding my eyes with my hand, I crouched further back into the pen.

"Who are you?" a woman's voice hissed.

I spread my fingers to see who was in the doorway. The flashlight in her hand blinded me for a moment, but I could see her shoes. They were the same black ones the nice lady with a baby had on at the market. Hearing only her ragged breaths, I guessed that she was alone.

"Ma'am, can you lower the flashlight? I can't see." After the initial spike of my heart rate at being discovered, I breathed easier and had spoken calmly.

When the woman lowered the light to the grass, I saw that

she held a pitchfork in her other hand. It wasn't a coincidence that she'd walked in on me. She knew I was here. The realization made my legs a little weak. I was so sure no one had spotted me.

"You haven't answered my question. Who are you, and why are you inside my coop at midnight?"

The strained sound of the woman's voice gave her away. She was more freaked out than I was. The woman wasn't wearing a cap, and her long hair was loose on her shoulders. For being the middle of the night, she was bright-eyed.

I took a step forward and lowered my hands so she could see my face. I'd rehearsed what I would say when this moment arrived. Now, I found myself at a loss for words. A dozen thoughts flicked in my mind. With a throaty breath, I decided to be as honest as I could be. This woman had been nice to me. She was kind.

"We met last week at the market." I took another step closer as the woman stepped back. "You gave me two fried pies, but I never got to eat them."

The woman inhaled sharply and narrowed her eyes as she studied my face. Her back snapped straight when recognition dawned on her face. "Oh my. This is a surprise." Her jittery voice quieted. "It's awfully stuffy in there. Come out." She gestured me to follow her, and I did.

After the dust and mold inside the coop, I breathed in the night air deeply. Moonlight illuminated the woman. She still held onto her pitchfork, which made me smile.

"I'm sorry about this." I flicked my hand at the coop. "I was hungry. Your eggs were all I could find. Well, I tried to eat the cat food, but I couldn't keep it down. The tomatoes were next on my list."

The woman's face dropped. My words had the effect that I had hoped for. Then her gaze shifted to the dress I had on. Her dress. "Oh, thank you for letting me borrow this." I pulled the sides up. "My clothes were soaked"—I looked down at a bare foot as I extended it and dug my toe into the grass—"and bloody."

She visibly swallowed. "What happened to you?"

I inhaled a shaky breath. "Dillon—the guy you saw the other day—attacked me when we got home. He kept me locked in the bedroom for days without food or water. I managed to get away and walked for hours and hours. When I recognized Goliath, I thought it was a sign from God that I would be safe here."

The woman frowned and then thrust the pitchfork into the ground. "You poor thing." She shook her head, pressing her mouth into a thin line. "You've been on my mind ever since that horrible man dragged you away." She lifted her arm. "Let me get you something to eat."

I hesitated. "Are you sure? I don't want to put you out or anything. I was just going to rest in your barn for a few days."

She flicked her hand and began walking. "The barn? My, you are resourceful. It will be my honor to feed you." She glanced down at my feet. "We can get you cleaned up and your wounds taken care of."

Letting out a breath, I lengthened my stride to keep up with her. "You're an angel!"

"Huh. Far from that, but I do my best." She stopped and turned. "The way that man treated you wasn't right. You're well rid of him." I nodded, and she thrust her hand out. "I'm Lucinda Coblentz, by the way."

I took her hand and shook it with a smile on my face. "Charlie—Charlie Baker."

11

LUCINDA

I placed the warm coffee mug in front of James and pulled up a chair next to him. "You're awfully quiet," I said.

Through the kitchen window, I saw the thin line of sunlight grow over the rugged hills beyond the community as the sky turned a buttery gold color. The light breeze hardly stirred the curtains. It would be another hot one. I rubbed my eyes. When I looked up, James watched me closely.

"I know you want to help her"—he brought his hands up—"and I understand that, but she's not a stray dog or a lost kitten we can take in. She's an adult woman—an Englisher you found disguised in Amish clothes in our chicken coop." His voice had risen steadily, then he caught himself, glanced into the dark hallway leading to the staircase, and whispered, "I have a bad feeling about it—about her."

My tiredness diminished as I stared back at my husband. "Ack, you haven't even met her yet. I told you what the girl told me. Her boyfriend abused her, and after witnessing his treatment of her firsthand at the market, I believe her. She borrowed my dress because her clothes were ruined. I washed them myself, so I can say she doesn't have mischief in her heart." I swayed closer, took James' hands into mine, and looked him in the eye. "She's all alone and needs our help. We prayed for her, James, and the Lord brought her to us. How can you question His will?"

James looked away. "She's English. It is not right for her to be here. If she has no family or friends, there are government programs for wayward people like her, shelters and such. You can make a few phone calls this morning and help her find shelter someplace else."

My husband was a sensible man but too stubborn in his ways. He didn't understand the situation because he hadn't seen how Charlie had been treated. I had to convince him that it was our calling to help her. "She's a lost soul. The outside world hasn't been kind to her. She had nowhere else to go. It's only for a few days until she gets her feet firmly planted on the ground and her wounds heal. I'll do some research to find the right place for her. I think there are centers around here for abused women, a place where they offer lodging and counseling. I promise she won't stay long. Please give me a chance to help her without rushing things."

James blew out a long breath, and I held mine. He was about to give in; I could feel it in my bones.

"What if someone sees her or the bishop finds out we're harboring an English woman? It could bring the entire community down on us. Is Charlie Baker worth all that?"

I stood and walked over to the sink to get a better view out the window. A glorious golden sunrise took up the entire sky, ushering in a new day. "In my heart, I believe it's what we should do. If anyone asks, we'll tell them she's a cousin visiting from Ohio."

"It frightens me that you can lie so easily—"

I spun around, dabbing at the tears in the corners of my eyes. "That girl had been reduced to eating raw eggs and cat food in a stranger's barn. She's bruised all over, and I sense her soul is greatly troubled. A small lie to protect her is a sin the Lord will forgive."

James rose and joined me at the window. He spread his arms, and I sagged into them. His scraggly beard tickled the side of my face.

"My dear Lucinda. If it is that important for you to assist this young woman, then so be it. She may stay until the end of the week. That should be enough time for her wounds, both inside and out, to begin the healing process."

With my ear pressed to his chest, I listened to the strong thumping of his heart. "Thank you, James."

The sun was high in the brilliant blue sky when Charlie came through the doorway onto the porch. I set down the dishcloth I was crocheting onto my lap and paused from pushing the porch swing. Josh and Sarah sat on the steps, snapping beans. Phoebe was taking her nap.

"Charlie, have you ever snapped beans?" I asked.

The girl's gaze shifted to the children and the basket full of beans between them. "Can't say that I have."

While Charlie had taken her bath, I'd tossed the pink dress into the laundry, replacing it with a light green one that complemented her greenish-brown eyes. Although her bun was a bit messy, she'd done a fair job affixing the cap to it. I put my work aside and left the swing. "Charlie, these are my other two children—Sarah and Josh."

"Pleased to meet you," Charlie said, sitting down next to Sarah. Dottie's tail wagged wildly as she greeted Charlie. The sneaky dog must have met the Englisher already.

"I already explained to them that you're visiting from Ohio for the week." I made sure to raise my brow when Charlie looked over. She gave a slight nod.

Sarah handed Charlie a bean. Then she picked another one up and snapped the ends off, tossing them into a separate basket. "We'll give those to the chickens later," she told Charlie.

Charlie quickly got the hang of it, and a moment later, had placed a handful of beans into her lap to be snapped.

Josh had been silent up until then. "Why did you arrive in the middle of the night?"

Charlie didn't look up from her work, and I answered for her. "Her driver had engine problems."

Josh pursed his lips. The smart lad didn't believe me. It was probably a good thing that I wasn't a proficient liar.

"You and Da never mentioned Charlie before..." He continued to stare at Charlie, and she ignored him.

"Last minute plans. No reason to think too hard on it, Josh." I sighed. "Since Charlie is here to help with the beans, you're free to ride your horse."

Josh jumped up. "Really?"

I nodded.

He snapped the bean in his hand first, then raced to the barn.

"Not fair," Sarah muttered.

Charlie found her voice. "Now that he's gone, we can talk about girl things."

"Like what?" Sarah turned to Charlie.

Charlie reached up and scratched her head, dislodging the cap so that it flopped sideways. "Is that your pony out there?" she pointed into the pasture.

The child nodded enthusiastically. "His name is Buster," Sarah's voice climbed higher. "He tries to buck me off sometimes, but I always hold on."

"I've never ridden a horse," Charlie said. She didn't stop snapping beans while she talked.

"You can ride my pony!" Sarah offered.

"I'll think about it." Her voice was subdued, almost melancholy.

I knelt behind her. "Here, let me fix your cap." I didn't want Sarah to wonder why Charlie had done such a poor job with her hair and made up a quick story. "The community Charlie hails from wears a different type of cap, like the ones in Lancaster. Do you remember?"

Sarah gave a quick nod. Our trip to Pennsylvania to visit James' relatives was still fresh in her mind. "What happened to your feet?"

Charlie drew her legs in, concealing her feet under her dress. "I fell out of a tree," she lied.

"What were you doing in a tree?" Sarah craned her head to see Charlie's feet.

"I like to climb trees." She rounded on Sarah and the child jerked back. Charlie tugged one of Sarah's cap strings and added, "I bet I can reach the top of a tree faster than you."

It was a clever distraction, but I interrupted. "Charlie, dear, your feet must heal properly before making challenges like that." Once I had tucked Charlie's loose brown strands under the cap, I pulled several pins out of my pocket. Holding them between my teeth, I began pressing them through the cap, into the bun.

"Ow!" Charlie exclaimed, reaching for the top of her head. "Why are you sticking pins into my skull?"

I held in my smile. English girls had no idea the pains we went to in order to keep our caps on. "It's the way to manage your cap, so it's neat and snug. I'm sorry. If you don't use pins, it will blow off with a strong breeze."

Charlie dropped her hands to her sides. "Oh, I see," she mumbled.

Sarah laughed and patted Charlie's arm. "You're funny!" She looked up at me. "Mama, can I ride my pony now?" Tipping the basket to show that it was almost empty, she gave me her most pouty look.

Wanting to speak with Charlie alone, I relented. "Go on." Sarah darted off the steps. "Be careful!" I warned the child before returning my attention to Charlie's cap. I stuck the last pin in. "There you go. Keep in mind you have six pins, so you can count them as you take them out. That will save you from accidentally poking yourself if you're in a hurry undressing."

I sat down in the spot Sarah vacated, and Charlie turned to face me.

"Do you have to wear these things on your head all the time?"

I could hear the angst in her voice, and it made me chuckle. "Yes, unless we're ready for bed, we wear the caps. You never know who might show up for a visit." I picked up the last handful of the beans.

"But why?"

I noticed the light peppering of freckles over the bridge of her nose. Combined with the perplexed look on her face, she seemed younger than eighteen, and even more vulnerable than she had in the dark of night. I recalled her smudged face as she'd ripped off large bites of the sandwich I'd made for her. She was rail-thin, but now that her belly was full and her body clean, I noticed her subtle beauty. She'd been blessed with a smooth complexion and wide-spaced, large eyes. I'd needed extra pins to hold her thick hair inside of the cap. The girl might be down on her luck, but she was strong and would regain her health quickly.

I watched Josh and Sarah hiking through the pasture to catch their mounts. The warm wind picked up a tad, causing the windchimes to tinkle. It was a soothing sound. "Our people strictly follow the teachings of the Bible. Scriptures say women must cover their hair. It's about modesty. The same for the dresses."

"And you're okay with that?"

Charlie wasn't being rude. English women had asked me versions of the same questions before. I understood how it would be difficult for others to grasp the reasons we did things the way we did. The outside world was all about comfort, efficiency, and freedom. Those were things we Amish had willingly forsaken.

"Yes, I am now. When I was your age, I went through a period of disgruntlement with the community rules." I eyed Charlie with a lift of my brow. "I even considered going English."

Charlie leaned in. Her already huge eyes widened. "What made you change your mind?"

"James. I fell in love. Since he was content with the Amish

lifestyle, I decided I could be as well. I wouldn't change a thing now. Family, faith, and community mean everything to me."

Charlie stretched her legs back out and crossed them. "I thought Amish kids were allowed to run wild before they settled down."

"Some communities do that. Ours does not. The bishop thinks we're opening ourselves up to sinfulness by allowing such behavior."

A crow cawed overhead, and both of us looked up. Two smaller birds chased the larger black one. The crow had probably gotten too close to a nest, and the pair were protecting their brood.

"Your people sure do talk a lot about sin." She faced me, and a flash of fear showed in her eyes. "Do you believe God's watching everything we do?"

The question came out of the blue, but the way Charlie waited for my response with a gaping mouth and searching eyes, I knew the answer was important to her. I set aside the basket, then laced my fingers on my lap. "Like I said, my people follow scripture, and the Bible tells us that the Lord is indeed with us all the time." When her mouth snapped shut, I quickly added, "But our Father is forgiving." I placed my hand onto her shoulder and squeezed. "Whatever sins you've committed, there's always salvation if you ask for it."

Charlie inhaled deeply and turned away. The tinkling of the chimes sounded distant, and a chill raced up my spine for no reason at all.

Before I could collect my thoughts, the sound of pounding hooves reached my ears. My hand flew to my chest. A lone rider on a bay horse galloped up the driveway. "Go into the house, Charlie," I ordered.

Charlie bolted to her feet and ran to the door. It slammed shut behind her just as the rider slowed to a trot, then stopped at the foot of the steps. It was Marvin Miller. The lad was only a few years older than Charlie, but I hadn't looked closely at him in a while. His shoulders were broader, and the bristles on his chin more pronounced than I remembered. Even from several feet away, his light blue eyes were dazzling.

"What brings you by in such a hurry, Marvin?" I half expected him to bring more ill news like Martha had the day before.

Marvin caught his breath. "Da sent me to visit everyone in the community. The ball game has been changed to tonight. Da fears the forecast of rain will cause us to cancel for a third week in a row if we wait until tomorrow. Can you and James attend?"

With his reins raised in his hands and his heels brushing the heaving sides of his horse, the lad was clearly making the rounds. Josh and Sarah were too young for the baseball and volleyball games that the teenagers looked forward to each month, but James and I were signed up as chaperones, so our presence was needed at the events. I crossed my arms, fondly recalling the excitement that had rushed through me for youth night when I was a young'un. The ballgames hadn't interested me in the least. I was not one of the athletic girls, but they were the only gatherings where young people could socialize. It was the place to meet the boy or girl you would court and eventually marry. Zeke Miller was right to insist on rescheduling if there was a threat of canceling once again. It was one of the few things the teenagers looked forward to.

"Aye, no worries. We'll be at the schoolhouse."

Marvin's smile lit up his face. He tipped his hat then his

gaze darted to the door. I looked over my shoulder and found Charlie standing there. My mouth dropped open. I couldn't say anything to her in front of Marvin. My heart raced. Why had the girl shown herself?

"Cousin Lucinda, will I be able to attend this ball game thing?" Charlie pushed away from the door until she reached the porch railing and leaned over it.

I looked back at Marvin, but he only had eyes for Charlie. "I didn't know you had visitors, Lucinda."

"It's only me," Charlie said.

I licked my lips. Of course, Marvin knew every teenager in the community. A fresh face, especially a pretty one, would stick out. "Ah, Charlie came for an unexpected visit." I turned back to the girl. "With the way you've been feeling lately, it's best you skip the ball game."

Charlie dropped her head and sighed loudly. Marvin, being a helpful boy, quickly offered a solution. "If you're not feeling well, Charlie, you can sit beneath the trees at the edge of the field. It's shady and a short walk into the schoolhouse."

"That's kind of you, Marvin, but—"

"I think some fresh air would make me feel a lot better, cousin. I do want to go." Charlie smiled sweetly, and my stomach twisted.

The two young people looked at me for confirmation of the plans. When I finally nodded, Marvin raised his hand at Charlie.

"I'll look for you tonight!" He whirled the horse around and bumped its sides.

I watched the gravel kick up behind him as he flew down the driveway, but my mind was elsewhere. I'd caught the look on his face before he'd reined his horse. It was anticipation.

I felt sick to my stomach. For all my ideas about keeping Charlie's presence in the community hidden until I could spirit her back to the English world, she now had an admirer— and the bishop's only son, nonetheless.

12

SADIE

With a two-car wreck on State Route 43, I needed Buddy in Possum Gap. Russo volunteered to join me on the thirty-minute trip to neighboring Wilkins. He had his head buried in the file from the time we hurried out of my office until we were on the road. Clouds once again built to the west as the sun set behind the long ridge of hills that surrounded a third of Possum Gap. I lifted my face to the cooler breeze, ignoring Russo's fluttering papers.

When he looked up, he said, "Do you mind closing the windows and turning on the AC?"

I rolled my eyes, but he couldn't see because I still had on wide aviator sunglasses. "Natural air is refreshing, especially after the scorcher we had today." We passed a ramshackle white house, and I took a double-take at the two giant pigs tethered in the only part of the yard where junk cars weren't parked.

Russo turned to gawk at the swine. "Are those pigs?" He didn't try to hide the astonishment in his voice.

"What else could they be?" I smirked.

He whistled, then settled back in the seat, closing the file folder. "They look like prehistoric creatures. Why would they be tied up in the front yard like dogs?"

Russo wasn't being funny. His face was long and serious. I shook my head. How this city boy ended up in rural Kentucky still baffled me. "They might be pets or dinner. Around here, it's a toss-up."

The sky was losing light fast. I removed my sunglasses and we drove another mile in silence, which I was enjoying when Russo started talking again after we passed by a single-wide trailer where the attached carport was overflowing with trash. Several scary-looking dogs skulked under the security light. A large red *No Trespassing* sign hung from the gate by the road.

"Why do people choose to live that way?" he asked.

This was the first time we'd spent any amount of time alone. I guessed since I'd been close to the previous coroner, accepting Russo—who was completely different from his predecessor—was hard. Johnny Clifton had been a quiet and unassuming southern gentleman that had a way of calming me down when I got anxious. Russo had the opposite effect. His never-ending questions and overflowing energy put me in an agitated state half the time.

Drawing in a deep breath, I tried to be patient and answer in a simple way. "Poverty does this to people. A long time ago, there were good jobs in Possum Gap. That all changed when the coal mine shut down. The following year, the paper mill moved out of state. Not being able to properly provide for your family can cause all kinds of problems. Alcoholism, drugs, domestic abuse, teen pregnancy, crime—it's all the result of the loss of hope."

"That's depressing," he said quietly. "Why don't people move away to more prosperous areas?"

I snorted out a laugh. "Look around, Russo. Possum Gap isn't the only town suffering in these parts." I shook my head, slowing down to make the turn onto the road that would take us into Wilkins. "Besides, kids like to stay close to family. Not everyone can be like you, up and leave everything you've known to start fresh somewhere far away."

"It wasn't easy. Just something I needed to do." His shrugged his shoulders as he stared out the window.

By the time we reached Wilkins, it would be dark. The dull gray light over the wooded countryside made the view gloomy and even a little sinister-looking.

A wave of sympathy coursed through me and I felt compelled to talk to Russo. "Do you like living in Possum Gap?"

He turned and gave me a slight smile. "Yes, I do. You see only the bad things. I guess we all do that—focus on the negatives about the place we grew up. Sure, there's poverty and way too much littering, but the people are so friendly. The other day, I had a flat tire. No more than thirty seconds after I pulled off the road, a pickup truck stopped. The man inside was old enough to be my grandpa. He offered to help, and before I could decline, he'd stiffly gotten out of his truck." Russo's smile deepened. "So, here's this old dude showing me how to properly use the jack when another pickup shows up. This time, a couple of teenaged boys got out. They introduced themselves, chatted with the old dude like they all know each other, and got to work. I was convinced the party couldn't get any larger." He tilted his head back and snickered. "A man and woman pulled up next. The man hollers out greetings to everyone by name, and then he parks. It took twenty minutes to put the spare on, and I'd made five new friends. Unbelievable. That sort of thing doesn't happen everywhere, sheriff. It's a gift. Like this gorgeous countryside—the green hills, tall trees, and rich croplands are special. You don't always find that kind of peace in urban areas."

I mulled over what he'd put so eloquently. People were suffering everywhere, just in different ways. "So, this isn't a quick one-year stint for you, Russo?" I glanced his way. "That's my problem. Not many people move to Possum Gap. You're an outsider. I hate to invest too much in our relationship if you're leaving us soon."

Russ laughed. "I like your bluntness, sheriff. You'd fit in well with the Italian side of my family. The best relationships are those founded on trust, and I want to have a good one with you. When I took this job, I planned it to be here for the long haul. The only thing that might change my mind is if the job is dull. I like to keep busy, and if this week is any indication, Possum Gap is a small town with a lot going on."

The fact that Russo looked forward to murder cases and I despised them, proved just how different we were. That didn't mean we couldn't work together to get the job done, though. Our differences might even help. "I'm afraid you could be right. Violent crime is on the rise. I really hope triple homicides do not become the norm."

When we arrived at our destination, a gray-haired woman came out of the Birdie residence, meeting us on the walkway leading to the two-story brick home. It was a nice house in a nice neighborhood. Unfortunately, things weren't always what they appeared to be. Why would a man who lived in such a straitlaced place get shot to death in a rundown trailer? There was no doubt in my mind that Randall Birdie was up to no good when he visited Possum Gap.

"Mrs. Birdie?" I asked, stopping in front of the slender woman.

She snorted and gave a shake to her head. "No, Leana Grady, Carolyn's mother. She's the one married to Randall." She snorted again. "Since he's dead, I should rephrase that—used to be married to him."

Russo and I looked at each other. I'd learned a long time ago to pay special attention to how people reacted to a family member's death. A lot of information could be gleaned in a situation like this. By Leana's cold, almost bitter attitude about Randall's death, she didn't like her son-in-law very much. But why?

"I'm Sheriff Sadie Mills from Possum Gap, and this is Raymond Russo, our coroner. Is your daughter home? I'm sure this is a difficult time for her, and we don't want to burden her further, but there's a few questions we need to ask her to investigate the case." Leana crossed her arms snugly over her chest and cocked her hip, but she didn't say anything. Her initial outburst of emotion had lured me into thinking she'd be open to talking freely. Now, her steely silence made me not so sure. "We're going to do our best to find Randall's killer and bring justice—"

I didn't get to finish my sentence when she interrupted. "Justice? That man deserved what he got."

Now we were getting somewhere. "What did he do to your daughter, Leana?"

"It's hard to stomach a damn cheater, but that man went out and paid for it."

Her loud revelation acted like a shot of adrenaline. "Is that why he was in Possum Gap—for a prostitute?"

Leana nodded her head firmly.

Ted's tip about the trailer being connected to prostitution in Possum Gap was correct, and the business had spread over county lines. "I really want to talk to Carolyn about it. You never answered me before. Is she home?"

"Honey, she done took some pills to fall asleep. Even though her husband was a dick, she's still upset about his death. She should be in a better emotional state by morning."

"Maybe you can help us out," I suggested. Leana gave me a small nod, and I pulled out my notebook from my pocket. "What did Randall do for a living?"

"He owned the Quick Oil Change over yonder next to the Super Mart. He inherited it from his daddy. He certainly didn't have the gumption to start up a business on his own."

Randall had a wife, a nice house, and his own business. And yet he got mixed up in shady dealings for sex with a stranger and wound up dead. It was hard to grasp. "Do you have any idea if Randall knew anyone over our way?"

"Randall had friends"—she made quotations sign with her fingers—"all over. Recently, though, Carolyn mentioned he'd been hanging out with a fellow named Dillon. She said the guy gave her the creeps."

"Did she say why exactly?"

"She sure did. He had this teenaged girl in the backseat of his car, and he'd tell her to wait in there, even if it was pushing a hundred degrees outside. Carolyn thought it was some kind of abusive situation."

"Do you have Dillon's last name?"

"Carolyn didn't say. Terry Wallace might, though. He's Randall's hunting buddy." Leana's smile was crooked. "Or he *was* Randall's hunting buddy."

I got it. If Chloe's husband cheated on her with prostitutes, I'd be glad to see him permanently out of the picture. "Where does Terry live?"

"On the other side of town, but he's probably working at this hour."

"Where?" I poised the pen over the paper.

"At the police station. He's one of Wilton's fine officers." Leana snorted, then shook her head.

When we got back into the car and I started the engine, Russo finally spoke. "This might get tricky."

Yep. I was glad the coroner understood Leana's implication. Wilton, just like Possum Gap, was a small town. Everyone was into everyone else's business. Who you associated with said a lot about your own character. If Officer Wallace hung around with a man soliciting prostitution and who had been caught up in a deadly shootout, it didn't look very good for his reputation.

"Let's see what the officer has to say. I know how to handle crooked cops." I glanced at Russo, who stared back. "You have organized crime and mobsters up north. The good ol' boys' club is a thing in the south, Russo. On the surface, these guys are upstanding citizens. They have pretty wives, straight-A kids, and they go to church every Sunday. They'll do anything to keep up appearances while in the shadows they're getting into all kinds of crap. And they protect their own. If Officer Wallace knew about Randall's extramarital activities, he'd be inclined to keep it secret for his dead friend's sake. We have to tread lightly. I'll do the talking."

After the introductions, Officer Wallace led us into a conference room at the Wilkin's police department and closed the door. The room was slightly larger than the one we had in

FREE FROM SIN

Possum Gap. When Officer Wallace faced us, I noticed several things at once about the cop. His black buzzed hair was peppered with gray, he was muscled enough to say he worked out at a gym, and either his twitching eye was a regular thing for him, or it was a sign that he was nervous.

"Please have a seat, Sheriff Mills and Mr. Russo." He sat down in the chair farthest away. "It sounds like you all have had a busy couple of days over there in the Gap. What brings you out our way?"

He knew why I was here. That he was acting dumb was more than a nuisance. Officer Wallace was blatantly letting me know that he would not be helpful to my investigation. "You don't seem too tore up about your friend being murdered." His eyes widened, but only for an instant, then his face went blank. "Especially in your line of work. I'd think you'd ask me about the evidence we have and how long it's going to take us to nab Randall's killer."

Officer Wallace's lips thinned as he visibly took a deep breath. He crossed his arms on the table. His gaze flicked to Russo. "I'd rather speak alone, sheriff. If you don't mind."

"I do mind. Russo is working the investigation with me. Whatever you say to me, I'll tell him, so let's cut to the chase and save some time by getting on with it."

Officer Wallace grimaced and dipped his head. "I heard you were hard ass. Guess the rumors are true." He lifted his hands and sat back. "I've known Randall for thirty years. We played ball together as kids. Our wives are friends, we grill out, that sort of thing. I hated to hear he'd been caught up in nefarious dealings in your county but wasn't really surprised. Randall's impulsive. Always has been. I worried that someday his running around would get him into trouble."

"Running around? Can you clarify what you mean?"

Officer Wallace looked me in the eyes. "Women. Randall couldn't keep it in his pants."

"You think he was killed because he slept with the wrong woman?" I wanted the officer to be the first one to mention prostitution.

He shrugged. "Could be."

"Okay. That doesn't explain why you don't seem too rattled by his violent death."

"Like I said, it was just a matter of time. Really a shame, too. He had a good thing with Carolyn. I never understood why he wasn't satisfied keeping it at home, you know?"

Officer Wallace was creating a narrative that Randall's murder was due to his infidelity. But I was sure he knew more than he was saying.

"Randall hung around with a man named Dillon. Do you know the guy?"

The officer's eyes shot upwards. He knew him.

He shook his head, looking past me. "No. I never heard of him."

I glanced at Russo. A smug smile formed on his mouth. The coroner was enjoying this too much.

Leaning forward, I tapped the pen on the tabletop, staring at the officer. We were in the same line of work but that was where our similarities ended. I believed no one was above the law, and I acted the same way I expected from the citizens in my jurisdiction. Officer Wallace was a fraud.

I set the pen next to the notebook and folded my hands over them. "I have a triple homicide back home. Believe me, Officer Wallace, I intend to find out exactly what happened in that rundown trailer, and when I do, arrests are going to be made. I don't care who goes down in the process." I paused, letting my words sink in. "I'm aware that prostitution was taking place there, and it's come to my attention that some high-profile locals might have frequented the trailer for sex. My interest in those Johns is to get to the bottom of the murders. I'm not looking to embarrass anyone or ruin their life. I think Dillon is a key player, and I need to know his last name. If you can help me out with that, I won't work too hard to uncover every man who might have gone to that trailer for sex." I rose, picking up the notepad and pen. "I'm persistent. I'll find out one way or another. If I get the name on my own, I won't be so discreet with the information that pops up. Are you following me?"

Officer Wallace nodded slowly. "Cunningham. The name's Dillon Cunningham."

13

CHARLIE

James left the job of tying up Goliath to Josh, picked up Phoebe, and hurried towards the schoolhouse. I shifted my gaze to Lucinda. After her scolding a few hours earlier, she'd barely spoken to me. Now, she watched her husband's long, brisk strides with a raised chin. Hearing the couple argue when he arrived home tied my stomach in knots. I waited in the guest room until it was over. In the end, James relented to my presence at the ballgame because he didn't have a choice. Marvin would be looking for me. If I didn't show, Mr. and Mrs. Coblentz would have to come up with a story about my whereabouts. I got the feeling Marvin would be insistent to find out the truth, and Lucinda sensed that as well. It was a slippery slope for all of us, but I didn't care. My time among the Amish would be short-lived. My days of being locked in a room were over.

Toying with the annoying cap string between my fingertips, I stepped out of the buggy. My butt was sore from bouncing on the hard, blue velvet-cushioned seat, and I was sweaty from being squeezed into the back between Josh and Sarah. The cooler evening breeze outside gave me an instant energy boost.

Holding Sarah's hand, Lucinda leaned in close. "Please try to behave yourself. The less you say, the better."

When she searched my eyes, I felt kind of bad. "Don't worry. I'm just a cousin visiting for the week. I won't do anything to get you or your family in trouble."

Lucinda pointed out the field next to the long shed where the horses were tied. "The girls are setting up the nets now." Her eyes and voice softened. "I'm glad you'll get to have some fun for a change."

My eyes misted, and I quickly reached up to rub the wetness away. "Thanks. I appreciate what you're doing for me."

Lucinda nodded and turned to leave, then paused and looked over her shoulder. "I'll be in the schoolhouse if you need anything. The other ladies and I are making sandwiches for a snack."

I watched the Amish woman and little girl walk away before I went to Goliath's side. I didn't get too close. He was so big. "Will you tie him over there?" I pointed at the shed full of horses.

"Yah." Josh left the harness on Goliath's back and disconnected him from the buggy.

"What are those?" I asked.

He puffed out his chest. "It's called the breeching."

"How old are you?"

"Ten." He stretched to his full height.

"You know an awful lot for a little kid. That's the same age as my sister and all she ever did was play with dolls."

"That's what girls do," Josh said with a shrug. His eyes were suddenly keen. "What's her name?"

My face cooled, and I backed away.

Ignoring his question, I headed in the direction of the volleyball nets. I quickly counted fourteen girls. Their colorful dresses flapped in the breeze like a moving rainbow. Some looked younger, but I judged most to be close to my age. A girl in lavender lifted her head from the stakes and saw me. She dusted the grass off her dress and walked straight over. Her determined strides forced me to slowdown.

"You must be Charlie." She came to an abrupt stop in front of me. Something about her dark hair I could see poking out from beneath her cap, high cheekbones, and light blue eyes was familiar, but I'd never seen her before. Before I could say a thing, she continued, "I'm Rachel Miller. You met my brother today—Marvin."

I let out the breath I'd been holding. "You two look alike."

"Everyone says that." She smiled.

A short, rounder-bodied girl in brown appeared at Rachel's side. "Charlie is a strange name for a girl," she said without introducing herself.

"It's short for Charlotte."

"Oh, like the spider in the pig book?"

Several girls folded in around me. The girl who had made the spider remark was a slender blonde with gray eyes. She had on the same frumpy-styled dress as everyone else except it looked a lot better on her. Her words and the curl of the side of her mouth made me instantly hate her.

"The book is called *Charlotte's Web*, and it's one of my favorites. I'm kind of surprised you know about it. That means you actually read, and you don't seem smart enough for that."

As I talked, the blonde girl's eyes grew larger and larger. One of the girls snickered; I couldn't say which one. For a moment, we stared at each other. I narrowed my eyes, daring her to make a comeback. The other girls remained silent. I was vaguely aware when the sun dipped below the hills, bathing the grassy field in dull light.

Our stare-down ended when the other girl forced a smile. "That's funny. I'm Vivian Hershberger. Pleased to meet you."

When she left, several girls went with her. The only ones that remained were Rachel and the pudgy girl. Rachel leaned in. "Don't mind Vivian. She's not as bad as she seems." Her mouth trembled until it broke into a mischievous smile. "This is my best friend, Delilah Schwartz."

"Sorry I asked about your name," Delilah said while staring at her shoes. "Rachel is being too nice. Vivian is as bad as she seems."

A laugh bubbled out of Rachel's mouth, and I couldn't help but join her. As the girls led me over to the nets, they bombarded me with questions: how old I was, what community in Ohio did I live in, am I courting. It went on and on. I was careful to respond with the pre-practiced answers Lucinda had drilled into me, and by the time Vivian tossed the ball my way, I half believed my own lies. My life with Dillon had made me a good actor or maybe just a fantastic liar. Either way, I was sure the girls were fully convinced that I was Amish.

"Do you play ball?" Vivian called out. Everyone's eyes turned my way.

I wouldn't admit that I had never played any team sports in my life. The idea of spiking the ball over the net seemed simple enough. Doing it in a dress and with the annoying cap poking into my skull might make it more challenging, but I wasn't about to let Vivian outdo me.

Taking my place with the girls on the closest side of the

net in the same row as Rachel and Delilah, I tossed the ball into the air and struck it as hard as I could. The ball whooshed through the air straight at Vivian. She lost the surprised look and recovered quickly, hitting it back. The girls played well, and their dresses didn't stop them from jumping into the air or skidding into the grass. I was rather impressed with their enthusiasm. I managed to hit the ball a couple of times but found myself out of breath halfway through the game. The black tennis shoes Lucinda let me borrow fit perfectly, but my cut up feet still hurt. Although I'd been eating well for the past twenty-four hours, my limbs were still scrawny and weak. I passed by Rachel, telling her I would take a short break, and she waved me on.

A cooler sat next to the field, and after a glance around and seeing no one was paying any attention, I opened it and pulled out a bottle of water from the ice. Dropping into the grass, I took a long drink and stretched out my legs. I inhaled the sweet scent of mowed grass. The temperature was just right. Still a little warm, but enough of a breeze to quickly dry the sweat from playing the silly game. I wasn't a fan of physical exertion, and other than wanting to hit Vivian's face with the ball, it wasn't my thing. But the other girls were enjoying themselves immensely, judging by their giggling, shouts, and huge smiles.

They were carefree, and I hated them all for their happiness. Those smiles wouldn't be on their faces if they'd been with Dillon for the past two years, spreading their legs for up to ten guys a day on the weekends in exchange for a little bit of food and a crappy place to live. In a few days, I'd be gone, and these girls would continue living their quaint lives in this picture-perfect place.

"Hey, I'm glad you made it."

I looked up, and Marvin Miller was standing there. He was taller than I thought he'd be off the horse. Before I could stand, he knelt beside me in the grass. Something funny happened in my stomach. It was like a million butterflies' wings pounded frantically. All the times that I'd been with guys, this had never happened before.

I felt warm and agitated at the same time. "I'm glad I came." Marvin didn't stop looking at me, and his intense blue-eyed gaze made me squirm inside. I looked ahead, pretending to watch the girls play.

"I saw you in the game. You're good." Marvin was intent on keeping the conversation going. He'd also just admitted that he'd been spying on me.

I glanced back at him and had to look away again. Maybe I never had a real boyfriend, but I knew that look in his eyes. He wanted to kiss me.

"This is the first time I've played." I'm not sure why I said it.

"You caught on quickly then." Marvin made a smacking noise. "So, what do you do you like to do in Ohio?"

I stared straight ahead, afraid that facing him would cause the uncomfortable sensations in my stomach to return. What should I say? That I didn't have favorite things to do because I'd basically been a prisoner for the past two years? I gave my head a small, frustrated shake. It didn't matter what I said. I'd never see this boy again. "I enjoy taking walks, and I used to read a lot when I was a kid."

"The last book I read was about a boy who had adventures on a riverboat. I think I was twelve."

"*Huckleberry Finn?*"

"Yah, that's it."

"I didn't think you all read regular books." I realized my mistake and scrambled to fix it. "I mean, uh, Kentucky Amish." I risked a glance his way. He was grinning.

"Well, us Kentuckians do know how to read and write, even though we do it all backward."

I saw the good humor in his eyes, and I swatted his arm. "Oh, you're a clever one, huh?"

Marvin's smile quickly turned into a frown as he looked down at the place on his arm where I'd touched him. I glanced away, and after glancing around, I noticed something that I hadn't before. The Amish—the teenagers, children, and adults—were separated by sex. The males hung out together and so did the females. Marvin and I were the only people of the opposite sex talking. Maybe I wasn't supposed to touch him either?

Marvin finally collected his wits. "Your community must be pretty laidback."

"Ah, yeah. We do stuff none of the other Amish do." I breathed a little easier knowing that I suddenly had a plausible excuse for my ignorance.

"I can see that." He nodded at my exposed calves.

Feeling my cheeks burn, I reached down and straightened my dress out to cover the pale skin.

"Don't worry, no one else saw. Be careful, though. Some of the girls like to gossip and cause drama." He cocked his head at Vivian. "Don't trust Vivian. She'll rat you out in a heartbeat."

I had never considered that there was backstabbing among the Amish. I assumed such a strict religious group of people would get along fabulously. If the kids ratted on each other, I'd bet the adults did as well. That's why Lucinda had tried hard to keep me from coming here tonight. If I messed up my disguise, someone might tell on me, which could be a problem for the little Coblentz family.

"This community is uppity, isn't it?" I tried to turn the tables.

"I guess it's stricter than yours." He winked, and the bubbly sensation in my belly happened again.

The girls finished the game with Vivian getting a point. A few started taking the nets down while Rachel, Delilah, and Vivian walked over. All three pairs of eyes swept from Marvin to me. Rachel's grin made her look like she'd just heard a funny joke. Delilah's mouth hung open in shock, and Vivian glared at me.

"Marvin, you kept Charlie from getting back into the game." Rachel lifted the side of her hand to her mouth. "He talks way too much." She raised her chin at her brother.

Marvin stood up, and I followed him, brushing the grass clippings off the green dress.

"Eh, don't listen to Rachel. She likes to pick on me since I'm the only boy out of the six of us." Marvin smiled.

"You have five sisters?" I asked.

"I sure do."

Rachel shook her head. "We don't tease him for being the only boy. It's because he's full of himself."

Marvin raised a finger and opened his mouth to protest when a dinner bell rang out. All at once, everyone started walking up the hill to the schoolhouse.

"Chow time," Marvin said. "I'll see you later, Charlie." He hesitated for a second, then jogged away, catching up with three boys.

Marvin hadn't said goodbye to the other girls, and when I

glanced at Vivian to see her reaction, she had already started walking away. Satisfaction made my steps light, and I didn't hide the smirk on my face.

"Vivian is mad," Delilah said, stretching her legs to keep up with me and Rachel.

Rachel looked sideways. "She's always upset about something. Don't let her bother you." Rachel glanced over her shoulder, then leaned in close and whispered, "Marvin likes you."

My face warmed, and I dropped my gaze to the ground. "He's just being friendly."

"Uh-ah. He's careful not to talk to girls." Rachel's side bumped mine, and she kept her voice low. "He says he doesn't want to lead on any of the girls that he's not interested in. Since he considers himself handsome and an amazing catch, he thinks all the girls like him."

"They do," Delilah cut in. "And he *is* handsome."

The dreamy, saggy look on Delilah's face made me giggle, something I hadn't done in ages. "I agree. He's cute."

"Will you court him then?" Rachel asked.

I didn't understand the Amish culture at all, and I wasn't a normal girl to begin with, but I thought Rachel was out of her mind. Snorting loudly, I glanced at her hopeful face. "What are you talking about? We just met today, and I'm only visiting for a week."

Rachel grasped my arm and pulled me to a stop. She shooed Delilah away, saying, "We'll meet up with you in a minute."

Rachel waited for a cluster of girls to pass by, and we were alone on the grassy slope. It wasn't quite dark yet, but the full moon shined high in the sky.

"Please don't think I'm kidding. My brother turns twenty-one next month. Most men his age are already married or at the very least courting. You're the first girl I've seen Marvin pay attention to. I think you've inspired him."

"He doesn't even know me," I argued. The sentiment was flattering, but I wasn't Amish.

Rachel gave me a knowing smile. "Don't you like him?"

"Ah, well, I guess. He seems like a nice guy." I'd liked Dillon at the beginning. Then he showed his true rotten self. Over the past couple of years, I'd seen how disgusting guys were. They'd cheat on their wives and girlfriends to sleep with a teenager. I had a hard time trusting anyone.

"Believe me, Marvin is super. He'll be a wonderful husband and father one day." She saw the shock in my eyes. "Since our father is the bishop, it's important for Marvin to finally grow up and begin courting. My parents are frustrated with his lack of interest in settling down. Ma mentioned several prospective girls in the community to him, and he laughed at all of them. Marvin can be a little stuck up. Sometimes, he acts like a boy instead of a man."

"Twenty-one is pretty young. Maybe you all are pushing him too much. If you stop talking about girlfriends and courting, he'll come around on his own." I grunted, then elbowed her side. "You know how guys are. When he's horny, he'll find himself a girl."

Rachel's mouth dropped open. She looked horrified, and I wanted to kick myself for what I'd said. The only good thing was that she probably wouldn't want me as a sister-in-law if she thought I was crude. "I'm sorry I said that out loud," I said through gritted teeth.

The shocked look on Rachel's face lessened, and the

corner of her mouth trembled. A few long, awkward seconds passed, and then she started to laugh. Seeing that Rachel thought it was funny, I let out a breath and relaxed again.

When she'd calmed herself, Rachel said, "You're different than any girl I've met."

"Uh, well, I sometimes—"

Rachel held up her hand. "No, don't say anything. I like that you're different. I never know what you're going to say. You keep me on my toes." We started walking again. "Come on, Charlie. We'd better hurry before all the sandwiches are gone."

That made me speed up. Just a couple of days earlier, I'd been starving. Now, I could eat whenever I wanted, and the food wasn't spoiled. Already, I felt stronger. My head wasn't fuzzy anymore, and when I had woken that morning in the soft, clean bed in the Miller's guest room, I'd thought I was dreaming. Nothing good had ever happened to me, and here I was, making new friends and playing sports. It was weird being surrounded by Amish people. Seeing the buggies whisk by on the road made it feel like I was still in a dream. I could pretend that I was someone else and I liked that. But it wouldn't last forever, and that caused my stomach to churn.

Rachel led me through the doorway into the metal building that looked more like a barn than a schoolhouse. Wall lamps flickered dully, and as we passed them, I noticed they were just like the gas ones inside of the Miller's house. Instead of hitting a switch, each of them had to be lit individually with a lighter. There was a faint, unfamiliar scent from the burning lamps that made me wrinkle my nose as I looked around the large, open space. A line of tables had been set up for the young people to sit at. Most of the benches were full, but

Rachel didn't seem to care as she guided me over to the counter where a few bologna sandwiches were left. A wrinkled-faced woman behind the counter poured us cups of water, and after putting two sandwiches on the plate, I picked up a cup.

"My, for such a skinny thing, you eat a lot," Rachel commented when she saw my plate.

I would never pass up free food again. When we went to find a seat, Delilah waved at us. She poked the girl sitting next to her, and like a domino effect, all the girls on the bench shifted a couple of places to make room for us. The girls sat on one half of the long line of tables and the boys had the other. I raised my gaze, searching the masculine side, and quickly found Marvin Miller. He stared straight at me, and when our eyes met, he smiled back. I didn't like the feeling of burning cheeks and a frantic stomach, so I focused on Rachel's back until we reached the opening on the bench and climbed over it. As I settled onto the hard bench, the hair on the back of my neck rose, and the breath caught in my throat. I looked up to find Vivian sitting across the table, scowling at me. I frowned back at her challenging eyes before she dropped her gaze to her sandwich.

Vivian didn't know it yet, but I would be her worst nightmare if she messed with me.

The kitchen bustled with women. Lucinda oversaw washing the platters. Her brows arched when I bent around her and asked if I could help.

"Yah, of course." She handed me a dishtowel, and I started drying the platters off. "Are you having fun?"

Fun? It had been a strange evening, that was for sure. "It's good to be out doing something. Dillon never let me have girlfriends."

Lucinda's face tensed like she was conflicted about something. She finally found her voice. "I saw you sitting with the other girls. It looks like you've made some friends."

"Maybe. I like Rachel and Delilah. Vivian, not so much."

Lucinda chuckled. "It's your way to be direct, but perhaps you can try to keep some of your thoughts to yourself." She dropped her voice. "You wouldn't want anyone to hear you say something like that. It might cause hurt feelings, right?"

Ah. It was a teaching moment. "Oh, yeah. Sorry about that. I'll keep my mouth shut next time."

"That's not what I meant." She sighed. "Strive to say only positive things."

I nodded. A round-faced woman with auburn hair jutting out from beneath her cap stepped up to us. "This must be Charlie. In only a few minutes, Rachel told me all about you."

The pretty-faced woman shifted her gaze to Lucinda, who looked like she might throw up. She recovered quickly enough. "Charlie, this is Susan Miller, the bishop's wife."

So, this was Marvin's mother, the lady who wanted to get her son married off as soon as possible. "Hello." I lifted my hand to shake hers, but when her hand didn't move, I waved instead.

"I grew up in Holmes County, Ohio. Exactly where is your community?" Susan suddenly resembled a hawk staring down at me from a powerline.

Lucinda quickly came to my rescue. "Far from there, closer to the Ohio river." She grabbed a garbage bag out of a trash can and tied the top. "Charlie, there's a dumpster behind the building. Please take this out for me, will you?"

"Of course!" I took the bag and smiled at Susan as I skirted around her. Her brows shot up, but she didn't say anything.

It took longer than I expected to reach the door. The boys had finished folding the tables and stacking the benches. Now they were playing basketball in the same space with the homemade-looking hoops. Groups of girls stood to the side of the court that was marked with orange cones, watching the game with keen interest.

"You're not leaving, are you?" Rachel snuck up behind me.

"Not yet. Lucinda asked me to put this"—I lifted the bag—"into the dumpster."

"Right. Come back in when you're done," she told me.

I nodded and hurried on. Between the number of bodies and the many gas lamps, the inside of the schoolhouse was suffocating. It was a relief to escape through the doorway, out into the thinner air. The moon lit my way along a dirt path that led straight to the trash dumpster. I stretched to lift the lid and tossed the bag inside.

Placing my hands on my hips, I studied the moon. It was so bright. I could see the dark ruts on it clearly.

"Hello again."

I whirled around, clutching my chest.

Marvin stood there, grinning.

I exhaled loudly. "Don't do that!"

"You're awfully jittery, Charlie." He glanced over his shoulder, checking to see if anyone was sneaking up on us.

"I think you're the nervous one." I walked around him. He caught up, matching my strides.

Marvin stepped in front of me. "Do you want to see my horse?"

I glanced down at the long wooden shed where all the

horses were tied. Squinting my eyes to see better, I caught a glimpse of swishing tails, but the interior was mostly dark. Marvin Miller really wanted that kiss.

"Sure."

I walked quickly to keep up with his long strides. Once we were inside, he led me to a horse that wasn't as tall as Goliath.

"This is Sierra." He patted her neck and looked back at me expectantly.

My heart raced, but I forced my legs to take a step closer. Stretching, I touched the brown fur lightly. "It's a girl?"

"Yah, she's a mare." Though a shadow covered half of his face, I caught the rise of his brow. "Do you like horses?"

"I like them very much, but I'm not around them very often." I was getting tired of pretending. "Other

people take care of them where I'm from," I said lamely, hoping he wouldn't ask me any more questions.

"Rachel doesn't handle the horses either."

We stood in the shadows, petting his horse, and I waited for him to pull me into his arms. But he didn't move. Maybe Marvin's mind wasn't in the gutter, and he really did want to introduce me to his horse.

"Do you ride?"

I shook my head, pausing my hand on Sierra's warm side. "I'm kind of afraid of horses, but when I was a kid, I used to dream about galloping through a grassy field on one." I glanced up. "Dumb, huh?"

His brow furrowed, and I couldn't look away. Damn. Marvin Miller was a good-looking man. I was seriously disappointed he wouldn't just give me a kiss.

"What are you doing tomorrow?"

Answering honestly, I said, "I have no idea. Why?"

"Our driver has an appointment, so I won't have to go to work." He shrugged, not taking his eyes off me. "I thought about going for a ride." Licking his lips, he let out a breath. "Do you want to go? My old gelding is very gentle. I can give you a riding lesson. It'll make your dream come true."

My mind clouded, and I couldn't see Marvin anymore. A vision of me riding his horse flashed in my mind; then I saw Dillon's face, red and angry. A blurry face hovered above me as a man's weight pressed me down onto the dirty mattress, and I felt pain between my legs. Then there was blood. Blood everywhere. And a scream.

I wobbled, and Marvin's hand caught my arm. Blinking, he came back into focus.

"Are you all right? I thought you might faint there for a minute." When he seemed sure I wouldn't topple over, he let go.

"I'm fine," I snapped. Marvin leaned back, and I forced a smile. "I'd love to go for a ride with you."

14

LUCINDA

James closed the Bible and leaned back on the pillows with a heavy sigh. It was late. We should be asleep, and here I was, brushing my hair, James staring at the ceiling, shaking his head. I felt bad that my actions had caused him so much grief.

"Don't fret so. In a few days, Charlie will be gone," I told him firmly.

He met my gaze. "I fear this situation is out of your hands."

There was a shuddering in my chest. I stretched to set the brush onto the nightstand. "How so?"

James rubbed his face. His distressed state was making me feel sick. "You insisted bringing the girl to the ballgame would not cause a stir." He inhaled deeply. "Well, it has. Marvin Miller has taken a fancy to her, and his mother knows about it." The groaning noise he made was loud enough to wake the children. "Susan surely has told Zeke by now."

"It doesn't matter if Marvin is sweet on Charlie. He won't see her again before she leaves. The bishop has more important things to focus on than a girl visiting the community," I insisted, hugging a pillow to my chest. My own words didn't convince me.

"Ack, Lucinda. Your gentle spirit is muddying your thoughts. Marvin hasn't shown interest in courting until Charlie came along. If it comes out that she's pretending to be Amish and we've facilitated the lie, Zeke and Susan will be furious. I wouldn't be surprised if they asked for our punishment before the congregation." He pressed his fingers into the sides of his forehead. "We'll be shunned for sure. And all for a stranger."

"Charlie isn't a stranger to us anymore. She's our guest and she needs our help. We're doing the right thing, although"— I took a quick, sharp breath—"perhaps we went about it the wrong way."

"What's done is done." His expression was grim. "The girl should go tomorrow. I'll meet with Zeke, explain the circumstances, and beg for forgiveness. That's our only salvation."

Hot blood surged to my head as I rounded on him. "What about Charlie's salvation? Does her life not matter to you?"

"She's a troubled Englisher." James realized how high his voice rose and dropped it with a quick look toward the door. "Charlie Baker is not our concern. Especially when this ruse is dangerous for our standing within the community. She's devious, Lucinda. Can't you feel the touch of the devil inside our home since she came here?"

I pushed off the covers and swung my legs over the side of the bed. The hardwood floor was cool on my feet as I padded across to the window. Fast-moving clouds blocked out the moonlight, and the yard was dark. The tinkling sound from the windchimes grew louder with the increasing wind. Lifting my face to the breeze, I thought back to finding Charlie standing next to Goliath. She had appeared small and lost at the great horse's side. A connection with the girl had formed in that instant, one that only grew stronger when her boyfriend manhandled her, shoving her into the car, and hauling her away like she was nothing more than a goat. The memory infuriated me, and now I turned my wrath onto James.

Shutting the window, I paced back to the bed and crossed my arms. "The only evil clinging to that poor girl is the man who abused her. I told you earlier that I called social services and was informed the office wouldn't reopen until Monday. I've hired a driver to take Charlie and myself into town. That's when I'll make other living arrangements for her." I sat on the edge of the bed. "You must be patient."

My impassioned words didn't sway him. "We don't have that kind of time. If the girl hadn't revealed herself to Marvin, the situation wouldn't be dire. She could have stayed the week, hidden in the house, resting up for the next leg of her journey to a better life. But her own actions put us in peril. I don't trust her. She has a wicked agenda. I suspected it before, but after tonight, I'm sure of it."

I threw my head back. "You sound foolish, James. She's a teenager who's had a rough life." I sighed, thinking back to the way Marvin had looked at her. "It's unfortunate that she's not Amish."

"What?" James' voice pitched again, and this time he didn't care. "That's a crazy thing to say."

"Why is it so crazy, huh? Englishers sometimes go Amish—"

"Ack!" He held up his palms. "Is that what you and the girl schemed all along? That's why you dressed her up in our clothes and turned her loose in the community?"

I huffed out a breath. My head felt thick. We'd never argued like this before. Working hard to regain my composure, I stared at the picture of a rustic white farmhouse on the wall. The Bible scripture in the corner read: *When anxiety was great within me your consolation brought me joy, Psalm 94:19.* I closed my eyes and said a silent prayer, asking for strength and wisdom. When I opened them, the crushing burden had lightened a little.

"I'm sorry for taking pity on an English girl. I did not lie to you the other day when I said I gave Charlie some of my clothes to wear because hers were ruined. At that moment, my only intention was to get her into something clean and without blood on it." I brought my leg up and rested it on his so that I could fully face him. "Charlie doesn't have family or friends in her life who will help her. She appears to be alone. If the outside world has been so cruel to her, why not invite her to join ours?" James opened his mouth to speak, but I tilted my head, frowned, and continued speaking. "If Marvin has taken a liking to her, and she likes him, why not trust in the Lord that it was His plan all along to unite them?"

From the roll of James' eyes and his heavy breaths, I knew he didn't like what I'd said, but his jaw wasn't as tight, and when he spoke, his tone was flat. "Problems will arise from such a union. Charlie isn't only an Englisher, she's tainted. I see it in her eyes." He met my gaze with a softer one. "But if your prayers have brought you to this conclusion, I won't stop you from talking to her about the idea—on one condition." I lifted my brows and gave a nod. "That we tell Zeke and Susan the girl's story right away. Harboring the girl secretly in our home for a short time is very different than knowingly passing her off as something she isn't. Our lies are sinful." He sat back, and when I continued to toy with a piece of my nightdress, he asked, "What do you say, Lucinda?"

The thought of facing Susan made my stomach roll. The bishop and his wife would not understand. They'd be furious. Even if James' conscious was lightened, I had to talk to Charlie and think more about what we were doing. My impulsive behavior is what caused our grief in the first place. Taking it slower from now on might be the way to go.

"That is agreeable to me, but I ask once again to give me until Monday. Charlie needs to talk to a social worker and hear her options before she makes the drastic choice to become Amish. If she decides to return to the outside world, the discussion with Zeke and Susan will not be so turbulent. I'd think their relief at learning that the English girl their son liked was gone for good might surpass the angst they'll feel for our mistake."

James shook his head. "It's bad all around. Marvin will be disappointed to find out Charlie is English. I feel for him."

Sensing my husband had given up on his plans to race over to the bishop's house in the morning with the sordid details, I could finally breathe freely. It would be a good time to distract him from any thoughts about Charlie, Marvin, and all the unintentional lies we'd weaved in only a couple of days. I firmly believed it was alright to fib when it served a greater good. Surely, the Lord would forgive us.

Lifting the blankets, I crawled onto James, straddling his waist. When I lowered my mouth to his, he parted his lips. Our kiss was hungry. James didn't like fighting any more than I did. Our minds might not always agree, but our bodies would come together in joy. The sun would rise on a new day, and everything would be alright.

But as James' hands roamed my body and his skin rubbed mine, I couldn't forget about the English girl in our guest room. James was right. No matter how it turned out, I sensed trouble was on the wind.

15

SADIE

"**D**illon Cunningham is not the owner of the Malibu, and he has an extensive criminal record." I tossed the file onto my desk. Russo picked it up, sat down, and started reviewing the notes. Buddy leaned forward in the other chair, rubbing his palms together.

"Start with Cunningham's record," Buddy said.

I used my fingers to count each charge. "Burglary, drug dealing, assault"—I paused for emphasis—"and pimping. He served four years jail time for his latest arrest for possession of heroin and petty larceny."

"What's his age?" Russo didn't lift his head from the materials in his lap.

"Thirty-six. Never been married and no social media presence." I folded my arms on the desk. There's a bench warrant out for his arrest in northern Kentucky for punching a woman at a bar. Turned out the woman was prostituting for him."

"Who owns the car then?" Buddy's brisk voice showed his impatience.

"Denton and Camille Baker from Covington, Kentucky. Cincinnati is right across the river." I glanced out the window. The sun fought with dark-rimmed, gray clouds and was losing. It looked like it would be raining within the hour.

"Have you contacted them?" Russo asked.

I pulled my gaze from the window. "That's where it gets interesting. The license plate on the car is a fake. The only reason I found out about the Bakers is because there was a hit in the database for a brown Malibu. Authorities in northern Kentucky have been looking for it."

Russo's head snapped up. The sharp lines of his face were tight, and his eyes alert. "What kind of crime are we talking about?"

"All I know is the vehicle was involved in a felony crime."

"Good Lord," Buddy muttered. "This is getting worse by the minute."

"Are the Feds involved?" Russo set the folder back on the desk.

"Agent Nick Makris is driving down here this afternoon. Whatever's on his mind, he didn't want to say it on the phone." I toyed with a pen, twirling it between my fingers. Buddy made a long, low, groaning noise. We never looked forward to outside law enforcement coming into the jurisdiction, especially from metropolitan areas.

"The plot thickens," Russo commented, looking past me in a distracted way.

"We also have a possible identification for the redhead." I'd already talked to Buddy about the guy, but this was news to Russo. His gaze widened exactly the way I expected it to. "Jax Dover—a twenty-six-year-old local boy. After graduating from Possum Gap High eight years ago, he worked in the coal mine until it shut down. He had a run-in with my predecessor after a physical fight with his girlfriend. Did four months in lockup and has been cruising under the radar since his release one year ago."

"Sounds like you have the victim pegged. Why the *possible* remark?" Russo asked.

"His name only came up from his prints due to the prior arrest. No one has come forward about him, either as a missing person or concern, after reading the Possum Gap Ledger article and our printed description." I pursed my lips and shook my head. "I've never seen anything like it."

Russo's mouth spread into a loose smile. He was amused. "Sounds to me like there's a coverup underway."

"What would a family have to cover up? Jax Dover is a supposed victim." I had a bunch of repugnant ideas swirling around in my head, but I was curious about what Russo had to say.

"The name Dover doesn't ring any bells?" Russo asked.

"Of course. Our main eyewitness is a Dover, but that's a common name around here."

Russo nodded. "Perhaps...although what a coincidence."

Buddy spoke up. "When are they coming to ID the body?"

I glanced at Russo. He looked expectantly back at me. "At two o'clock. It's going to be a busy day."

He smirked. "Just the way I like it."

Darcy walked in. Her eyes flicked to Russo, and even though her skin was dark, I could have sworn she blushed. When our eyes met, she flashed me her usual please-say-yes expression. "Can I steal the coroner for lunch?"

Three murders, a possible link to a prostitution ring, a car with ties to a crime in the big city, and an inbound federal agent shouldn't keep anyone from lunch, right? I chuckled at my inner dialogue. "As long as he's back before two, sure, go ahead."

"No worries." Russo stood up and stretched as if preparing for a lunch date with Darcy was comparable to a marathon run. "This is one corpse viewing I don't want to miss."

"Buddy, go ahead and make the rounds in town. This case can't distract us from all of our usual duties."

"I'm on it."

When I was alone, I rubbed my forehead. I'd checked in with Sandra earlier in the morning, and Chloe was still skulking, but fine, otherwise. Sending my daughter a text seemed a little too impersonal under the circumstances, but I wasn't sure if I could deal with her sullen attitude at the moment either. "What the hell, might as well begin mending fences before I pick her up on Monday," I said to myself and reached for my cell phone.

"Woo wee, is it time for a break yet?"

The perky voice broke through my dreary thoughts, and I set the phone down. When I saw what my best friend, Tanya Beaumont, had in her arms, I sighed happily, pushing the files out of the way to make room on my desk.

"Girl, I thought you might need a mid-day pick-up." Tanya set down the shopping bag from my favorite café in Possum Gap. It was actually the only café in Possum Gap, but that didn't take away from its excellent espresso and delicious cinnamon rolls.

"You're an angel, Tanya." She sat in Buddy's chair while I pulled the tall cups and box out of the bag. I popped the lid and closed my eyes, savoring the aroma before I took a sip. "Seriously, I needed this."

Anyone could tell Tanya and Darcy were sisters separated by about a decade. They had the same oval, smooth faces, and large brown eyes. Tanya had a bit more meat on her bones and was slightly taller than her younger sister. She also left her shiny black hair bushy and artfully wild, whereas Darcy liked to straighten hers or keep it pulled back neatly. Tanya wiggled a small bottle out of her purse and wagged it in the air. "Want to spruce up your coffee with a drop or two of this?"

We'd graduated together nearly twenty years ago, but the mischievous smile tugging my friend's mouth made it seem like we were back in high school sneaking a few drops of Jim Bean into our milk cartons during lunch. We were naughty back then. I opened the box with the rolls and got my fork ready. "Not today. I have a meeting with a federal agent later, so I better be on my game."

She slipped the bottle back into her purse and dropped it to the floor. I handed her a roll, and she dug in. "Bless your heart, you've got quite a mess on your hands." She cocked her head, a fork full of gooey roll suspended in front of her face. "Darcy told me all about it." She looked back at the door that was slightly ajar and whispered, "Even the sex stuff."

I held in a smile, not remembering discussing any *sex stuff* with Darcy. The secretary/receptionist had her fingers on the pulse of the office, that was for sure. I might have to have a talk with her, but as long as she only shared the information with Tanya, I was fine with it.

"You aren't kidding. The dead guy from Wilkins had his own business, an attractive wife, and a couple of kids. Yet we found him in the middle of nowhere in a trailer that any decent human being would be leery of approaching, let alone going into." I took a bite, chewed, and swallowed. The dark conversation didn't affect the mouthwatering taste of the cinnamon roll. "I'm sure the bastard was there to buy sex. The only problem is that no women have turned up."

Tanya grunted. "Maybe it's a guy-on-guy thing, you know?" She lifted a brow, dead serious.

"Naw, I doubt it. But I'm missing something. Hopefully, after I speak to the agent, I'll have something to go on."

The window rattled, and I looked over at the raindrops pelting the glass. "Great, just what we need, another storm."

Tanya took a sip of her brew and eyed me. "How's Chloe doing? That girl was in a mood when I picked her up from the pool."

I let out a breath and set my cup down. "Not much better. She didn't want to stay with Ted and Sandra. I have too much going on this week to get her back and forth to work, let alone feed her, and stuff like that."

"Why didn't you call me? I would have been happy to have her—bitchiness and all."

"I would have, but it's about time Ted stepped up and became a real dad because it seems that one parent in the picture isn't cutting it." I leaned back and watched the water making trails down the glass. "It's my fault. I'm hardly ever home, and when I am, I'm exhausted. This job takes a toll."

"Ah, don't be too hard on yourself. You always do the best you can. Being a single mom isn't easy. It's been hard enough for me without kids to get through a damn divorce, and I'm just a realtor. I don't know how you survived this shit."

Tanya wasn't one to sugar coat anything. "With your help, that's how I made it through. And I'm going to be there for you too. Once things settle down here, we'll have a night with adult beverages and binge one of our favorite shows."

"I'm fixin' to hold you to it." She pointed at me.

"When will the divorce be finalized?"

"Well, it would have been last week except for Joey dragging the case out. He wants the damn RV, and the judge is going to have to make that decision. I'm not just handing it over to him. I think it's worse that he hired your ex as his lawyer. It's almost as if Ted is egging him on."

"Wouldn't surprise me. Being my friend goes against you. But it's a small town, and you're a popular woman. If it gets out that Joey's giving you a hard time after his fling with the Sunday school teacher, he'll get an earful." I knew my smile was wicked. "I can help spread the word."

"Ha." Tanya wagged her finger at me. "That's why you're a good sheriff. You get things done." She picked up her trash and tossed it into the can. "I better get a move on. I have an appointment to show a house on Mulberry Road, and with this rain, I should leave a little early."

I came around the desk, and when I hugged her, I caught a whiff of her signature perfume. It was a familiar smell and a burst of normalcy. "Be careful. The roads are bound to be slick."

"Sure thing. Hang in there, girl. I'm betting you'll have those murders solved by next week."

Tanya's optimism about my abilities was flattering but not realistic. Sometimes cases like this took years to figure out. Plopping back down in my seat, I swiveled the chair to stare out the window. The dreary day matched my mood.

A sense of foreboding settled over me as I watched the rain come down. Whoever shot those men were out there somewhere. Was it Dillon Cunningham? If not, then who? I also had the gut feeling that there were others in that trailer the night of the murders.

And if I was correct, more lives could be in danger.

16

CHARLIE

I tiptoed down the stairs, pausing on the last step. Clinking noises came from the kitchen, and I guessed Lucinda had started the canning she'd talked about at breakfast. Holding my breath, I continued padding quietly across the foyer and out the front door. When I got the door closed, I sagged against it, letting out a long breath.

"Where are you going?"

My heart leaped into my throat, and I spun around to find Sarah staring up at me. She resembled her mother right then, with her arms crossed over her chest and her face laced with concern.

I forced a wide smile. "Oh, it's such a nice day, I thought I'd take a walk around the farm."

The little girl's brows knitted. "It's getting ready to rain."

My smile faded. I bent down to look the child in the eye. "I like the rain, and if I want to take a walk, it's none of your business."

Sarah wasn't intimidated. "Mamma told you at breakfast not to leave your room today."

The stubborn lift of her chin made me clench my teeth. I grasped her skinny arm and squeezed. "If you tell your mom you saw me outside, you'll regret it."

"You're hurting me," Sarah whined as she tried to tug her arm away.

"You'll hurt a lot more if you don't keep your mouth shut. Got it?"

Sarah's lip trembled, and she dropped her head. "I won't tell."

I let go and left her behind as I jogged down the porch steps. I didn't like being mean, but I wasn't going to be held prisoner inside the guest room for the next few days either. Mr. and Mrs. Miller thought they could keep me hidden away, like Dillon had, but they were wrong. I had an idea that might be my salvation, and no one was going to stop me.

Just like we planned, when I turned the back corner of the barn, I saw Marvin sitting atop Sierra. A long lead line stretched from his hand to another horse, one with large white splotches covering its brown coat. The bossy kid was right. Gray clouds were low in the sky, and the wet smell of rain hung in the air. Not wanting the weather to cancel our ride, I walked forward quickly, stopping next to the new horse. "He's beautiful," I said.

Marvin dismounted. He smiled broadly like he always did when he looked at me. "That's Rebel. Don't let the name fool you. He's a good boy, and he doesn't have a rebellious bone in his body." He tilted his head to the sky. "We might get rained on. Are you alright with that?"

"A little rain won't kill us. As long as the horses don't mind." My heart beat faster when I reached out and stroked Rebel's neck.

Our shoulders brushed as Marvin stood next to me, tightening a leather strap on Rebel's saddle. "I think they like the rain, especially during the summertime when it's hot."

Marvin stepped back and flicked his hand at the stirrup. It felt like my heart would explode out of my chest, and the inside of my mouth became chalky. Swallowing with difficulty, I glanced at Marvin. His gaze sharpened with understanding. He pointed to the stirrup again. "Put your left foot in here and grasp the saddle horn with your left hand and the cantle with your right, then pull yourself up."

I still didn't move. A week ago, I'd never petted a horse; now I was supposed to ride one? If I refused to get on the horse, Marvin would have no reason to stay. He might even be mad that I'd wasted his time bringing Rebel to the Coblentz farm.

"I can help you," Marvin coaxed. He stepped back to search toward the house. "Is anyone here?"

I nodded slowly, continuing to stare at Rebel. "Lucinda, Sarah, and the baby. Josh went with his father to the feed mill."

"Come on. We don't want anyone to see us. My da will have my hide if he finds out I'm secretly riding horses with you before we're courting."

His words jabbed my mind. *Courting?* The sound of it made me imagine long-ago days where women wore fancy gowns and carried umbrellas. And did he mean that he planned for us to court? I had many questions, but one popped right out of my mouth. "You're almost twenty-one, and you'll get in trouble for horseback riding with a girl?"

The corner of his mouth scrunched, and he narrowed his eyes. "You're so different, Charlie. From your name to your overly laidback community and now your ideas. If I didn't know better, I'd think you were an English girl in disguise."

My heart stopped beating. I was sure of it. It was hard to laugh, but I forced myself to. "That's ridiculous. Boys where I come from are encouraged to have some fun before they settle down."

He snorted and grinned at the same time. "Your elders must allow Rumspringa. That makes sense."

I had no idea what he was talking about but needing him distracted and feeling a raindrop hit my face, I inhaled deeply and lifted my foot into the stirrup. Before I could change my mind, I placed my hands onto the saddle the way Marvin had shown me and hoisted myself up. My quivering legs were almost my undoing, but Marvin came to my rescue. He grasped my hips and lifted. After I threw my leg over, straddling Rebel's back, I remembered I was wearing a dress. This one was blue, and because Lucinda was a few inches taller than me, the bottom of the polyester dress was long enough to cover most of my pale calves. It would have been considered extremely modest by anyone's standard, at least, anyone not Amish.

Marvin must have seen the concern on my face. He patted my tennis shoe. "No worries. We'll stay hidden in the trees. No one except me will see your legs." He hesitated, looking up under thick lashes. "Is that all right, Charlie?"

It was strange for a guy to ask me if it was okay to look at my legs. I could only nod my head firmly, and when his hands hovered over mine as I gripped the saddle horn tightly, he asked, "May I?" Again, I couldn't speak and nodded my response. "Here, hold the reins. I'll lead Rebel, but just in case, you should always be able to take control." Since my white-knuckled grasp of the horn wouldn't relax with gentle hands,

Marvin pried my fingers apart to stuff the leather reins into them. He smiled up at me. "You're going to be fine. Relax."

He pulled Sierra closer, then swung up in the saddle. By the time we were moving, a drizzly mist fell on our heads. My scalp itched beneath the cap, but I didn't dare reach up to scratch it. The back-and-forth swaying movements had me hunched over and clinging for dear life with my legs as Marvin led Rebel along a narrow, dirt path behind the barn. He aimed for the corn, and within minutes, we reached the cover of the tall stalks. The last time I'd come through here it had been raining, but unlike today, I had been hungry and my feet were killing me. Feeling a little bit more convinced that Rebel wasn't about to kill me, I loosened up enough to wiggle my toes and arch my heel inside the tennis shoes. I could feel a trace of discomfort but nothing like before. My wounds were healing.

Marvin glanced over his shoulder. "How do you like it?" He sat confidently in his saddle, moving with the horse like they were one and the same.

I drew in a breath, swatting at the sharp leaves smacking my arms. "It's bouncier than I thought it would be."

Marvin laughed. "Now, this is bouncy." He clucked to the horses and they sped up.

A screech escaped my lips, and I clung to the saddle with every muscle I had. Marvin's laughter kept me from cussing him out. I'd really blow my cover then. Besides, I didn't want him to think I was a complete wimp. The effort to stay on and the cramping pain to my side kept my mouth closed.

"We're almost there," Marvin said, pointing to the fast-approaching tree line at the end of the corn rows. Once he tugged Rebel beneath the branches, he pulled the reins back, and we slowed back down to a walk. Marvin was right. Walking was a lot less bouncy.

It was drier beneath the trees and a shade darker too. I inhaled the scent of the pine. All was quiet except the squeaking of the saddles and the breathing of the horses. Not even a bird chirped. "I love the forest," I said.

Marvin slowed Sierra until Rebel walked alongside her. Our knees bumped and the twittering sensation in my stomach I'd experienced the night before returned. He looked sideways, and I went on, "You asked me things I like to do." I breathed in deeply, then exhaled. "Trees make me happy."

Marvin's eyes wandered over my face and his mouth lifted. "Me too. I'd like to build a cabin in the woods someday—a place where I can take my family for the weekends."

A picture of Marvin's idyllic future sprang to life in my mind. The cabin would be made of logs and have a porch swing like the Coblentz's had on their porch. Smoke would puff out of a chimney, and graceful deer would step right up to one of the windows for treats.

"That sounds wonderful," I breathed.

Our horses walked in sync, and the soft bumping of our knees continued. My breaths were shallow. I was afraid I'd mess something up. I shouldn't have stressed about it. Marvin had other things on his mind.

"When's your birthday?"

The abrupt question erased the hazy forest around us, bringing the brown trunks and green leaves sharply back into focus. "November 2nd. Why?"

"I want to get you a present." Somewhere along the way, he'd snatched a long stem of grass, and now he balanced it between his lips.

The racing of my heart and the butterflies in my stomach made me feel woozy. "I won't be around when it's my birthday," I replied. For all he knew, it was the truth.

"We'll see about that." His jaw was set.

Even though the air was cool and wet, warmth spread through me. "I wouldn't mind staying in this community, but I'm not sure how that would work."

"If the Coblentz family sponsors you, my da would allow it."

Marvin had put some thought into this already. He sounded awfully confident. We walked and talked until the terrain became steep, and my focus to stay on the horse took all my energy. I even closed my eyes sometimes when we rode along the edge of a rocky cliff or crossed the fast-moving, shallow creek. Rebel never faltered, and by the time the horses stepped into a flat grassy area, I had let go of the saddle horn. Tall grass surrounded a wooden structure. It was square-shaped and likely had only one room inside. "What's that?" I was struck at the rustic prettiness of the lonely little cabin in the woods.

"Members of the community use it for hunting. There's a table...and a bed in there."

I cupped my mouth to keep my smile hidden. "Can we check it out?"

"Of course."

Marvin dismounted before me, tying the two horses to the hitching rail. Then he came around Rebel's side. He braced the saddle with his left hand and offered to help me down with the other. I couldn't wait to get off the horse but was surprised when my leg shook like jelly as I brought it back over Rebel's rump. Marvin once again, without shyness, placed his hands on my hips while I stepped down. He didn't immediately let go, and I looked up at him.

"I'm really glad you came to Possum Gap, Charlie." The emotion in his voice was unmistakable. It convinced me I was doing the right thing.

"I want to look inside." I didn't take my eyes off Marvin's face. I saw the apprehension there when his gaze flicked to the shed's door and back at me. His confidence wavered. Poor Marvin looked frightened.

I took his hand and led the way into the shed. The door scraped across the wooden floor, and my nose filled with a musty smell. Dust particles danced in the shards of light streaming in through the one tiny window. The bed was rough looking, but a lot better than the dirty mattresses I was used to laying on.

Marvin closed the door and faced me. For once, he wasn't smiling. There was a mixture of hunger and anticipation in his eyes. He dropped his gaze when he began unbuttoning his shirt. I didn't stop him. Tugging the bottom of his shirt from his pants, I quickly finished the job for him. He gasped when I touched his bare chest. My fingertips held a power that I hadn't thought about before that moment. The realization made me brave.

I swayed closer and lifted my chin, parting my mouth slightly.

"Are you sure, Charlie? I didn't show you the shed thinking about us doing…anything." He sounded flustered, his words bobbing in the air.

"It's what I want." I pulled the dress over my head, then slipped off the bra, dropping both things onto the floor.

Marvin blew out a breath and lowered his mouth to mine. The touch was light at first. When I slipped my tongue into his mouth, he groaned into mine. Then his arms looped around me, his hands squeezing and moving up and down my back.

Everything had worked out perfectly.

17

SADIE

The faint scent of formaldehyde made me exhale. I hated the smell. It added to the discomfort of the cold room in the basement of the morgue. The walls were a glaring white, and the body drawers, stainless steel. Coming down here never got easier, especially on the rare occasions when a body had to be identified. Most families were distraught, and the emotional aspect added a sickening realness that the corpse on the table used to be alive. The times when the family members were reserved, callously so, made it worse. Like now. I crossed my arms as I stood to the side, hugging myself.

This was Russo's territory. I gladly let him take charge of the scene. He carefully draped the paper blanket back, revealing a redheaded man in his twenties—Jax Dover. His skin would have been tanned when living. A large red birthmark covered part of his left cheek. His hair had been pulled back in a ponytail when we'd bagged him at the trailer. Russo had let it down, showing its long length. Jax was tall and lanky. He would have stuck out in a crowd.

I studied the woman and man who stepped forward. They were his mother and stepfather—Geraldine Dover and Jessie Dixon. Her hair was gray at the roots, but the ends were the same bright color as Jax's. The man's bearded face was indifferent, but the mom sniffed a couple of times. They were both dressed like they'd just returned from a hike in the woods. It seemed people from the Dover clan were more at ease outside in nature than hemmed up in any room.

"Yep. That's him," Jessie said with no emotion at all.

Russo lifted the blanket to cover the man back up, but Geraldine stopped him.

"Wait!" She moved to her son's side, bent forward, and kissed his forehead. "You're a good boy, Jax. You done right. The family is grateful."

Her mountain accent was thick, but I understood her plainly, and it caused my heart to stutter. What a strange thing to say to her dead son.

Russo eyed me as he finished covering Jax. He'd picked up on her statement as well.

I came forward and placed my hand on Geraldine's shoulder. "Let's go into the other room." She let me guide her out of the morgue while Jessie and Russo followed behind. The conference room was small, but at least it had a coffee machine. "Would you like a cup of coffee?" I glanced between Geraldine and Jessie.

He gave a brisk shake of his head, and she said, "That would be appreciated."

I started the coffee brewing and sat down across from the couple. "I'm very sorry about your son. We'll release him tomorrow to the funeral home of your choice."

"We're taking him straight home. There's a family plot on

Jewelweed Hill. Like all our kin, he'll be laid to rest in a pine box there."

Burial laws in Kentucky were fairly lax, so I let it go. "I'm sorry to talk about anything upsetting, but I do have a few questions about Jax, if you don't mind."

Geraldine looked at her husband, but he didn't say anything. She pursed her lips and nodded. "What do you want to know?"

"How was Jax doing since he was released last year?" I didn't use the word prison on purpose, trying to show some respect to the woman's son.

She swallowed. "He kept to himself mostly. Picked up vaping and lost a lot of weight. Frankly, I was worried about him." She shook her head and stared at the tabletop between her hands. "He got clean in the joint, but since he's been out, I think he was using again." She paused, and I had another question fired up, but she continued. "The last couple of months, Jax was better, though. He'd been spending time with his cousin, Christen, and I think it helped quiet his mind and urges."

"Christen Dover?" I remembered her. She was a year older than Chloe and a cheerleader at Possum Gap High School.

"That's right. She's a blessing, that one. Easy going, not like her fool mother," Geraldine said.

I also knew her mom. We'd gone to school together, although I'd lost track of her years ago. We didn't hang out either. She was a hill girl, through and through. When she hadn't been jumping a girl in the hallway for glancing at her boyfriend, she was in detention for something else. She also had the signature Dover red hair.

Come to think of it, I hadn't noticed Christen at the last few football games. "Is Christen still cheering?"

"She was until—"

"She quit." Jessie interrupted without looking at his wife. His deep frown caused me to lean over the table and direct all my attention to him.

"Why would she do that? Wasn't she one of the captains?"

Geraldine opened her mouth to speak, but Jessie beat her to the punch. "Her business is none of yours. I thought we were here about Jax," he said with a snarl.

Okay. Jessie had a secret to hide. Why else would he be so blatantly hostile?

"All right. I'll get to the point. Do you know why Jax was in that trailer when he was shot?"

Jessie answered. "Your guess is as good as ours. That boy had issues. We tried to guide him in the right direction, but he was hard-headed and never took advice."

I looked at Geraldine. Her lips were pressed firmly together. She blinked her eyes. The woman was in distress. It could be that she just saw her son's body, but my gut told me there was something else bothering her. The way Jessie worked hard to keep Geraldine from talking put him doubly on my radar.

"Have you heard of Dillon Cunningham?" I caught the flaring of both pairs of eyes. "He might have been Jax's friend."

"Never heard of him." Jessie finally acknowledged his wife and asked, "You?"

She shook her head stiffly.

Jessie pushed away from the table and stood up. "Anything else?"

I rose and leveled a hard look at him. "Usually, when people are murdered, families beg me for justice. They call me every day asking for news. Not you two, though. No one in your entire family came forward. We had to come to you. Why is that?" I fixed my gaze on Geraldine. "Weren't you wondering where Jax was these last few days?"

Jessie started to bark something out when Geraldine raised her hand. Surprisingly, he did what she wanted and snapped his mouth shut.

"Jax hadn't come around the house for a while. It was like him to up and disappear. We didn't even know he was missing." She sounded defensive.

Jessie nodded vigorously as if cheering her answer on.

"Aren't you at all curious about who murdered him?" I said bluntly.

Geraldine swallowed. Her gaze wasn't misty any longer. "Good luck finding that out, sheriff."

Russo's eyes bulged, and his mouth dropped open. I felt the same way but tried harder not to show it. The couple left the room without another word and I sunk down in the chair, lost in thought.

"They're hiding something," Russo said.

Yes, they were. Geraldine's challenge just upped the chances of me unraveling the truth. The hills that the Dover clan claimed as theirs were well within my jurisdiction.

"I believe, after we talk to the federal agent, we'll make a trip out to Jewelweed Hollow."

18

LUCINDA

Martha folded her hands on her lap and looked expectantly at me. Not only was she my friend, but Martha also had a head full of common sense, and she wasn't prone to being judgmental or—perhaps more importantly—she wasn't the gossipy sort. She would keep a secret. I just had to figure out exactly what to say.

The rain persisted, and James had mentioned more stormy weather was on the way. It was appropriate weather for my gloomy mood. Strangely, it had rained almost every day since Charlie had arrived.

Meeting Martha's focused gaze, I decided to be as honest as I could be without telling her the full truth. James wouldn't want me to say too much anyway. "It's about Charlie." I paused and let out a rough sigh. "She's a troubled girl. I wanted to help her, and that's why she's staying with us. But in a few days, she'll return home." I glanced through the spindles of the front porch railing. We were alone. Phoebe napped, and Charlie rested in her room. Josh was with his father and Sarah had gone over to the neighbor's house to play. I shouldn't be so nervous to have the conservation with my friend. "Have you heard about Marvin Miller being sweet on her?"

Martha nodded. The corner of her mouth curved up. She was slow to respond, thinking carefully about her words. "Marvin is a fine young man. Perhaps a relationship with him will help your cousin with whatever ails her," she suggested.

Yes, that would have been the case if Charlie was Amish. But she wasn't. It wasn't the time to enlighten Martha either. "I can't tell you everything. It's not my"—I fidgeted with a hem of my blue dress—"place to give too much away. A match between Marvin and Charlie is out of the question." I slumped in the rocking chair. "I fear that the situation is out of my hands."

Martha swatted her hand in the air. "Eh, when it comes to romance and young'uns, we don't have a lot to say." She tilted her head, and her expression sobered. "I can tell you that I heard the bishop and his wife are amiable to courtship between them. Especially Susan. She's thrilled for him to finally have an eye on settling down."

The back of my throat was dry. The gossip line was already revved up. Everyone's tongues must be wagging. "What am I to do?"

Martha gave me a half-smile. "If telling the entire truth is out of the question, then you should explain the situation to Susan the same way you did for me. She's usually a reasonable woman, and she knows you are the same. If it were me, I'd assume a courtship would not be in the best interest of my son if you said so." Martha stood up, raising her finger. "A word of advice, if it's possible to send her home early, you should do so. The longer the girl is here, the more likely a budding relationship between her and Marvin will grow."

She was right about that, but I'd made a promise that I couldn't tell Martha. She wouldn't understand my dilemma without knowing the entire story. "You have to go so soon?"

I followed her down the porch steps. "I told Lydia I'd babysit her little ones while she went to a doctor's appointment. I don't want to be late. The poor woman is a nervous ninny most days. I shouldn't add to her stress level when she'll probably have her blood pressure checked."

I smiled at Martha's back. She never said no to anyone, but she was likely to complain a bit for her effort. "I'll see you at church."

Martha paused with one foot on the step into the buggy. "Call me if you want to talk. I'll be home this evening."

After we said our goodbyes and I made my way slowly back up the steps to the front porch, my eyelids grew heavy and my limbs more so. I'd barely slept a wink the night before. James and I had hardly talked. He was still upset about Charlie, and he had a right to be. I despised conflict, but even more, I hated the sense of dread that had been building inside of me over the past couple of days. There were no easy answers. I'd started out trying to help an English girl in need, and now I had troubles with my husband, and soon, the community. What a mess I'd made of things. I should have listened to James at the get-go. Charlie's problems were beyond me. She was better off with her own people.

The sound of the telephone ringing in the shed came through the open doorway. Feeling a burst of energy, I spun around and jogged back down the steps and across the yard. An umbrella wasn't necessary. The rain had tapered off to a hard drizzle. It was still stuffy inside the shed when I picked up the receiver.

"Hello." I pressed my backside against the table that the telephone sat on.

"Mrs. Coblentz, your message was passed along to me. I don't usually work Saturdays, but I can absolutely meet with you tomorrow. Do you want to bring the girl into town, or should I make the trip out to the settlement?"

The social worker's words were music to my ears. "It's best if I hire a driver and meet you at your office. Does late morning work for you?"

"It does. I'll be in the office catching up on paperwork until around one o'clock. Call me if you change your mind."

"I will. Thank you." When I hung up the phone, I made a little hop and threw my head back. Tomorrow, the uncomfortable mess I'd gotten myself into would be over.

I jogged back to the house as quickly as I'd left it. Once through the front door, I slowed and inhaled deeply, collecting my thoughts. It might not be so easy to convince Charlie that leaving the following morning was for the best. I dreaded the conversation with her and dragged my feet up the steps to the second floor. Quietly, so I didn't wake Phoebe, I softly rapped on the guest room door. *Better to get the discussion over with*, I told myself.

Several knocks later and no Charlie, I turned the handle and peeked in. She had blankets covering her head, and the book I lent her sat unopened on the nightstand. A flutter of annoyance churned in my stomach. An Amish girl would never sleep this late, even on her day off from chores.

I silently crossed the room. When I reached the bulge of blankets, I went to gently shake Charlie awake. My hand sunk into the bedding. I flung the blankets back and discovered an empty bed.

Hurrying out of the room, I first checked all the rooms upstairs, even at the risk of waking Phoebe. Charlie wasn't on the second floor. I descended the staircase, holding my breath. Searches of the kitchen, family room, bathroom, and basement came up with no sign of her.

By the time I stepped back into the kitchen, my heart pounded furiously. "Where can she be?" I muttered to myself, grasping the edge of the tabletop. All kinds of mischief flashed through my mind, quickly followed by stifling worry. Charlie might be anywhere.

A rap at the door spun me around.

"Hullo, Lucinda. Do you have a minute? I'd like to talk."

It was Susan Miller. Her maroon dress and smiling face appeared through the screen. I drew in a deep breath, gathering my wits. Pretending nothing was amiss would be difficult. Susan was a perceptive woman, and being the bishop's wife gave her authority over me. The day couldn't get any worse. "Of course." I hurried to the door screen door and opened it. "I'm surprised you took the buggy out in the rain."

Susan swept into the kitchen. She smelled like cookies, and there was a smudge of flour on the side of her dress. She held a tin container in her hands.

"I'd prefer not to travel alone in foul weather, but I couldn't pass up the opportunity to bring your family these snickerdoodles I baked this morning."

Susan set the container onto the tabletop. Her smile broadened, and my heart froze.

"That's very kind of you." I glanced away, searching for Charlie in the yard through the window. The haziness of the rainy day made it difficult to see the barn clearly. "I hate to rush you off, but there's something I'm working on that I should get back to." I regretted the sound of my voice and what I'd just said. I worried that I'd sounded rude. Normally, I would have invited Susan for a cup of tea, and we'd leisurely chat around the kitchen table, but not today.

"I'd be happy to help with your endeavors. My afternoon is free for a change." Susan stared back at me with the look of someone daring me to turn her away after her generous offer.

Rubbing my sweaty palms together, I realized that it would be impossible to get Susan to leave until she was ready to. Swallowing was painful. "I suppose I can take a quick break. Would you like a cup of tea?"

Susan immediately pulled up a chair and sat down. "I'd prefer coffee."

I nodded, then went directly to the stovetop while making small talk. "Hopefully, this horrid rain will stop soon. I imagine the creek on Butler Road is flooded. The Schwartzs might not be able to cross the bridge this evening."

"That is a distinct possibility." Other than the sound of raindrops striking the porch's tin roof through the screen door, there was a moment of ponderous silence while I busied myself at the counter with my back to Susan. "Where's Charlie? I'd like to visit with her."

I closed my eyes, taking a calming breath. "She's napping. I had her up early this morning doing laundry, and when we finished, she didn't feel well, so I told her to rest for a bit." The lies flowed too easily from my mouth. When I turned around, Susan's brows were raised. She looked disappointed.

"That's a shame. I hoped to get to know her better."

Playing dumb seemed to be my best option. "Whatever for?"

She scoffed. "Surely the girl has mentioned her interest in my son?"

I shook my head, pressing my lips tightly together.

"Hmm. That is odd. Marvin hasn't stopped talking about her since yesterday."

The pot whistled, and I fetched it off the stovetop, glad for the opportunity to look the other way and gather my thoughts. I returned to the table with a mug of coffee that I set down in front of Susan. She kept her hands folded on her lap, and I pulled up a chair. I avoided looking her directly in the eye. "Ah, you know how girls are at that age. They don't know if they're coming or going half the time."

Susan leaned in. "I'll be frank with you, Lucinda. After several years of pestering Marvin to pick a girl to court—and him ignoring me—a girl has finally captured his eye. That girl is Charlie." A frown formed on her suddenly stern face. "If the girl isn't interested in a union with my son, you must tell me immediately." Her wide-eyed expression made it obvious that she'd have a hard time believing that any girl would turn down Marvin. She sat back, but her posture was still tense. "Is there another boy back in Ohio who has captured her heart?"

Oh my, James was so right about the troubles we would encounter by bringing Charlie into our home. Helping the girl was my desire, but in the process, more people would be hurt—like Marvin. His heart would be broken when Charlie left tomorrow. Susan and even the bishop, would be mad at me and James, and we'd be lucky if we weren't punished for our deceit. I was tempted to tell Susan everything right then and there. I could beg for forgiveness, but my stomach did a somersault at the thought.

"Honestly, Susan, Charlie came to stay with us for a quick visit because she's had difficulties at home. She has a rebellious streak." I didn't have to work hard to look sympathetic.

"It's best if Marvin forgets about her. She's leaving tomorrow anyway."

"Tomorrow?" Susan pressed her hand to her chest. I wasn't expecting such a passionate reaction. "Poor Marvin will be downtrodden for sure." She shook her head, drawing in a hasty breath. "I'm surprised you'd speak ill of your own cousin. We were all a tad rebellious in our younger days. It's nothing new. A courtship is the perfect solution for an unsettled mind, don't you think?"

"It's not that easy." I stood up, wringing my hands and not able to keep my eyes from straying out the window. "Trust me, Susan. Charlie isn't the right girl for Marvin. He might be disappointed, but it's for the best to end the infatuation right away rather than cause him more grief down the line. Now, if you'll excuse me, I should check on Phoebe and get on with my day."

Susan rose more slowly. Her brow knitted. "Actually, I thought I might see Marvin over here. He left on his horse early this morning, and he took his old pinto with him on the lead line."

My heart thumped madly. It made perfect sense! Charlie had snuck out to be with Marvin. As quickly as my chest inflated with relief, it collapsed again. The English girl would not follow our hands-off courting rules. She'd likely tempt Marvin, and being a young man, he might not be strong enough to resist her charms. I clutched my neck. What if they were together? But that would mean they'd gone riding. Surely, the rain would hamper a trail ride. But then I remembered something, and I let out a ragged sigh. I could breathe again.

"Charlie is afraid of horses. She wouldn't be riding with him," I said.

Susan tilted her head. "I never said anything about them riding together. I assumed he might be taking the gelding over to the Yoder's farm. A while back, he'd promised to lend the horse to Tim's little girls to play with for part of the summer." Her eyes narrowed into dark beads. "Didn't you say Charlie didn't feel well and was asleep?"

Susan's sharp mind was the Lord's way of teaching me a lesson for all my lies. Ack. This day kept getting worse, but perhaps I could turn this in my favor. "I wasn't honest with you earlier, hoping to save my cousin from wagging tongues and you from worrying." I drew in a deep breath. "Right before you arrived, I discovered that Charlie was missing. There's a distinct possibility she feigned illness and made up her bed to disguise her absence because she went with your son."

There, I'd said it. I gripped the back of the chair.

Susan whirled away, heading for the door. "Marvin is just shy of his twenty-first birthday. We can't treat him like he's a surly teenager. He is a grown man. Any courtship will be short, and we'll support his choice fully." She stopped when her hand closed around the doorknob. "The bishop and I will expect this incident to be kept between you, James, the couple, and us." She looked over her shoulder with a set jaw. "Is that agreeable?"

"Of course," I replied quietly.

"Good. This is a hiccup in the road, nothing more." Susan went through the doorway, picked up her umbrella, and made her way back to her horse and buggy at the hitching rail.

My head dropped. If Susan knew the whole truth about Charlie, she'd realize it was much more than a hiccup. If I had my way, Susan, the bishop, and everyone else in the community would never find out Charlie was an Englisher.

Tomorrow, she'd be gone, and everything would go back to normal. The hours would pass slowly, I knew, but they would pass. All I had to do was be patient.

19

SADIE

I could have pegged Nick Makris as an agent a mile away. His navy-blue suit didn't have a single wrinkle, and he wore a Rolex wristwatch. The stylish eyeglasses sat primly on the bridge of his nose as he looked over the report I'd generated.

Raindrops continued to streak the window glass in my office. It rattled occasionally from the wind. My mind wandered back to Geraldine Dover. Why wouldn't she want us to find her son's killer? What could she be hiding?

Russo had suddenly become extremely busy when Makris arrived, hurrying back to his office in the basement. After exhibiting intense curiosity about the case, the way he'd blown off meeting with the federal agent was strange. He wouldn't be the first person spooked by a fed, but he didn't strike me as a cowardly type.

"This is definitely the car." He pointed to the picture. "That little dent there is in the exact same place of our victims' car." He dropped the picture on the desk, and I reached for it.

"Tell me about the victims." The words were thick in my mouth. I hadn't expected such dark news about the owners of the car.

"Denton and Camille Baker's bodies were found in their bed. They'd been shot to death while they slept. The ten-year-old girl, Lucy, was discovered in the garage. She had also been shot, but unlike her parents, whose bodies hadn't been disturbed after the slayings, the girl had been wrapped in a blanket. The teenager—Charlotte Baker—was never found, but it came to light during interviews with neighbors and school officials that she didn't get along with her stepfather. Abuse, possibly sexual, was suspected but never investigated."

His words didn't sit well with me. "How old was Charlotte?"

"Sixteen. She'd be eighteen now."

"At the time of the initial investigation, did you have any suspects?"

"No. That's what makes this case so unusual. I don't know if you've been up that way, but like most small cities, Covington has an impoverished area, and that's where the Baker family lived in a rundown, one-story house. Neither parents nor the kids had active cell phones. We couldn't find any social media presence, and friends and extended family didn't have much to say about the murders or that the teenager was missing."

"When no one talks, it usually means they're complicit in some way, or they believe the murders were justified. Since there's a dead child, it's hard to believe it's the latter." I cocked my head, staring at the agent. "What do you think happened?"

Makris grunted. "I don't know. My department worked with local law enforcement in Kentucky and Ohio on the case and came up empty. We suspected a burglary gone bad, but only prescription meds were found in the house. Nothing was stolen either. There wasn't any obvious evidence that the teenager ran away either."

"And yet she's never been found—alive or dead." I tucked my hair behind my ears with my fingertips while I thought about the girl. "From your telling, sounds like the older daughter's boyfriend knocked off the family, and she left with him."

"Well, yes, we'd thought of that too. It might be true, but why kill the little girl?"

Makris was several years younger than me—a newbie for all intents and purposes. Even if he'd worked the beat as a police officer before being promoted, he might not have seen some of the horrendous things I had. Human nature was complicated. People murdered for all kinds of reasons—jealousy, personal gain, sport—you name it. Too often, cops got bogged down in their thinking because they couldn't accept that some suspects were downright evil. It wouldn't surprise me at all if a teenager was involved in the murder of her parents and little sister.

I shrugged. "The kid probably saw something, or it might have been a personal grudge. Siblings don't always love each other."

"Her teachers described Charlotte as kindhearted and spunky. Although, as we compared notes from middle school and high school, the girl's personality changed as she grew older. She went from talkative and friendly to introverted and anxious. A neighbor mentioned that Charlotte argued with the stepfather often. There definitely were problems in the home."

"Can I keep the file? I'd like to talk to a couple of your witnesses."

Makris gave a slight nod. "Those are copies. You're

welcome to them. I doubt they'll do you much good." His voice was sullen. This guy wanted all the glory for solving the cold case.

"You might have missed something. I'd also like to have the state lab compare gunshot forensics on the Baker family and my trailer victims."

"We never recovered a weapon, but I suppose the lab techs can use the data collected from the wounds and gunshot ballistics on the walls." He paused, glancing at his cell phone. "Do you think our cases are related?"

"The Bakers' car being at my murder scene points to a strong connection, don't you think?"

He grunted. "The car might have been dumped a while ago and picked up by someone else—that's what usually happens. I think it's highly unlikely that whoever murdered the Baker family also shot up your drug dealers two hundred miles away."

Makris wasn't a creative thinker. "Once someone put an old Kentucky license plate on the car, it wouldn't have been noticed unless the driver made a traffic violation in front of law enforcement, especially around here. Cheap, dented cars with bad paint jobs are common in Possum Gap. There's enough evidence to at least raise suspicion that there's a connection."

He stood up, grabbing his coat off the back of the vacant chair. "Well, keep me posted. It sure would be nice to bring justice to the family, especially little Lucy." He gave a brisk shake of his head. "It leaves a bad taste in my mouth when kids are murdered."

Yeah, mine too.

When the door closed behind Makris and I was alone, I sifted through the papers until I found the ones I looked for.

I positioned the pictures on my desk. The first one showed Lucy's body tightly wrapped in a floral blanket. The second one was after the blanket had been pulled back. The poor little girl had been shot once. The bullet took off most of her face.

Whoever shot Lucy Baker had been in a rage. It was personal.

20

CHARLIE

I pulled the blue dress over my head, then went about stuffing my hair into a bun and pinning the cap back on, watching Marvin dress the entire time. Once the sex ended, he'd been too shy or guilt-ridden to look at me until I had clothes on. He sat on the edge of the bed, his back to me, while he laced up his black boots. Rain still loudly drummed the tin roof, and the window was fogged up.

He found his voice. "What are your plans this evening?"

Poor Marvin was so clueless. I wasn't sure what I would do minute to minute, and he expected me to have plans. "I don't know. Why?" I couldn't help it if I sounded suspicious.

He pivoted to face me. "School begins next month. I signed up with several other young people to clean the schoolhouse and make some repairs. You can come, too." When I didn't say anything and continued to stare at him, he quickly added, "It will give us a chance to see each other again."

I crossed my arms as my skin heated. "Is that the only way we can get together—by volunteering?"

A look of confusion flushed his face and darkened his blue eyes. Now that we'd done the deed, I wasn't sure if I wanted to continue with the charade of being Amish. It was exhausting, but it might be too soon for Marvin to hear.

"There are rules we'll have to follow while we're courting, you know that. We should talk to my parents about setting a wedding date right away. That way, we won't have to sneak around like this." He gestured at the bed with his hand, then waited for me to respond.

Thoughts pierced my mind in quick succession. Marvin was ready to get hitched right away just because we'd fucked. It was kind of flattering, but the Amish really were backward in that regard. He had only met me a few days ago. For all he knew, I could be a psychopath. It worked perfectly with the wispy idea in my head, though, so I went with the flow.

"Sure. I'll go." I glanced out the window, trying to gauge the time. It was too overcast to tell. "Can I ride Rebel to the schoolhouse? I'm afraid if I go back to the Coblentz's, Lucinda will come up with a stupid reason why I can't go." I reached back up and fidgeted with the pins poking my head.

Marvin dropped his gaze. "I have to bring him back home first. If anyone sees us alone together, there will be trouble." When he saw me slump in disappointment, he quickly came up with a solution. "We can take the trails behind the schoolhouse, and I'll drop you off at the edge of the forest. There's a woodshed you can wait in. Once everyone starts arriving, you can make your way up the hill and join us."

He sounded so proud of his brilliant idea, I had to smile. I'd picked a smart one. "Perfect." I scooted forward on the bed and flung my arms around his shoulders. "I love you, Marvin."

A raspy sigh escaped his lips. "I love you, too."

※

The rain had turned to a smattering of droplets by the time I jogged the short distance from the cover of the trees to the woodshed that Marvin had pointed out to me. Once inside, I leaned against a stack of logs and looked out at the water-drenched field that we'd played volleyball in the other day. Marvin had assured me that people would start arriving within the hour, and he'd return as soon as he could. After the busy day and a mostly sleepless night, a wave of tiredness washed through me. My eyelids felt heavy until they fluttered closed. I listened to a cow mooing in the distance. A few minutes passed while I thought about the familiar floral pattern of the blanket in the cabin before a memory flooded my mind.

"What was that noise?"

I spun around. Lucy stood in the hallway, rubbing her eyes.

"Go back to sleep, now!" I ordered.

"Is that a gun?" Lucy stayed rooted in place, staring at what I held in my hand. "What did you do?" The demanding sound of her voice jabbed my insides painfully.

I charged, and Lucy ran backwards until she bumped into the door leading into the garage. The kid was fast. I made a grab for her but missed. She opened the door and went through.

"You hurt them, didn't you?" Her hair bounced on her shoulders as she shouted at me. There was nowhere else to run.

Dillon would be at the end of the driveway any minute now. I didn't have time to deal with the brat. "They deserved it!" I screamed back at her. "*And I did it for you. Denton would have been climbing into your bed after I left. Mom would ignore it, just like she's done for the past three years with me.*"

"*You're lying! You always lie!*"

Lucy was so spoiled and stupid. She didn't know anything.

"*Mommy!*" *she shrieked.* "*Mommy!*" *When no one came, tears dribbled down her red cheeks. Her hysteria didn't bother me as much as her narrowed eyes.* "*I'm going to tell on you!*"

"*No, you won't.*" *I advanced on her, and this time, she held her ground.*

"*Everyone is going to know what you did! Mommy!*"

"*Stop it! Stop it!*" *I grabbed her arm. She jerked it up and down, trying to rid herself of my tight grip.*

"*I hate you, Charlie!*" *she screamed.* "*I hate you!*"

Clip clop, clip clop, clip clop.

The fog lifted, and my mind cleared. I blinked until the damp grass came back into view. On top of the hill, I saw several horse-drawn buggies along the roadway. They slowed, then one by one turned into the driveway leading to the schoolhouse.

I rubbed the tears away vigorously and sucked in a sharp breath, filling my lungs until they felt like they'd burst. *It's not my fault. If Lucy had stayed in bed and not argued, it never would have happened.* I exhaled loudly, then gasped out another ragged breath.

Hearing voices, I pressed my hand to my mouth, took a few steps to the opening of the shed, and peeked out. Buggies were being parked, and some of the boys had already led their horses to the long barn to tie them up. I couldn't see Marvin, but several girls milled around on the hillside. Their brightly colored dresses stood out in the sea of wet green grass.

I patted my cheeks until they were dry and spit the mucus out of my mouth. I exhaled a long, steady breath. When I stepped out of the shed, it wasn't raining anymore. The clouds lifted, and the sky over the western hills turned a pinkish-orange color as the sun made a brief appearance before disappearing. The air was fresh and cool on my face, and the remnants of the awful images in my head were pushed back.

Putting one foot in front of the other, I slowly made my way to the group of girls. When Delilah saw me coming, she waved and stepped away from the group.

Before she reached me, I asked, "Is Rachel here?" I didn't care at all about Rachel. It was her brother I was interested in, but I couldn't come right out and ask if he had arrived.

"Not yet." She smiled, not having a clue. "I didn't expect you to clean the schoolhouse."

Glancing at the roadway, I answered her in a distracted way. "Why not?"

Delilah's smile disappeared. "Oh, well, it's something the local teens take care of. Since you're a visitor, I thought you'd be busy with your relatives."

I studied the girl's face. It was a plain face. I remembered how flustered she had been when Marvin had appeared the other night. Delilah had a crush on him, just like Vivian. That bothered me.

"I'm staying."

Delilah's eyes grew two sizes larger. "What?"

"Since Marvin and I are dating, it only makes sense, right?" Crossing my arms, I challenged Delilah to argue about it.

"Dating?" Vivian appeared from behind me. "Don't you mean courting?"

I shrugged. "Same thing."

Vivian's mouth pursed. "Maybe if you're English."

Delilah's hand flew to her mouth. "How can you be courting? Have the bishop and Miss Susan agreed to it?"

I made the mistake of pausing to come up with a suitable reply when Vivian jumped at the chance to give her opinion. "It wouldn't happen that fast." She took a step closer. "Maybe you aren't acquainted with our ways enough to know that."

My skin prickled, and the muscles through my back and neck turned to stone. "Can we talk alone, Vivian? I have something I need to tell you in confidence."

Vivian's eyes wandered to Delilah's surprised face and back to me. She hesitated, and I added, "Please."

"Fine. Just for a minute." She flicked her hand to Delilah. "Go on and get started without me. I'll be there soon."

We walked side by side towards where the buggies were parked, not speaking. She stopped beside the first buggy she came to, and I kept walking. "There's a shed down at the bottom of the hill. It's a good place to talk."

I didn't look back. After a few long seconds, she rejoined me, and we continued until we stepped inside the dim interior of the three-sided wooden building. With the darker sky came a cooler breeze and a lot of flying insects. I swatted two away from my face as I turned around to face Vivian.

She stood with hands on her hips. Her dress was a light pink color that I thought was pretty. I also envied how she managed to get her white cap fitted perfectly to her head. Maybe if I'd grown up Amish, I'd be better with the pins and everything else.

For the first time in days, a small, throbbing sensation shot through my left foot, right where the cut was healing. Horseback riding and walking up and down the hill in one day had been too much. My feet were killing me.

"What do you want to say?" she asked impatiently.

Vivian stared at me with a high-browed look of superiority. It wasn't the first time someone gave me a haughty gaze. Around a year ago, Dillon had let me go with him to a grocery store for supplies, and a woman had looked me up and down, then hustled her little boy away as if she feared they'd catch whatever I had if she stayed in my presence for more than a moment. For as long as I could remember, people treated me like I was trash. After my real dad ran off, Mom had been too lazy to get a job, so I couldn't dress in clothes that were stylish or even fit me. She and Denton spent all their money on cigarettes and alcohol; that left me in rags most of the time. No one wanted to hang out with a homeless-looking girl.

For the first time in a week, I longed for a cigarette. I swallowed down the dry taste in my mouth and lifted my gaze to Vivian's face. If I hadn't arrived, Marvin would have probably hooked up with the Amish girl eventually. She was the type of girl who got everything she wanted. And she wanted Marvin.

"Stay away from Marvin. He's mine," I said in a low voice.

"No, he's not. His parents and the congregation will have to agree, and I don't think they will," she said smugly.

My hands trembled. I took a quick breath. "Why is that?"

"Because you aren't Amish." I opened my mouth to respond, but she plowed on, "One of us would never talk that way. I overheard what you said to Rachel as well. I don't know what kind of mischief Lucinda is up to, bringing you into our community, but I'm going to get to the bottom of it. When I do, whatever lies you've told Marvin to trick him into liking you will be exposed. Then it will be over."

My vision of Vivian was marred by purple dots as blood rushed to my head. I jerked my dress off my shoulder, exposing skin. "Why don't you come over and take a sniff, Vivian. If you do, you'll smell Marvin all over me because guess what? He fucked me a few hours ago. Not once, or even twice." I raised my fingers and counted. "Three times he fucked me."

Vivian swayed. Her voice came out in a whisper. "Don't talk that way—"

I stepped forward. "Oh, but you're so smart. You figured out I'm not Amish because of the way I talk. Why can't I say what I want, huh?" I took another step and reached back; my hand folded around a piece of firewood. "How does it make you feel to know that Marvin's lips were all over me as he pushed inside me?"

"You're sick." Vivian spun around, but I was quicker.

I grasped her arm with my left hand and brought the wood down hard with my right hand. The first strike knocked Vivian backward, but she managed to reach out and steady herself with a post. Blood stained her cap, which amazingly was still pinned in place. I watched in fascination as the blood spread on the course, white material. Vivian wasn't so pretty anymore. She grimaced and reached for her head. When she looked at her bloody fingers, she made a wet, choking sound.

Our eyes met, and I saw a combination of panic and pleading in hers. But she was going to give me away and ruin everything. Her people would believe Vivian over me. I had no choice. This was the only way. I struck again. This time, she was ready and tried to block the blow with her hands. She lost her footing and fell to the ground. A puff of dust sprayed out around us as I followed her down, swinging again—and again—and again—until she was silent.

21

SADIE

I glanced in the rearview mirror. "Where'd you get that gun?" I asked Russo. Buddy turned around in the passenger seat to see what I was talking about.

"Don't worry. It's completely legal." He continued to carefully load the bullets into the .38 Special, a handgun that packed a powerful punch but a weapon I'd also deem more for gals than guys.

"What the hell?" Buddy said.

"Like I already informed you, going out to the Dover homestead in an isolated location at dusk is a really bad idea. Those people are dangerous. Anyone can see that." Russo pushed the barrel back into place and set the gun down on the seat beside him. "I don't want to die today."

Buddy huffed, and I chuckled. "Are you prejudiced against country folk, Russo? Because it certainly sounds that way." I made the turn onto the gravel road that wound through a dense stand of trees in Jewelweed Hollow. The canopy of leafy branches eliminated the last of the day's light, making the drive suddenly much darker.

"Yeah, well, I admit to some frightening preconceived notions about hillbillies living in places called hollows. Don't they all have a shotgun propped up next to the door?" He grunted, and I saw him lean sideways to look out the window. "Whenever someone refers to their family as kin, I get worried."

"Dammit, Russo. We're going to have a look around and ask a few questions," Buddy insisted. "The judge signed the search warrant, so we're all good."

"Oh, I'm not concerned about the legalities. What's bugging me is that there's just the three of us in one cruiser for the mission."

"I already explained that we don't have the manpower on a weekend to bring more officers with us. Besides, Buddy's right. The Dovers have no reason to be hostile towards us. They're close-knit, and we're investigating the murder of their relative." What I wasn't admitting was that my heart rate spiked higher the closer we got to the compound where two double-wides and six single-wide trailers were situated in a cleared field at the narrow base between two wooded hills. After the evasive way Jessie and Geraldine behaved, I really didn't know what to expect, but we had no choice except to go in and check things out.

"Ha. The Dovers aren't going to like this visit. Be prepared," Russo said. He rapidly tapped his fingers on his thighs, belying the calm, level tone of his voice.

"Make sure you keep your gun hidden," I remarked to Russo.

"You're going to allow him to be armed?" Buddy sounded incredulous.

"He's right. It's a good idea to be ready for anything." I

slowed the cruiser to a crawl, maneuvering around the water-filled ruts the best I could. At least the rain had finally stopped. That was a plus.

"What are you thinking, Sadie?" Buddy asked. "More than likely, Jax and Billy got involved with Randall Birdie over drugs or prostitution. Something went wrong, and they wound up dead. End of story."

I smiled at the simplicity of Buddy's statement. If it were only that easy. "Then who shot them?"

"We'll know better when the forensics come back, but I'd bet good money that they shot each other. The only evidence someone else was in the trailer is from John Dover. He might be protecting his cousin, Jax, for all we know."

"The DNA on the cigarettes and the mattresses will show that there was at least one woman inside that trailer. I'm sure of it. Where did she go?" I grunted and eyed Buddy. "Where are the murder weapons?"

Because of his massive size, whenever Buddy made a noise, it came out sounding like a grizzly bear's growl. "Maybe your mystery woman shot them all."

It had crossed my mind.

Russo spoke up. "My initial examination of the trailer and yard says that someone escaped out the back window. I stand by that now. Which means whoever that person was didn't shoot all the men because Billy Becker was taken down in the front yard."

"It's all conjecture," Buddy argued. "The shootings could have happened in a dozen or more ways."

That was also true, but as we left the cover of the trees and pulled into a flat patch, I felt my pulse quicken. Every inch closer to the Dovers we came, the more certain I was that we were getting closer to the truth. I caught a strong, tangy whiff of hickory smoke. A full moon hung in the grayish, milky sky right over the handful of homes scattered throughout the meadow. The barely-contained creek to our right tested its edges, but since the rain had stopped, I was confident it would stay within its banks. The raging sound of water was impressive, and so was the hill that jutted out of the trees beyond the compound. A beautiful location that was marred by junk trucks, plastic toys, and a couple of trash-filled yards. It didn't seem right calling them yards since most of them hadn't been mowed all year if the knee-high grass was any indication.

"Damn!" Russo exclaimed in a whisper. "This is worse than I dreamed it would be."

I ignored his comment, driving past the single wide-trailers and a few wild-haired gawking kids who were barefoot and in dirty clothes to reach the highest sitting doublewide. It was the only residence with a mowed yard, and other than a few plastic flamingos, a statue of Jesus, and two car dealership-sized flags—one American, the other Confederate—it was tidy.

"What's that?" Russo asked, rolling down the window in the backseat and pointing at an acre or so of bushy plants in neat rows.

"Hemp. You can apply to Kentucky's Department of Agriculture for a growing license. CBD oil is becoming a big cash crop around here."

I'd only been back in the hollow one other time, and that was before I became sheriff when a feud had been brewing between the Dovers and the Cliftons. Like a scene straight out of the Hatfield and McCoy war, the families were going to shoot it out over marijuana growing operations. Since the previous sheriff had been up to his neck in illegal shenanigans with the locals, he was able to talk both sides down, working out a plan whereby everyone profited. Back then, growing pot or anything similar was illegal. Nowadays, state officials profited directly from the taxation of CBD oil companies and their legal leases with farmers to grow cannabis. No one really paid attention to actual marijuana plants anymore. I reckoned within a couple years it would be just as legal to grow the stuff in Kentucky as it was in numerous other states. There weren't enough officers to enforce the laws on the books in all the nooks and crannies of the Kentucky wilderness, which was vaster than outsiders knew. As long as no other crimes stemmed from the production of weed, just like my predecessor and to keep peace within the county, I looked the other way.

"I'm sure that's not all the Dovers are growing back here," Russo said as he swiveled in the seat to watch the giant flags flap in the wind. "That's not something you see every day."

"Stay sharp." I nodded at a large, redheaded man walking our way. We hadn't made it to Jessie and Geraldine's home, and already a crowd had formed in the driveway, blocking our way.

Buddy's hand went to his sidearm, but he didn't pull it out. "Maybe we should come back in the morning," he suggested.

I ignored him and rolled down the window, waving the group out of the way. Not surprisingly, they didn't go anywhere, and I was forced to stop the cruiser. The large redhead bent down next to the driver's side window and looked in.

"What do ya want, sheriff?" His voice was even; not friendly, but not irate either.

"We're here to take look around and ask a few questions.

It's for Jax." I focused on the man's wide face, but I was well-aware of his bulbous gut and the combination Confederate-American flag on his t-shirt and the saying, *American by Birth, Rebel by Choice,* in bold, red print. I'd already counted eight rifles in the hands of not only the men but a few of the women in the group as well. They held the weapons casually, either slung over their shoulders or propped against their legs.

"That's not a good idea." The man wiped his nose with the back of his hand. "We're still grieving and all."

"What's your name?"

"Summit Dover," he volunteered easily.

"Summit, I have a search warrant, so let us do our job and get the fuck out of our way." I kept my voice neutral, but my words didn't faze the hulking man who rivaled Buddy's size.

"Let's not go there, sheriff."

I felt my face flush. As I gripped the door handle, Buddy grasped my arm. He shook his head slowly. When I turned back to Summit, I dropped my voice, "We don't care about anything you might be growing up here, but if I return to my office and make a few phone calls, truckloads of state badges are going to descend on your mountain, and they'll take everything from you."

Summit stared at me. I felt the strings of tension pulsating between Buddy and Russo as they sat stone still in their seats.

"Then let them come." Summit pushed off the cruiser and walked into the group of what was now around fourteen adults and too many kids to count.

I deliberated while Buddy and Russo waited for instructions. Turning back was the last thing I wanted to do, but Russo was right. The three of us weren't equipped to deal with this kind of resistance. The Dover clan's bad behavior had served one purpose. I was more certain than ever that they were involved in Jax's killing.

Putting the car into reverse, I placed my arm over the seat and looked back, avoiding the relieved look on Russo's face. Hoots and whoops followed us as we retreated like cowards back down the bouncy gravel road.

Damn rednecks.

Once the gathering was out of sight, I backed into a narrow pull-off and let the vehicle idle.

"What are you doing?" Russo pressed up against the partition, frowning.

"Do you think we're going to run away with our tails between our legs like whipped dogs?"

Buddy knocked his head back against the headrest. "Not sure if sticking around is well advised, boss."

My first deputy's tired voice drew my gaze. "They can't get away with it, Buddy. If we're not careful, the thugs will be running the town."

"They already do, and you know it." Buddy sat forward again. "I get it. You're fully invested in this case, but we don't have evidence that the Dover clan is involved. The judge gave you the warrant as a favor for not arresting his wife when you pulled her over for drunk driving last spring."

"Damn, sheriff," Russo said. "And you had the nerve to talk about how corrupt the cities are."

"It's not like that. I know Judy, and she's a good woman. She'd been drinking because her dick husband had been cheating on her. That's why the judge signed the warrant. It doesn't hurt to have a few cards in the back pocket. I'm only trying to do my job the best I can."

Buddy groaned. "Now what? Shall we sneak back in there

and do some snooping? I guarantee we won't get very far. The kids are lookouts."

A sound reached my ear, and in a fluid movement, I was out of the cruiser with my gun drawn. I saw a flash of color through the branches, and then they parted. A teenager showed herself. Her long reddish-brown hair fell over her left eye, but I could still tell that it was black and blue. The side of her face sported a large purple bruise. I recognized this girl. She was skinnier than the last time I saw her, and she stood awkwardly like she was in pain.

"Christen?" I lowered my gun as I glanced toward the road. Buddy and Russo were out of the car, looking around with tense movements.

She nodded, flicking her fingers to come closer, which I quickly did.

"You have to help me, sheriff. Please, help me get him out before they kill him." Christen talked in a wispy way, breathing hard. She must have chased after us at a full run.

"Who are they going to kill?" My heart pounded as I searched the trees past Christen's shoulder.

"I don't have time to explain. I think I can get you back to where he's locked up." She glanced at Buddy and Russo. "Not them. He's too big, and that one would never make it in the suit."

"If the sheriff goes, so do I," Buddy insisted.

I lifted my hand to cut him off without turning my head. "Okay, we'll do it your way, but you have to tell me who I'm going after."

"My boyfriend—Dillon Cunningham."

22

LUCINDA

"What do you mean? Vivian is missing?" I set Phoebe down in the playpen and turned to stare at James.

He removed his hat and ran his hand through his hair with a rough tug. "Samuel caught me at the mailbox. He says his daughter didn't come home from the schoolhouse tonight. She left her horse at the hitching rail, and there's been no sign of her since around six o'clock."

"That's odd." My stomach constricted uncomfortably. Vivian was a sensible girl, not the type to sneak off or do anything without talking to her mother first. "Louisa must be in a panic." I handed Phoebe a cracker as I gazed out the window into the darkness. "Has Samuel talked to the other girls? Perhaps she went home with a friend and forgot to mention it to her parents?"

"Why leave her horse unattended then?" He paced across the room, rubbing his chin. "Yes, he spoke with Rachel Miller and Delilah Yoder. Delilah mentioned that Vivian had been at the schoolhouse when everyone arrived, but when the girls became busy with the cleaning, they didn't notice Vivian wasn't among them until the job was finished. Rachel is the one who called Samuel on the school phone after she saw Vivian's horse still tied up, and the girl was nowhere in sight." He stopped beside the playpen, placing a hand on Phoebe's head. "Josh, bring Goliath in from the pasture and hitch him up to the buggy." Josh ran out of the house without question, and James cocked his head back to me. "The bishop called a meeting of the congregation at the schoolhouse in one hour."

I let out a breath, hurrying to the peg on the wall where my jacket was hung. "What about the children? Shall we bring them?"

He shook his head. "Parents only. The English girl can stay with them until we return."

I clutched the jacket to my chest. "Actually, I wanted to talk to you about Charlie—"

"Is something amiss?" He stopped in the middle of the kitchen, the crinkles at the corners of his eyes deeply etched. He looked like he'd aged several years overnight.

I swallowed down the spit that formed in my mouth, trying to ignore the rapid beating of my heart. With so much going on, it didn't feel right to complain too much about a girl who I had insisted on bringing into our home. Still, James needed to know some of it. "Susan stopped by for a visit today. She says Marvin would like to court Charlie and that she and Zeke approve."

"What?" he hissed the word out, then clutched the side of his head as he shook it. "So much for keeping the girl's presence secret until you could help her find her way back to the outside world."

An urgency to speak the truth made me blurt out, "That's not all. After feigning illness, she snuck out today and met with Marvin. I'm sure of it. Somehow, she ended up at the schoolhouse this evening. After helping the other girls clean, Marvin escorted her home in his buggy." The sudden widening of James' eyes prompted me to quickly add, "Rachel was with them, and it's acceptable for a sibling to chaperone, so that part isn't a problem." My shoulders curved, and I brought my fingertips to my lips. "It's what mischief they might have gotten into if they were alone earlier that worries me."

James crossed the room and picked up my hands. "The girl must go as soon as possible. I know you only wanted to help her—the same way you wish to aid anyone in harm's way—but her presence in the community is causing chaos." His eyelids drooped while his thumb swirled against my hand. "Originally, I worried about the consequences for us and our family if we were discovered to be hiding an Englisher in our house. It's not about us anymore. If Marvin is infatuated with Charlie, his heart will break when it's revealed that she's English."

I reminded him of what I'd already suggested. "What if she converted?"

James let go and paced to the playpen again. "That never works, and even if Charlie made a go of it, Zeke and Susan will not approve of their only son's involvement with an Englisher turned Amish." He leveled a hard look at me. "She has to go, Lucinda, and right away."

I leaned against the counter. "I talked to the social worker in town. If we can arrange a driver, she said we can take Charlie to meet her tomorrow. The woman is willing to come here too, but I thought that wasn't a good idea."

James shook his head. "No, no, it isn't. I'll make a few

phone calls in the morning. I'm sure one of the drivers will be willing to take a quick trip up the road. I'll offer double pay to hire someone if needed."

Sarah burst through the door. She had been locking up the chickens in the coop. "I saw Josh bringing in Goliath. Where are ya going?"

I had been telling enough lies lately, so I let James handle the response.

"A meeting has been called that your ma and I have to attend," he said smoothly.

Sarah was very inquisitive. Meetings were seldom thrown together last minute, and even more rare after night fell. "Why?"

James looked away. How do you tell your eight-year-old daughter that a teenager from the community had disappeared? I decided it best to avoid the truth altogether. "Never mind. Come wash your hands and put on your nightdress."

"Are we staying alone while you're gone?" she asked as she skipped her way to the sink.

"Where are you going?"

I pivoted on my heel. Charlie stood in the opening to the hallway. She'd changed into a different dress than she'd worn earlier, and she'd removed the cap. Her skin seemed paler than usual, and her eyes even larger. Guilt squeezed my insides that we planned to take her into town the next day. It felt eerily similar to when I'd picked up a skinny stray dog on the way home from the market one day. She was such a sweet dog and friendly with the children, so I took pity on her. After a fair amount of begging, James had reluctantly agreed we could keep her. I hadn't anticipated that Dottie wouldn't like the newcomer, and to keep the dogs from fighting, I had to lock Dottie up in the barn. The very first night on the farm, the stray killed two of our chickens, and that was the last straw. James insisted I hire a driver to take her to the animal shelter in Possum Gap the very next morning, which I willingly agreed to. The stray would never fit in, and worse yet, she had been a danger to our other animals. But that bitter knowledge didn't make it any easier when it came time to coax the unwitting dog into the car, shut the door, and walk back into the house without looking back.

Charlie was a lot like that poor pup—as much as I wanted to save her, I couldn't. The sad realization made my eyes water. I quickly wiped the tears away before she could see. "James and I must go to a parent gathering at the schoolhouse." I glanced at James, and he gave a brisk nod. "Will you keep an eye on the children while we're gone? We shouldn't be too long."

Out of the corner of my eye, I saw Sarah's head drop and heard her dramatic sigh, but my focus remained on Charlie's drawn face.

"Sure, I'll take care of them." She walked into the kitchen and straight over the refrigerator. After she poured a glass of milk, she opened the tin container and pulled out four of Susan's snickerdoodle cookies. "Is the meeting about Vivian?" she asked without looking up.

I flicked my hand at Sarah. "Go change." The girl didn't move, and I raised my voice. "Now!" That got her going.

James watched Charlie eat the cookies but didn't say anything.

I waited until Sarah disappeared into the hallway and closed the distance to where Charlie stood at the counter. "How do you know about Vivian?"

She didn't hesitate. "The other kids were talking about it while we left the schoolhouse. Rachel suspected Vivian snuck off with a boy." Charlie looked up at me under long, dark lashes. "She does that all the time, you know."

James erupted. "Do not speak ill about Vivian Hershberger! She's a respectable girl."

Charlie's brows raised, but she didn't look at James. The corners of her lips twitched. "The adults are the last ones to know."

"Stop it, Charlie!" I took a breath to steady myself. "Why didn't you mention Vivian when you returned?"

Charlie shrugged. "I didn't think it was important."

James and I exchanged glances. "There's something we need to discuss with you—"

The front door flung open, and Josh ran through it. "The buggy's ready!"

"We must go, Lucinda," James said.

I turned back to Charlie. Her hand slipped into the jar for another cookie. "It will have to wait until later." I nodded at Phoebe. "She's ready to go in the crib. Sarah and Josh will show you what we normally do."

"I'll take care of the kids. You don't have to worry." Charlie chewed on the cookie, staring at me.

I slowly followed James out the door and straight to the waiting buggy. Goliath nickered, and I touched his velvety nose as I passed by. Once inside the buggy, James snapped the reins, and the buggy lurched forward.

I looked over my shoulder at the house. The dim light shining through several windows drew my attention. A whip-poor-will repeated its chirpy noises, causing an icy chill to sweep over me even though the air was thick and warm. I shivered.

Hearing the bird's song near the house was an omen of death. The clouds spread to reveal a bright, full moon. The sudden spray of light eased my fear somewhat. I didn't look away until James turned the buggy onto the roadway, and the farmhouse disappeared from sight.

23

SADIE

It was hard to keep up with the teenager in the dark. My foot caught on a raised root, and I stumbled forward, righting myself just before I hit the ground by grabbing a low-hanging branch. We never strayed far from the fast-moving river, and its constant whooshing roar drowned out any occasional words coming out of Christen's mouth. When there was a gap in the tree line, moonlight broke through, lighting the way for short bursts of time. The scent of damp leaves flooded my nostrils, along with the occasional sharp wood-burning smell.

None of these sensations were foreign to me. I'd grown up exploring the hilly wilderness with friends. Summertime campouts and fly fishing in this very same river were so familiar, almost like spending time with an old friend. Back then, my biggest worries were chiggers, ticks, or running into an ornery mamma black bear protecting her cubs. This journey was very different. My heart banged in my chest not only from the strain of dashing through the underbrush without breaks but from fear of what I was about to face.

Christen's urgency made me less careful than I normally would be. I liked well-thought-out plans with several layers of back-up contingencies. Flying into a scene like this was terrifying, but it was also exhilarating. The adrenaline rushing through my veins sharpened my senses, giving me the illusion of invincibility. I was well aware that it was just that—an illusion. As headache-inducing as it was to think about, I could easily be shot out here, and my body disposed of in a way that it would never be found.

As I dodged branches and hopped over fallen tree trunks trying to keep up with Christen, Chloe invaded my mind. My kid was smart, kind, and independent. The perfect child, really. With each pump of my legs, I regretted our recent fight more and more. I might be a pretty good sheriff, but I'd failed as a mother. Ever since my folks had passed away and I got busy with a case, I would drop Chloe off at Tanya's or her dad's house and expect them to deal with her. She never wanted to go to Ted's, but when Tanya wasn't available, I had no choice. Deep down, I knew that all Chloe wanted was to spend more time with me and not always be second fiddle to the job.

Christen started to pull away, and I felt like my lungs would explode, but I found the strength to run a little faster without tripping on a gnarly root or a jutting rock. The girl I chased after was not much older than Chloe, and here she was, involved with a pimp and possible murderer. Whatever her family was up to would have drastic consequences for Christen. Was she being dramatic, like a typical teenage girl, or was there a real possibility that the Dover clan held a man captive with the intent of dispensing their own justice?

Even though I was sweating, a chill raced along my skin. Christen abruptly stopped, and I bumped into her back. Moonlight shined into a grassy space about twenty yards across. Jutting over the trees were well-known hilly ridges that gave me a good idea of approximately where I was in relation to the main road that led into Possum Gap. In the center of the clearing was a wooden hunting stand that reached approximately twenty feet in height. The small windows were boarded over. From this distance, I could see the shiny padlock on the door and at the foot of the ladder was a thin, scruffy-faced man. He clutched a shotgun in his hands, and I saw the puff of smoke from his cigarette. He was looking the other way.

Christen turned and whispered, "He's in there."

I bent over, carefully inhaling and exhaling. The guy had probably been stationed as a guard because of his alertness. If Christen and I weren't absolutely quiet, he might hear us. Whether he shot first and asked questions later was a toss-up. I breathed in the wood-burning scent that drifted in the dewy air, studying the south end of the clearing where smoke trickled into the sky. That was where the Dover homesteads were, and I reckoned it was a mile from here on foot.

Since Christen hadn't been restrained in any way, the Dovers wouldn't expect her to lead me to their prisoner. It was safe to assume the only person I had to deal with would be the guy at the base of the hunting stand. I blew out a quick breath as I deliberated. Buddy and Russo were waiting at the cruiser for my return or a phone call. They didn't know that I'd shut off my cell phone as soon as I started running in case it rang or buzzed, giving me away. Reception would be sketchy in these hilly woods anyway.

The best course of action was to incapacitate the guard and get Dillon away from here in a hurry. I was on my own.

I touched Christen's shoulder, leaned in, and whispered into her ear, "I'm going to knock that guy out and bring Dillon back to the car. Go to your house." I narrowed my eyes on the girl as she lifted her chin stubbornly. "If this doesn't work out as planned, you don't want to give anyone the heads up that you helped me."

She glanced between me and the hunting stand. When her gaze settled on me, I saw compliancy there. "Thanks, Sheriff Mills."

Like a spooked deer, she was off again, darting back into the trees without a sound. I returned my attention to the guard. I watched him slowly turn one hundred and eighty degrees. When he faced away, I pulled my 9MM from its holster and made my move.

The guy didn't even know I existed until I was a few feet behind him. His head shifted, and I sprang forward, focusing on the side of the man's neck. A strike downward with the grip of the gun was all I needed to hit his vagus nerve. The man wobbled in place and then went down. I replaced my gun and pushed his gun away with my boot. I dropped down beside him.

He would be unconscious for anywhere from one minute to a few, so I wasted no time patting him down. I felt something pointy in his pocket and pulled it out. Attached to a looped chain was a single key. I jumped back up and ascended the ladder as fast as I could. With a calmness of hands that my heart wasn't experiencing, I inserted the key and turned. It clicked, and the latch opened. Pushing the door inward, I was assaulted with the pungent odor of feces and urine. Wrinkling my nose, I whispered into the dark room, "Dillon, I've come to get you out of here. We have to hurry."

The wait was only a few seconds but felt longer. There was a scuffing sound and a groan. When an arm appeared through the opening, I grasped it, tugging him forward until he was fully illuminated by moonlight. I sucked in a breath. The man's face was hardly recognizable for all the puffy bruising and broken skin. Someone had given him quite a beating. He moved stiffly, but at least he could walk.

"Can you climb down the ladder?" I whispered.

He answered me with a grunt and a flick of his hand.

I went first, and once on the ground, I carefully sidestepped the guard, then bent down to pick up the rifle. I checked the chamber, and it was loaded. Dillon lost his grip on a rung and fell the rest of the way down. I returned to the ladder and grasped his arm, jerking him upright. Luckily, he wasn't much taller than me, and I was able to get him on his feet.

In a stern whisper, I said, "Look, if we don't get the hell out of here, we're both dead."

He gave a loose nod, and I gripped his shoulder, propelling him towards the trees. An invigorating breeze touched my cheeks, and I said a silent prayer of thanks when a dark-rimmed cloud drifted over the moon, giving us the cover of darkness we needed to cross the clearing. Once under the trees, I let go of his shoulder and took the lead. Given the mad run through the forest with Christen, I was still conscious of the boulders and larger-girthed trees we'd passed. Our fast-moving bodies had broken branches that I followed, and keeping the sound of rushing water on my left, I was confident I went in the right direction. The going was slower, and I had to stop a handful of times for Dillon to catch up and take a breath. The further we got away from his prison, the better his legs worked, and I fell in alongside him, keen that having him behind me wasn't safe now that he was revived.

After fifteen minutes of intermittent jogging and walking, I spotted a flash of light in the direction we were headed. It blinked out, blinked on, then out again. It was Buddy showing me the way.

The clouds separated, exposing the moon, and with its light, I spotted the cruiser's blue stripe through the trees. I dropped back until I was behind Dillon.

"I'm mighty grateful you came to my rescue, sheriff." Dillon finally spoke, his voice strained.

"How do you know I'm the sheriff?"

"I heard talk that Possum Gap's sheriff was an attractive bitch. You fit the bill."

We'd reached level ground, and just as expected, Dillon took advantage of it. When he whirled around, striking out with the stick he'd picked up earlier as a walking cane, I was ready.

Using the barrel of the rifle I still carried, I blocked his thrust successfully, tearing the stick from his hands. He raised them as I pointed the rifle at his chest. "Go on. Get moving!"

Dillon stumbled a few steps backward, then spun around. When he broke through the branches, he came face to face with the end of Buddy's handgun. Russo was also armed, and it surprised me how comfortable he looked with the little revolver in his hands.

"Read him his rights, Buddy, then cuff him." I walked around Dillon's side.

"You don't have anything on me!" Dillon shouted, gaining strength by the minute.

I snorted. Evidence mounted that Dillon was the shooter in the trailer, but I wasn't ready to press charges without talking to Ted first. The case had to be airtight. "You idiot. Swinging a weapon at an officer is grounds for arrest."

"Fuck that," Dillon snarled. Buddy easily overpowered the injured, smaller man, and within minutes Dillon Cunningham was secured in the back seat. Buddy had radioed in a backup cruiser without sirens, and it was on its way.

"I'm impressed," Russo stepped closer. I kept looking back up the road toward Jewelweed Hollow. I wouldn't relax until we put some miles between us and the hill clan.

"Turned out, it wasn't as difficult as it should have been," I said without looking his way.

"Even if you have your guy, how do you plan to deal with the hillbillies that held him captive?" Russo's voice was tinged with humor. I didn't have to look over my shoulder to know he grinned.

"A lot is going to depend on what"—I raised my chin at the cruiser—"he has to say." I snorted, finally eyeing the coroner. "We're missing something important. I can feel it in my bones."

Russo hadn't put his gun away. "I get the same feeling we're not in the right place."

Our eyes met, and for the first time since Russo came to town, I felt a kinship with him. He actually got it. "You know what we call a Yankee who moves down south?"

The side of Russo's mouth lifted. "No, what?"

"A damn Yankee." I chuckled and jabbed him with my elbow. He smiled back.

"Do you hear that?" Buddy interrupted the bonding moment.

I craned my neck, then I heard the roaring of engines. "Shit! Take cover behind the cruiser!"

The three of us barely got behind the car when seven four-wheelers emerged from the forest from both sides. The bearded guy who had not-so-politely asked us to leave was the first one I recognized. Eight more rough-looking men and two wild-haired women accompanied him. They all were either holding guns or had them strapped to their ATVs. It was like a scene out of *The Road Warrior*. The forty-year-old Buick creeping up the road towards us added to the surreal, movie screen feel of the moment. The wind picked up, bending branches and making the trees sway. I glanced over at Buddy and Russo. Buddy's gun was drawn. He was ready to act. Russo's pursed lips made him look annoyed. If my timing was right, backup would arrive within minutes, giving us the boost we needed to get out of here alive. Thoughts of a possible shootout made my heart bounce in my chest. When the approaching car finally stopped, I let out a breath and pushed up on steady legs. Buddy rose with me, but Russo picked up the rifle I'd set down and positioned himself behind the cruiser, peeking over the hood.

Holding my handgun up, I shouted, "Lower your weapons! Aiming guns at law enforcement will get you all jail time!"

"How about shooting them? What will that get me?" The voice came from one of the men in the front. His long blonde hair was pulled back in a ponytail, and his tanned face was covered with uneven stubble.

"In Kentucky—the death penalty," I shouted back.

24

CHARLIE

I looked up from the puzzle at Sarah, who sat across the kitchen table. "Why is Phoebe still crying?"

Sarah twirled a piece in her hand, staring at the half-finished picture of a field full of flowers and a couple of sheep in the middle of it. I never did a jigsaw puzzle before, and this one was a thousand pieces. Without a TV, cell phone, Xbox, or any other technology, this is what Amish kids did after dark. They liked to read too, but tonight, this was their choice.

Still not lifting her gaze, Sarah said, "She probably wants Mamma."

"They've been gone an awfully long time," Josh spoke up from the chair next to me. "What do you think they're talking about?"

I let out an agitated breath. "Vivian Hershberger is missing." I didn't care that both of the kids' eyes rounded and their mouths dropped open.

"Where did she go?" Sarah asked.

"If she's missing, that means no one knows, silly," Josh

said. He cocked his head at me. "I like Vivian. She always gives me peppermints before church."

"She's a fake bitch," I snapped.

Sarah gasped. It took a few seconds more for my words to sink into Josh's hard head, then he pushed his seat back and stood.

"Don't talk that way in front of Sarah!" Josh raised his voice. Phoebe must have heard him because her crying grew louder.

I rose and leaned forward, bracing my hands on the tabletop. He was a few inches shy of my height. Someday, he'd catch up to his dad, but right now, he was still kid-sized. "What are you going to do about it?" I challenged.

Josh puffed out his chest. "I'm not a snitch, so I won't tell on you."

"I will," Sarah's voice came out in a tiny chirp.

I rounded on her. "Oh, really? Why do you want to get me in trouble?" I tried not to shout but failed. "Are you trying to get rid of me—is that it?"

Tears bubbled in the corners of Sarah's eyes, then dribbled down her cheeks. "You shouldn't say bad words. It's sinning."

Since Marvin and Rachel had dropped me off, my head hurt, and I felt sick to my stomach. No one understood what I was going through—especially these spoiled kids. Sarah's cap was nowhere in sight, and her blonde hair fell in messy waves down her shoulders. I pointed a finger at the girl. "Don't you dare tell me what I should or shouldn't do. I'm older than you. Show some respect."

Sarah was full-blown crying now. Her shoulders lifted with each sobbing breath. "You're mean!" She forced the words out through gaping lips.

The pain in the side of my forehead intensified, and I pressed my fingers into the throbbing place. "Shut up!" I shouted.

"Leave her alone," Josh said. He inched closer to his sister. "Sarah, stop crying. It's only making her madder."

His stern voice had an effect on Sarah. She sniffed and wiped her face with her hand. When she'd calmed down, she said, "I'm sorry."

Dottie, who had been lying next to the door, raised her head and looked at me. The low growling sound was unmistakable. My jaw clenched, and I could barely breathe. I advanced on the dog, but Josh reached her first.

"I'll put her outside," he said as he grabbed her collar, opened the door with his other hand, and shoved her onto the porch.

When he turned back, his face was flushed, and he forced a smile onto it. "Let's finish the puzzle." He swallowed and looked at Sarah, then at me. "Okay?"

My lungs finally expanded, and the pressure in my head eased. I shifted my attention to Sarah. "Go see if you can get the baby to shut up," I ordered.

The girl dashed out of the room without another word.

The faint sound of a phone ringing reached my ears. Josh paused and cocked his head. He had heard it too. "I should answer that. Maybe it's Da or Ma calling."

The phone was in a shed about thirty feet from the house. It had an extra loud ringer so the Coblentz family could hear it from inside. Not only were the Amish not allowed to have electricity, but they also didn't have telephones in their homes. Lucinda had tried to explain it to me—something about evil traveling through wires into their lives.

I had chuckled when she'd told me that. Evil was everywhere. It had nothing to do with cords or tech. People carried it with them all the time. Usually, the ones who seemed the most innocent—like Vivian with her peppermints—were the most tainted.

The phone continued to ring. "Do you care if I get that?" Josh waited next to the door.

My chest and head felt heavy. They might have found Vivian and somehow figured out that I had been with her. Delilah knew I'd gone to talk alone with Vivian, but she was the only one. I was fairly certain that everyone had been busy and not paying attention to us, and I had taken care that the buggies blocked our view from the schoolhouse as we'd walked to the bottom of the hill. Plus, I had gone back into the woods and circled around to the road so no one would have seen me coming up from the shed.

The rapid fluttering of my heart made me feel like throwing up. Vivian deserved it. She had threatened to blow my cover, and she would have done it out of jealousy. This wasn't a game to me. My life was at stake.

The phone wouldn't stop ringing, and I covered my ears with my hands.

Do the Amish know that it was me?

"Charlie, are you all right?" Josh asked.

"Go answer it!" I shouted at him.

When the door closed behind him, my legs became weak, and I slumped into the nearest chair. "Please don't let the Amish know it was me," I muttered. It wasn't a prayer. God had abandoned me a long time ago.

25

SADIE

The moon cast enough light to see everyone's faces, and I imprinted them to memory. When the car doors opened, I shifted my gaze. Jessie Dover was the first to emerge from the shadows. Then Geraldine walked up. Neither one of them were armed. Jessie held a Budweiser. He lifted the bottle to his mouth and took a swig. The action calmed the tension considerably. Several men lowered their weapons at once.

"We want that man, sheriff. Hand him over," Geraldine said, stopping a dozen feet away.

Excuse me? The nerve of the clan's matriarch almost made me laugh. Having grown up side by side with Dovers, I knew that would be a mistake. They liked to be taken seriously, and me laughing would be considered impolite. Sensing all Geraldine wanted was an escape route where neither she nor any of her kin would lose face, the rapid beating of my heart slowed.

"You know I can't do that. This man is wanted in connection

to the murders of three men, including your son." My mouth twitched as I searched for the right words. "Don't worry. I guarantee you, if he's guilty, he'll pay for what he did to Jax." I spread my hands, feeling confident Buddy—and even Russo—had me covered. "You all don't have to risk your own freedom to get the job done."

Geraldine considered what I had said with puckered lips and steady breathing. She dipped her head, "Christen, come on out here, girl."

Christen exited the Buick. When she straightened up, her red cheeks were puffy and wet. As she walked up to her grandmother, she wiped her face and sniffed in fresh tears.

"Go on, girl. Tell the sheriff what happened to ya," Geraldine said in a coaxing yet firm voice.

Christen didn't look up. She scuffed the bottom of her tennis shoe across the stones while everyone waited with bated breath. "I done met Dillon a month or so ago at the bowling alley. He told me all about how he moved down here from Cincinnati 'cause he was looking for clean air and quiet. I liked him and all, so we started hanging out." She stopped talking and made a gurgling sound. She covered her entire face with her palms.

Geraldine grabbed Christen's hands and pried them away from her face. "Talk, girl," Geraldine ordered.

Christen's voice shook. "I wasn't happy here anymore, and Dillon said he'd take me somewhere else."

Geraldine shook her head when Christen said it. "And the smack, girl. Tell the sheriff about that."

Christen swallowed hard. "Yeah, I like me some dope. Dillon had that too."

"Where did he take you, Christen?" I already knew the answer, but I held my breath, nonetheless.

Geraldine grasped her arm and rubbed it up and down. "Go on, girl. Tell the sheriff everything."

Christen's eyes met mine. The defiance disappeared from her face. She looked defeated. "An ugly trailer at the end of Old Hollow Road. We partied there for a couple days, I guess. I can't remember how long. Dillon needed more money for the dope. He said I had to pay my way—earn my keep." Her gaze dropped to a puddle where she dug the toe of her tennis shoe into, not concerned that it was getting soaked.

I kept my eyes on Christen. "What did you have to do to earn your keep?"

A tear trickled down Christen's cheek, and she shifted her head so that her long hair fell over the side of her face, covering it.

I spoke gently. "We can talk in private—"

"No!" Geraldine objected. "The family knows everything. This is her cross to bear, and a good way to healing is by saying it out loud."

Geraldine's voice had taken on an evangelistic flair. Several of her relatives nodded in agreement.

"I had to turn tricks, but I didn't want to. That's what happened in that trailer." Christen flipped her hair back and lifted her chin. "John Dover suspected what was going on. He called our cousin Jax. That's why he came—to take me away from there."

I listened carefully, and my mind laced her story into the evidence I had already collected. So, Jax went in guns blazing. He popped two of them, but he was shot in the process—by Dillon or one of the other guys, that was still to be revealed.

Poor, dumb Jax. If he'd come to me first he would still be alive, but that's the way hill people operated. They took matters—and the law—into their own hands, then dealt with the consequences later.

"Was John Dover in the trailer when it went down, Christen?"

She shook her head. "No, I never saw him. I heard afterwards."

"Who shot Jax?"

Geraldine's eyes strayed to the cruiser. "That bastard in there."

My heart rate slowed. The pulsing energy in the air had dissipated with every word she said. I faced Geraldine. "Trust me, I will make sure Dillon pays for what he did to your granddaughter and Jax. Your family has suffered enough, don't you think? If you all do something stupid right now, law enforcement like you've never seen will descend on this mountain, and some of you won't see this beautiful place again. Concrete walls and iron bars will be your new home." I saw Geraldine take a long breath, and Jessie finished off his beer. He was letting Geraldine make the call. She was the matriarch of the family, and everyone would listen to her.

Geraldine lifted a brow and took the last few steps to stand right in front of me. "Do you swear to me on your mamma's grave, Sadie Mills, that Dillon Cunningham will never walk free again?"

I inhaled deeply, running every scenario through my head as quickly as I could. *Solicitation and facilitation for sex of a minor, selling heroin—and even if Jax's death couldn't be pinned on him or he claimed self-defense—there were the probable murders of the Baker couple and their ten-year-old daughter to pin on him.* I didn't like making promises I might not be able to keep—and if my mamma was included in the bargain, I had to make good on it, but the law was on my side this time. Geraldine trusted me to follow the same honor code she and her kin lived by.

"I promise, Geraldine, on my dear mamma's grave. Dillon will live out the rest of his days behind bars if I have my way." The matriarch paused, then gave a firm nod of her head. She was satisfied. "Are you willing to bring Christen to my office tomorrow to write up an official report? That's the first step in making my promise a reality."

Geraldine glanced at Jessie. He nodded, then walked back to the Buick. It was done. As Christen pivoted on her heel, I stopped her. "Wait. Christen, were there any other girls in that trailer with you the night of the shootout?"

Christen turned slowly. Her lips pursed, and her eyes flashed. "Charlie's not with you?"

My head felt light. "Charlie?"

"She was Dillon's other girl—his star employee, I guess you could say." She stared at me with a faraway look on her face. "I forgot all about her until now." She shrugged. "She was a crazy bitch, I'll tell you that."

Geraldine left Christen's side and returned to the Buick. The rest of the family followed suit. Engines roared to life, and gravel spit up from under spinning tires as the ATVs peeled out. "Why do you say that?" I followed Christen as she took two steps backward.

"Her eyes were dead, sheriff. That girl didn't have a soul."

26

LUCINDA

Samuel and Louisa Hershberger stood at the front of the large classroom. By the looks of Louisa's puckered face, she was trying hard not to cry. Samuel paced back and forth while rubbing his forehead. My heart went out to Vivian's parents. I remembered hearing about a young woman who went missing from an Indiana community while she'd walked home from church one Sunday. Her remains were found a month later next to a pond. That was fifteen years ago, and nothing like it had happened since that I knew of.

Martha elbowed me, then leaned over to whisper, "This is dreadful. I fear something terrible befell the poor girl."

I opened my mouth but snapped it shut when Zeke began to speak to the congregation. "Several of our drivers are searching the roadways, and a group of young men have gone on horseback into the fields and woods surrounding the school. We should take time to pray for Vivian's safe return."

I swallowed down the hot juices and stepped forward,

brushing off James' hand when he reached for me. "Bishop, I have a question."

Zeke's head swiveled in my direction at the same time as his wife did. I hadn't spotted Marvin and reckoned he had taken his horse out with the other riders to look for Vivian. It was an odd gathering of only adults with troubled faces.

"Yes, Lucinda, speak up," Zeke said. He walked closer, and the crowd closed in tightly around us.

"Have you called the authorities? They have resources, experience, and many people to aid us."

Zeke's lips thinned. Several heads turned his way, waiting for his answer.

"I discussed that very same idea with Samuel and the other ministers. It's best we wait until tomorrow morning to bring the situation to the attention of outsiders."

My skin tingled, and I glanced around. I saw surprise etched on many faces. "Why wait so long? This is an urgent matter. Vivian may be in trouble." I avoided looking at Louisa and kept my gaze glued to the bishop. James stepped up beside me, and Martha moved in closer.

Zeke inhaled sharply and twisted the end of his long, brown beard. "The girl is likely being reckless." He glanced at Samuel and grimaced. "I'm sorry, my friend, but perhaps she's run off to the English world. She's at an age when longing stirs in the hearts of some of our young ones. Odds are, Vivian is a runaway."

"No, no, no!" Louisa shook her head forcefully. "My girl loves this community and is content here. Thoughts of going English were never on her mind, I can assure you of that." She nudged her husband. "Tell him, Samuel."

Samuel was a weak man, more likely to side with the bishop

to earn his favor than to stick up for his wife and daughter. I watched the conflict of the moment twist his face before he spoke and held my breath, hoping I was wrong this time. "Dear, this is upsetting for all of us. Zeke has a point. We don't always know our children's hearts. They sometimes keep secrets." Louisa threw her hands up and dropped her head back as her husband rambled on. "It would be better if she ran off. At least her disappearance would be by her own choosing."

Louisa wiped the tears from her eyes, and Susan draped her arm over the other woman's shoulder snugly. "There, there, Louisa. All will be well. Vivian is a good girl. I'm sure she'll return to you once she sees how wicked the outside world is."

I flinched when Zeke looked my way and raised his voice. "It would hurt the girl's reputation if we created too much of a stir. When she returns, we'll discuss her punishment. That is the way we do things."

The bishop was around ten years older than me. He chose a wife later in life, and when I was only eighteen and he twenty-eight, he'd asked me to court. My parents were delighted as Zeke had become a minister at the age of twenty-five, and his aspirations of rising to bishop were well known in the community. His family operated a successful metal shop, and they owned a large portion of the community. I, on the other hand, had no interest in the older man. It wasn't his looks or even the age difference that mattered. I sensed his demanding nature and knew deep down it would not be a good match. James had also caught my eye, and even though he was a simple man from one of the poorer families, he had an abundance of humor and made me laugh. James always treated me as his equal, something Zeke, nor any of the other men in the community, would have done.

Gray hairs poked out of Zeke's beard, and the lines at the corners of his eyes had deepened. He reminded me of the bossy elders from my past. The frown he directed at me made me thank God that I had not picked him for a husband. I stared past his rigid body at one of the sconces on the wall. The light flicked and danced within the glass. I sweated beneath the coat. There were too many bodies crammed into the building, and the lights added to the rise in temperature. I heard the scuffling of feet on the floor, clearing of throats, and sniffling. Otherwise, my people were silent. No one dared question Zeke.

I blinked and returned my gaze to the bishop. "I know Vivian Hershberger well. Her mind and heart were set on a life within this community. I was privy to her interest in a certain young eligible bachelor as well." I narrowed my eyes, and Zeke's widened when he realized who I meant. I wanted to see Susan's reaction, but kept staring at Zeke. "Vivian would not leave us on her own. Something must have happened for her to be gone this long." I drew in a quick, sharp breath. "You should notify the Englishers at once. Our Lord tells us in Proverbs, 'Where there is no counsel, the people fall, but in the multitude of counselors there is safety.' I believe He means for us to seek assistance in times of need—like now—from those who are in positions of authority. The Englishers can help us. We should not wait another moment to reach out to them, for Vivian's sake."

Murmurs spread throughout the building. My breathing eased, and I glanced around to see men and women nodding.

Several smiled at me, including Martha. Louisa mouthed, *thank you.*

Zeke's cheeks darkened a shade, and the corner of his mouth twitched. He heard his people, sensed that he was losing them to me in the argument. "Order!" he called out. "English laws have no place in our community. We settle our own business, and this is no different. We shall wait until the morning to give Vivian a chance to turn up on her own before we seek help from outsiders. It has been decided." Zeke's voice gradually rose as he talked, reminding me of his Sunday sermons. He liked to be significant that way.

I rolled my eyes and turned to James. "This is a mistake. Something is terribly wrong. I know it."

Our people refrained from touching in public, but James wasn't a conformist. He did his best to follow the rules and walk the line of obedience, but at that moment, I saw the flicker of rashness in his eyes. Reaching out, he gripped my hand for a few seconds, then let go. I smiled sadly back at him, my racing heart not allowing me to enjoy the moment.

"Excuse me," a quiet voice said. I looked around for the speaker, and then the voice rose a notch. "Excuse me, bishop."

It was Delilah. The bishop finally noticed her and in his loud voice, he ordered everyone, "Silence!" All eyes were on the girl as she stepped up to the bishop, looking like a scared rabbit who after a mad dash though the meadow, found herself surrounded by foxes. "If you have something to say, speak up, girl," Zeke demanded.

Delilah shifted her weight between her feet. I felt sorry for her, but I didn't dare move. I wanted to hear what she had to say as much as the bishop and everyone else.

"It might not be important, but it's been on my mind all

night, and I need to get it off my chest. Do with it what you will." She sucked in a deep breath. "Earlier this evening, when we all arrived to clean, Charlie asked Vivian to talk with her alone. They went down the hill together and disappeared behind the buggies. After that, I saw Charlie again, but not Vivian."

Delilah had spoken in the simplest fashion, and I wondered why no one had questioned her before now. What she said made the air catch in my throat, and my muscles go weak.

Charlie was with Vivian right before she disappeared. The revelation settled over me with chilling force.

The room erupted in voices, and once again, the bishop quieted them with a shout. "Enough!" His head snapped in my direction. Before he could speak, Susan whispered something in his ear frantically. Zeke closed his eyes for a moment, then opened them. "Is this the same girl who is Lucinda Coblentz's cousin?" He directed the question at Delilah, and she nodded, not looking my way. This time, when his gaze met mine, his face wasn't so tight. "Where is Charlie now?"

I saw the pleading look in Susan's eyes, but it didn't sway me. "Your son and daughter brought her home in their buggy after the schoolhouse cleanup. She's been at our house ever since."

Zeke's head dropped, and he shook it lightly before running his hand through his hair. *Yes, Zeke, young'uns at this age are prone to rebellion and secrets. No need to look further than your own household.* I wanted desperately to say it out loud, but of course, I kept my mouth tightly shut.

"We must speak to this girl. If anyone knows where Vivian is, it would be her," Zeke said briskly. The situation was getting too personal for him, and I would have enjoyed watching him squirm if Vivian wasn't missing.

James found his voice. "We'll take you to our home now, Zeke. There's no time to waste."

Suddenly, a ragged scream rang out from somewhere outside. It was so loud that it sent a choking spasm up my throat. Everyone closed their mouths and stopped moving. The ghostly sound came again at an even higher pitch. Zeke and James rushed to a window to look out. Galloping hooves followed the wail and several men pushed the sliding door open to reveal the full moon shining on the hitching rail. A few seconds passed, and a rider appeared in the doorway. It was Timothy King. He was only a year older than Josh but an inch taller. His face was milky white, and his eyes were round saucers.

He reined the horse to a stop and pointed down the hill. "I found Vivian in the shed!"

"Praise be," Louisa called out, squeezing through the crowd to reach the door.

Timothy shook his head violently, and Zeke grabbed his horse's reins. "Spit it out, boy!"

"She's dead. Vivian's dead."

27

SADIE

Russo waited until the ATVs were gone and the Buick was bouncing its way back up the road towards the homesteads when he stepped out from behind the cruiser.

"Damn, sheriff, any more days like this and I'll be tempted to start drinking again," Buddy said as he holstered his handgun.

Most of the clouds had moved off to the west, letting the moon hang brightly in the sky like a lightbulb. I could see Dillon's silhouette in the back seat. I was fairly certain he wouldn't willingly corroborate what Christen had said. The man was a slippery slime ball who had lived a life of crime and abusing people, and he'd gotten away with most of it. It hadn't surprised me that he had used drugs to entice girls into the sex trade. What was baffling is that he got away with it for years.

Russo stepped up. "You handled that well, sheriff. This town is more entertaining than I ever dreamed it would be."

He flashed a grin, then sobered. "Do you know who this Charlie is?"

A gust of wind lifted my hair, and I looked back over my shoulder into the thick woods that Charlie would have fled into that night. Once she made it into the trees, she had disappeared into thin air.

"Charlie is a nickname for Charlotte. Charlotte Baker. Looks like we've found the missing Baker girl."

The interrogation room in the department was smaller than my office, which was tiny. Buddy stood by the door. His size and fixed frown made him intimidating to most people, but not Dillon Cunningham. He lounged in the chair across from me like he didn't have a care in the world. Buddy had escorted him into the bathroom, where he washed his face and changed clothes. The bruising didn't seem as bad as before, and the puffiness around his eyes had diminished somewhat. His breathing appeared normal as well. I didn't regret hauling him in for questioning before taking him to the hospital. If he was in good enough health to jog through a forest and attempt to knock me out, he could answer a few questions.

Without a murder weapon, it would be difficult to pin the shootings on him. I had to tread lightly in the hopes of getting a confession. "Dillon, if I hadn't shown up, there's no telling what the Dovers would have done to you. I'm guessing it wouldn't have been pretty."

Dillon chuckled, then winced a little. "I don't owe you anything."

The guy would not be easy to crack. Even if he wasn't

covered with bruises, he wasn't much to look at. He was physically fit; I'd give him that. Some women would find the elaborate designs scrawled along his upper arms and across his collar bone attractive. His square jaw and weathered skin made him look like a character who had stepped out of an old western movie. Sure, maybe a thirty-something-year-old divorcee would chase after him, but what did teenagers see in him? I could kind of understand it with Christen. Her family's lifestyle was rough, to say the least. She probably thought Dillon would rescue her from a life in the hill country. But Charlotte Baker was another story altogether.

I pulled her photo from the file left by Agent Nick Makris and held it up so that Dillon couldn't see it. Charlotte—or Charlie—was only fifteen in this school picture and not smiling. Her long, brownish-blonde hair hung limply around her slender, pale face. Her one striking feature was her enormous hazel eyes. She didn't look like a killer, but looks could be deceiving. The fact that when the opportunity presented itself, she had separated from Dillon was in her favor. My hopes were that Dillon was solely responsible for the trailer shootings and her family's murders. In this business, I'd faced the hard reality that things didn't always work out the way I wanted them to.

I crossed my arms on the table. "You can play the tough guy all you want. It doesn't make a difference to me 'cause you're totally screwed, you know that? At the very least, we have you on sex trafficking and rape charges, which carry up to twenty years."

Dillon stared back at me, stubbornly silent. The only way I might get him worried was to lead him to believe that Possum Gap was an Appalachian town that operated within its own perimeters and wasn't afraid to ditch the rules to make an arrest or get a conviction. We were ruled by common sense, the strong desire to protect our own and to keep our secrets hidden.

"Right now, there's an opportunity to tell me, in your own words, what happened in that trailer. Because believe me, we'll put together the forensic information and make a call that may or may not benefit you personally. You might as well talk while someone is willing to listen."

Dillon suddenly came alive, going from a slumped form with droopy eyes to wild-eyed and sitting upright. "Those people are insane. They barged into my home like a bunch of lunatics, shooting everyone in sight."

I had thought Jax acted alone. Not that I'd trusted anything Dillon said, but if it were true that several Dover family members were with him, it explained Geraldine's and Jessie's reluctance to push the investigation.

I pulled out my little notebook and poised a pen over it. "How many were there?"

Dillon relaxed a little. "Four. The long-haired redhead, a big guy with a red beard, a skinny, greasy looking one, and another guy with a scruffy beard. It was complete chaos. I don't know who shot who, but when the smoke cleared, one of them was carrying Christen out of the trailer, kicking and screaming, and the other two had tackled and bound me with a rope."

He talked rapidly while looking me straight in the eye. If he was lying, he had practiced the rant well and sounded believable. The next question was a little tricky, because in my opinion, it got to the heart of the matter.

I decided to be straightforward. "Where was Charlie during this fiasco?"

Dillon dropped back, folding his hands on his lap. He didn't answer right away. I had surprised him. I continued to stare at him. Patience was a virtue of mine.

He grunted, and his face twisted. "How do you know about her?"

I sighed at the cat and mouse game. "Charlotte Baker is an eighteen-year-old girl you've been traveling with for the past two years. She's a missing person from a murder scene near Cincinnati." He opened his mouth, but I raised my index finger and wagged it. "I have a witness that she was in the trailer the night of the shootout, so don't say different."

"I have no idea what you're talking about."

"That's funny, you've been driving her parents' car—her parents who were shot to death, along with her little sister." I leaned further over the table, conscious of the soundless tapping of my foot.

"I didn't do it." He cocked his head and smirked. "I want a lawyer."

I chuckled. The guy was smooth. "Agent Nick Makris came all the way down here from northern Kentucky to tell me about the murders and the missing teenager face to face. He ID'd the vehicle, the same vehicle that was parked outside of the trailer you were dragged out of by the Dover clan. None of that is disputed. Like I already said, I have an eyewitness that Charlotte was in the trailer during the shootout. She's missing again." My brow knitted as I made a confused face. "It seems to me that you're in a hell of a lot of trouble. Not only are you a suspect in the trailer slayings, but also for gunning down Charlotte's family."

Dillon rolled his head back. "I know how this works, and I'm not talking to you anymore without a lawyer."

I glanced at Buddy, who crossed his arms across his broad chest, then smirked. When I turned back to Dillon, I, too, was smiling. "You obviously don't know how things work in a small town like this. A lawyer isn't going to help you if you've murdered these people, especially a child. If you come clean here and now, you might not end up on death row."

"I have rights," Dillon argued.

He was persistent; I'll give him that. "Yes, you do, and I'm not taking those away. Look around, Dillon. Do you see a video recorder?" After he scanned the small room, his lips puckered. "Right now, it's your word against mine"—I tilted my head at Buddy—"and his. With your record and the crimes leveled against you, are you really confident that you'll be believed over us?"

Dillon let out a long, ragged breath, then cracked his neck. "What do you want from me?"

I did a happy dance inside, but outside, I remained cool. "To answer some questions about Charlotte and her family."

He chewed his lip as he nodded.

"Where is Charlotte?"

"I don't know. She was in one of the bedrooms when those rednecks busted through the door. Charlie is a smart one. I'd say she took the opportunity to escape."

"Escape?" I narrowed my eyes.

Dillon swatted the air. "From the chaos, not from me. We're friends."

I scribbled down what he'd said on my notepad. Glancing up, I said, "Friends, huh? I know that Randall Birdie was at that trailer for sex with a young woman—either Christen or Charlie. Around here, you don't pimp your friends out, Dillon." I watched his chest rise and fall with his breaths. I was beginning to get to him, so I plowed on. "From where I'm sitting, this is what happened. Two years ago, you somehow met Charlie and convinced her to run away with you. It wasn't enough to steal the girl; you killed her parents. The sister probably saw something, and you finished her off as insurance. After that, you sex-trafficked Charlie to make some money. Ending up here in Possum Gap a month ago, you lured Christen in the same way you had Charlie. But you didn't know about her crazy family which was a drastic mistake on your part." Dillon sat like a statue; only his eyes flicked at my words. "When we get the forensics back, I believe it will show that you also killed Jax Dover. That's four murders on your hands." I leaned back. "You'll be in solitary confinement, staring at four white walls for the rest of your life."

"It didn't happen that way," he insisted.

I gave Buddy a look, and he left the room for less than ten seconds. When he returned, he set the recorder down on the table. I pressed the button and looked at Dillon who stared at the machine. I held my breath until his shoulders dropped, and he began talking.

"I'm not the one you need to worry about. Charlie killed her parents and even the girl. She shot them dead all by herself."

My heart rate stuttered as I digested what he said. It wasn't unheard of for a teenager to murder their family, but it was hard to wrap my head around the possibility that Charlie had not only shot her parents, but also her sister. The more likely scenario was that Dillon was lying to protect himself.

One loud knock, then the door burst open, and all three of us turned to see Russo and Darcy barging in. Their wide-eyed looks brought me to standing in a hurry.

It was Darcy who spoke. "There's been a murder in the Amish community—a girl."

I couldn't speak at first, the shock was so great. Buddy stepped up. "I'll take Cunningham back to his cell."

I nodded absently as Buddy led a silent Dillon out of the room. I finally found my voice. "How was she killed?" I asked, picking up my jacket off the back of the chair and walking into the hallway behind Darcy with Russo right on my heels.

Russo answered. "Sounds like she was bludgeoned to death."

"In a shed out behind the schoolhouse on Horner Road," Darcy added in a voice pepped on adrenaline.

"Russo, you're with me." I turned to Darcy. "Field the phone. Tell Buddy to stay here for the time being." I stopped at the coffee machine and poured a cup to go. "Are the EMTs on the way?"

"They are." Darcy plucked the right number of sugars and a creamer out of the bowl and handed them to me. "Can you believe it? Three men shot last week, and now an Amish teenager violently murdered." She shook her head. "What is the world coming to?"

Russo waited by the door while I quickly prepared my coffee. I glanced at my wristwatch. Eleven o'clock. It would be a long night. "The world has always been an evil place, Darcy. And it's finally found its way to Possum Gap."

The moon had shifted considerably since my journey through the wooded hills with Christen and then Dillon, at Jewelweed Hollow only a couple of hours earlier. The bishop had requested we didn't use sirens or flashing lights when we entered the settlement, so even though we sped toward a murder scene, my cruiser was quiet and dark. I took a sip of coffee, then touched the brake when I spotted three deer standing next to the road in a grassy spot. Sure enough, one jumped right in front of the cruiser. I had to stop completely for the other two to make it across safely. I had barely accelerated when yellow eyes flashed from the tall grass. A pair of coyotes dashed after the deer. I hit the brakes hard and swerved to avoid hitting them as my seat belt tightened uncomfortably across my chest.

Russo gripped the seat. "Fuck!" he exclaimed. When the coyotes disappeared into the same brush the deer had, and I sped up again, I eyed Russo, who blinked back at me. "I'll never get used to wildlife in the road. Did you see that? Those wolves were after the deer, like in a wildlife documentary."

Some of the tension through my shoulders and neck disappeared. Russo was entertaining. "We don't have wolves around here. Those were coyotes, and yes, they eat deer."

"They were big," he said dumbly as he stared out the window into the inky darkness of a forested spot. "It's strange to think that while we're going about our daily business, there's large canines out here hunting." He scratched his head. "Anyway, what do you think we'll find in the Amish community?"

I let out a breath, maintaining a slower speed. Full moons not only brought out madness in humans, but they also riled up the animals. "I can't say, really. We've never had any problems with the Amish. They mostly govern themselves. I think the last time we were called in was when one of their ministers had a horse stolen out of his field. He suspected it was an Englisher, and he turned out to be correct. That must have been about seven years ago, before I was sheriff."

"I find the culture fascinating. Last weekend, I drove out to their market to have a look around. I've never seen so much deli meat and cheese in one place before. I bought a peanut butter pie, and it was beyond delicious."

"Yeah, the Amish know how to bake, that's for sure." I pressed the brake pedal when the triangular reflector on the back of a buggy came into view."

Russo lurched forward, not taking his eyes off the outdated vehicle. "That's amazing. They use the same mode of transportation we all used in the 1800s." His head swiveled my way. "Is that legal—just the one reflector light?"

Russo's excited voice bugged me. Not only did I have the crimes in the trailer under investigation, now a murder in the Amish community was on my plate. Not to mention Charlie Baker. Could it possibly be true that she'd killed her family? And where the hell was she anyway?

I drew on mothering experiences when Chloe used to repeatedly ask questions when I had other things on my mind to keep my voice steady. What I wouldn't give for my daughter to be as communicative nowadays. "Some of them have blinking lights, others don't. Occasionally, we deal with a vehicle/buggy accident. It's a disorienting juxtaposition that can result in tragedy. Last year, a mother and her youngest child were killed on Route 43 when a semi-trailer swerved onto the shoulder and struck their buggy. Two other kids were thrown from the buggy and survived. The horse had to be put down on the side of the road. It was awful."

"Why do they insist on living this way when it's so dangerous?"

I made a mental note that a buggy probably wouldn't be out this late normally. The entire community must be in a state of panic. Hearing the horse's hooves loudly strike the pavement, I carefully pulled around and passed it. Russo turned in his seat to stare at the buggy until it was swallowed by the darkness behind us.

I'd been asked the same question before, and I certainly wasn't an expert. "Some don't. A number of kids leave the ranks as teenagers. That's why I suspect they have such large families, to keep their numbers up."

"They're within your jurisdiction. You must know a little of what makes them tick." Russo sounded frustrated.

"Honestly, we don't get many calls out this way, and when we do, although polite, they're tight-lipped. I guess that's the way they keep their society going. The less we know, the better." The woods gave way to fields, crops, and fences. Amish didn't have security or porch lights, so the farms we passed were dark, except for the moonlight. "Believe it or not, I don't know any of them personally. I occasionally stop by the market or furniture shop, but that's about it."

We passed another buggy going in the opposite direction. The horse was black as the night and moving fast.

"I'd think you'd want to get to know them better. I know I would."

"You can be the goodwill ambassador, how's that?" I wasn't kidding.

Russo made a humming noise. "Looks like you're going to be knee-deep in their culture now." He leaned back. "Have you ever heard of an Amish murder?"

"Can't say that I have, but like everyone else, the Amish are as susceptible to crimes as Englishers."

"From England?" Russo asked in a perfectly serious voice.

"No, not real Englishers. That's what the Amish call

anyone who isn't Amish. There's a bunch of strange protocols and you can't make the usual assumptions with them. That's why this case is going to be so difficult. The cultural divide is challenging on any given day, but emotions will be extra high after one of their own has been brutally killed."

"So, you think it's an outsider?"

I could tell by Russo's hard tone that he wasn't convinced.

"I wouldn't bother to guess at this point. Up until a week ago, it was highly unusual for anyone in this county to die from murder. Now, we're dealing with four murders and a connection to a triple homicide north in the state. It could be anyone."

"How did the interview with Cunningham go?" His sudden change of subject was jarring.

The interrogation hadn't been far from my mind, even with the development in the Amish community. "He never admitted that he was pimping Christen and Charlie out or that he'd shot Jax Dover, but he insisted that he didn't kill the Baker family." I swallowed the lump in my throat. "He says Charlie did it herself."

"That's hard to believe."

The schoolhouse came into view. Lights shined through the windows, and a dozen or more buggies were parked in the gravel lot beside the metal-sided building that looked more suitable for storage than students.

I focused on drawing in normal breaths. This was not going to be pleasant.

"Lately, I'd believe just about anything," I admitted.

28

LUCINDA

"Just because she talked to Vivian doesn't mean she had anything to do with this tragedy," I told James.

He remained silent for a moment, snapping the reins over Goliath's hindquarters to make the horse move faster. My head still felt heavy, and even the night air blowing onto my face didn't wake me from the foggy feel of having a bad dream. Poor, poor Vivian. What wickedness had descended on her?

"You're thinking like one of us and not an outsider," he said.

"Most Englishers are not dangerous."

"True, but some are. It might have been one of the drivers or an English man who saw Vivian and became infatuated with her, but it's odd that it happened after she spoke to Charlie. And don't forget, Delilah said that the girls didn't get along."

"They'd only known each other for a couple days. How could that be so?" I thrummed my fingers against my cheek.

"You know as well as I do that Vivian was sweet on Marvin

Miller, and he had eyes for Charlie." He folded his lips together and gave a shake of his head. "A disastrous situation."

"I planned to tell Charlie that we'd take her into town in the morning when the call came about the meeting at the schoolhouse. She seemed perfectly normal, perhaps a bit sullen, but that seems to be her nature." I dropped my hand to my lap and rubbed the pebbly material of the dress. "If she knew something was amiss with Vivian, she would have said so."

James looked sideways. "You think so? She snuck out of the house without telling you and made up the bed to look like she was sleeping in it. I doubt you can trust anything she says, and remember, she isn't one of us. She could easily be capable of lying."

A police car passed by us, and I turned in the seat to look at it. "That must be heading to the schoolhouse." A tear formed in my eye and dribbled into my lashes. I wiped the wetness away with the cuff of my sleeve. "Did you see Samuel's face when he heard about Vivian? And Louisa's scream pierced my heart." I dropped my head forward, struggling to catch a breath.

"It's the devil's work, I tell you." James slowed Goliath to make the turn onto our road.

I closed my eyes and said a silent prayer for the safe passage of Vivian's soul to our Lord and to provide some kind of peace and healing for her parents. When I opened my eyes, we were almost to our driveway. "I'm glad you didn't go to the shed." I sucked in a breath. "Something like that will never ease from the minds of those who see it." Poor, sweet Timmy. Nightmares would rule his nights for a long time to come.

The rest of the ride, we didn't talk, but James did reach for my hand and held it for a moment. He stopped the buggy in front of the porch steps to let me out. Lights flickered from inside. I wondered what I would tell the children if they were still awake. And then there was the conversation to be had with Charlie. Vivian's death might delay her departure by another day, but that would be it. I was ready to be free of the entire affair, especially now that there was so much turmoil within the community.

"I'll unhitch Goliath and be right in," James said.

I grasped the door lever, and James' hand snaked out to grasp my arm. He pulled me back and kissed my cheek. "We must keep faith that the Lord will take care of everything," he said against my skin.

My body rocked into him. "Whoever did this to Vivian is still out there—"

James cupped my chin and searched my eyes. "Lucinda, you're safe. I'll protect you and the children."

"I know you will. It was good to see the police are here too. I pray they'll figure out who did this."

Slowly, I walked up the steps. Every movement was like trudging through deep snow. I cocked my head to listen for sounds from the children through the open windows, but all was quiet except for the whip-poor-wool chirping its ominous song.

When I pushed the door open, I found a jigsaw puzzle laid out on the tabletop, along with crumpled napkins and a half-eaten cookie. Seeing the milk jug flat on the counter and a stream of milk spilling out into a puddle on the floor, I mumbled, "What on earth?" I hurried over and picked up the nearly empty jug, setting it right-side up. The inclination to wipe up the mess was strong, but another emotion tugged at my insides. I spun around, stretching my legs to reach the staircase quicker.

I jogged to the second floor with a quivering chest and holding my breath. The first room I came to was Josh's. I pushed the door slowly open, not wanting to wake him. The bed was still made. No one had slept in it, and Josh wasn't in sight. I hurried out of his room, across the hallway, and into the girls' room. This time, I didn't hesitate and turned the knob, then flung open the door. My eyes burned behind gathering tears, and my heart shriveled in my chest. With no time to light the lamp and only moonlight shining, I saw that Sarah's bed was the same—made and unslept in. Her stuffed toy horse sat on her pillow, and the picture book about horses she had been looking at that morning was dropped in the same place on her nightstand. I held my emotions in the best I could when I peeked over the rim of Phoebe's crib. Gone.

I ran out of the room, pumping my legs as fast as I could until I reached the guest room. The door was shut. For a brief moment, I pictured the children inside with Charlie—she had read them a book, and they'd fallen asleep—and I was filled with hope. I grasped the knob with a sweaty palm and turned it until it clicked, then I pushed it open. Being on the east side of the house, the moon didn't shine here, so I felt around for the matches on the dresser drawers next to the doorway and quickly struck one. The lamp's wick flickered to life, and I could see.

The scream left my throat as I crumpled to the floor.

Empty. The room was empty.

29

SADIE

The girl's head and face had been reduced to mush and brain matter. I wouldn't have known the color of her hair except for a few long blonde strands that had escaped the bloody cap and were caught on a post. The murder weapon—a slender piece of firewood—was tossed to the side. Chunks of bloody flesh clung to it.

My stomach rolled, but I managed to swallow down the urge to vomit. Russo stepped carefully around the body while he put on his gloves, then squatted beside it.

"It appears we have the murder weapon there." He pointed at the log I'd already acknowledged. He swiveled in place. "The attack happened right here in the shed, and this is where she died."

Everything he said agreed with my initial cursory impression of the crime scene. While Russo collected evidence from and around the body, I turned to the bishop of the community. He'd introduced himself as Zeke Miller. His long, scruffy-looking brown beard was peppered with gray hairs, and his tan face was weathered from a life spent outdoors. The man was tall and thin, with a hooked nose and sharp, blue eyes. His manner was solemn. He stood alone in the opening to the shed, looking the other way. I didn't blame him for not being able to lay his eyes on the body. It was a difficult thing to do when you didn't know the victim. In this case, he did.

I left Russo to his work and joined the bishop in the doorway. It was after midnight, and dew had formed on the grassy field next to the shed. A thin, milky mist pushed out of the woods that was only around ten yards away.

I cleared my throat softly, and the bishop lifted his chin, eyed me, then returned his gaze to the empty field. A nightbird called, causing me to shiver. A whip-poor-will was nearby. So, the saying was true then—death followed the little bird like an unwanted shadow. The dark-clad man with his black hat and erect posture added to the overall creepy vibe of the place. Even if there wasn't a young woman's corpse behind us, I would still have felt uneasy.

"I'm sorry about your loss, especially in such a horrific way," I said quietly.

He faced me. "Who could do something like that? Vivian was a fine girl, one of our best young'uns." The pain was clearly etched on the man's slim face.

It was a question I'd heard before from other victims' loved ones. It never made sense, but as human beings, we clung to the delusion that there was always a clear explanation. Oftentimes, random misfortune had simply invaded their lives.

I pulled out my notebook. "I understand that you're distraught, but I have a few questions for you that will hopefully help us"—I nodded at Russo—"make sense of what happened here, and most of all, who did it."

The bishop nodded. "Yes, of course. What do you need?"

"What is Vivian's last name?"

"Hershberger. Her parents are Samuel and Louisa. They are in the care of family and friends inside the schoolhouse."

After this vicious attack, the parents would never be the same. "How old was she?"

"Seventeen. She would have turned eighteen this fall."

A year older than my Chloe and the same age as Christen. I closed my eyes for an instant and drew in a deep breath. When I looked back at the bishop, he waited for the next question. I got it. Answering my questions kept him from dwelling on the gruesome discovery of one of his congregation members. It also gave him a feeling of purpose.

"Did anyone see a stranger on the property today or recently?" I paused the pen over the paper. The scent of pine needles was strong in the air. It would have been easy for a person to sneak into the shed from the woods and disappear again after the attack. Whoever did this picked the shed for its isolated location and quick, camouflaged escape route. It would be interesting to see what Russo had to say, but I was betting the assailant knew the victim and had targeted her.

The bishop shook his head. "I asked the others the same question. Only our well-known drivers and the congregation have been on school grounds."

Russo spoke up from behind us. "You hire Englishers to drive you around sometimes?"

The heavy feeling of dread lifted ever so slightly. Russo had used the word Englisher like he'd always known what we were called by the Amish and hadn't just found out about it a little while ago.

"Yes, that's right, but none of our drivers would do something like this. Several are elderly, and the rest middle-aged women." The bishop sounded sure of the statement.

"How many people are in the schoolhouse right now?" I could see the silhouettes of people moving back and forth beyond the schoolhouse windows.

The bishop lifted his fingers, raised his eyes, and silently counted. "I believe forty-two. Some left after Vivian was found. Others heard of the news and came."

"What were you doing at the schoolhouse so late at night?" It was a question that had first come to mind when we drove up and saw the huge crowd.

"Vivian went missing earlier this evening. It was around six o'clock when it came to my attention. The news spread rapidly throughout the community, so I called a special meeting of all the adults."

I rubbed my forehead. There were too many people in this county that took matters into their own hands. "Why didn't you call us earlier?"

The bishop exhaled through pressed lips. "At the time, she was merely missing." He took two steps forward to stand in the grass. I followed him and was grateful to get away from the stale air in the shed. The ambulance sat a dozen yards away with the EMTs waiting inside for me to give the signal to transport the body to the county morgue.

Like the Dover clan, the Amish did their own thing, only calling the law if things were so bad they had no choice. It was unfortunate, though. The girl's blood was thin and after seeing Russo lift her limp hand to check her fingernails, I could see rigor mortis hadn't set in yet. She hadn't been dead long. If we'd been called immediately, we might have arrived in time to save her, but that was all conjecture and saying it out loud wouldn't help the girl now.

"Did Vivian have any enemies that you know of?"

He shook his head as he wiped his brow with a handkerchief. The questions were starting to get to him. I might have to finish the interview later if he cracked.

"How about a boyfriend?" It suddenly occurred to me that since she was Amish and they married young, she might be married. I added, "I didn't see a wedding band, so I assume she's not wed."

The corner of the bishop's mouth twitched. "Our people do not wear any jewelry, including rings. She was not courting either." He fully faced me. "I should get back to the Hershbergers. Their grief is raw and as the spiritual advisor of the community, it's my place to pray with them."

"Of course, I understand. We can talk more later, and I'd like to interview everyone who was here the last two days. Can you set that up for me when the sun's up?" He nodded, his face sagging with relief that I was through with him.

"What will happen to her body, sheriff?" he asked.

"We have to take her into town for an autopsy."

"Isn't it obvious how she died?" He frowned back at me.

"There are things the coroner, Mr. Russo, can glean from the body that might not be easily noticed. It could give us clues about who did this to her."

"When will we get her back? The family and congregation will want to bury her quickly. We have a community cemetery where she will be laid to rest, and it's our way to take care of the details as soon as possible after death."

The sadness in his voice was evident, but I also picked up on the subtle pressure on me. Bishop Zeke Miller was the leader of his community, and he was used to giving orders and having his people respond. He would be sorely disappointed by the meticulous slowness the autopsy and paperwork might take. "I'll do my best to bring her home promptly, but there's a killer out there—maybe someone you know. That needs to be your main focus."

"Are we in danger, sheriff?" The man's eyes widened with understanding.

"It's best if none of your people go off on their own until we find out who did this to Vivian. This could be a targeted assault, but just in case, we need to treat it like it might happen again. Keep your eyes and ears open." I handed the bishop a business card with my contact information. "Call me if you learn anything relating to Vivian that might be helpful. I'll be out again in the morning to conduct more interviews. I won't bother the parents right now, but if they know anything that will help the investigation, please encourage them to talk to me."

"I'll do all that you ask." The bishop stretched out his arm. We shook hands, then he turned away.

"One more question. Who was the last person to see Vivian alive?"

The bishop made a grunting sound of displeasure as he glanced back. "Another young woman. Her name is Charlie."

30

LUCINDA

James grasped my shoulders and gave me a shake to stop me from sobbing. I tried to speak, but the back of my throat was dry, and I couldn't form any coherent words.

"Lucinda, snap out of it and talk to me. Where are the children?" Even in my state, I could hear the panic in his voice.

"Gone." It was painful to draw in a deep breath, but I did it and wiped the tears from my eyes. "They're all gone—even Charlie."

"Where would they be at this hour?"

"I don't know, but I fear for the little ones." I pushed up off the floor, and James grasped my arm, helping me to my feet.

"Perhaps they went outside to play? It is a full moon. There's enough natural light to guide their steps." James had an optimistic soul. He was also practical to a fault.

"With the baby? Why on earth would they take her outside in the middle of the night?" I shook my head, and James held my arms. "Something is terribly wrong. I can sense it,

James—and after what happened to Vivian." Another sobbed rocked my body and I sucked in a wet gulp. "She went missing, then turned up dead."

"Don't say that!" James let go and crossed the room to the window. "That's completely different. She was alone—"

As if he suddenly realized what I had been thinking all along, he abruptly paused, and his wild eyes sought mine. "No, she was with Charlie. And now, so are the children. Good Lord!" James said, rushing into the hallway.

"Where are you going?" I chased after him, my limbs finally moving freely again.

"They might be in the barn or the coop. Maybe Sarah wanted to visit her pony in the field, and Josh took her. They wouldn't leave Phoebe behind if the babe was fussy."

James rambled on as he ran down the staircase and straight out the front door. I couldn't keep up with him and slowed to a walk at the paddock gate. My husband was distraught and trying to make sense out of the madness. I felt the Lord guiding me as I grabbed the halter and lead rope off the fence post and jogged into the field. My old riding mare, Gypsy, lifted her head as I approached. She nickered and tossed her head. Having her mistress run up on her in the dead of night was not usual for the horse. As I reached for her head, she sidestepped away, but I moved with her. Once the halter was secured, I tugged her into a trot, and we ran to the barn.

I tied the mare next to the tack room. It was too dark to see, but I felt my way around until I had the saddle pad and saddle off the rack and placed them on the mare's back. James sprinted up behind me, breathing hard. He grasped the mare's head as I tightened the cinch.

"They're not in the barn or the coop. I found Dottie locked

in one of the stalls." His gaze fell on the horse as if he finally noticed I had saddled her. "Are you saddling her for me?" He reached for the bridle, hanging on the peg. Like me, James knew the inside of the stable like the back of his hand.

"No, for me. I'm riding to the schoolhouse to get the police officers we passed."

"I'll go, Lucinda," James pleaded, grasping my arm.

I paused, my hands resting on the cool saddle leather. The Lord had cleared my mind and given me the strength to do what I must. "This is my fault, James. I brought that girl into our home." My voice trembled, and James' thumb made circular motions over my arm. It was something he always did to calm me down, like when I would give birth. Unlike some of our men, James had insisted on being by my side for the entire labor and delivery for each of the children.

"It's not your fault. You were guided by kindness." He drew in a jagged breath and closed his eyes. "It was the right thing to do at the time."

New tears streamed down my cheeks and his face blurred. "What if something terrible comes of it? First Vivian, now Josh, Sarah, and Phoebe."

"No, I won't believe it. The Lord will protect our children. Whatever mischief is in our midst, the Lord will take care of us all."

"He didn't protect Vivian." I swallowed the lump down. My hand shook as I grasped the stirrup. I tried to convince myself that I didn't mean it, but when I thought of sweet Vivian and her fate, I know I did.

"Do not talk that way. Have faith. We'll find them—"

"Will they still be alive, James?" I didn't want to strike out at James in my fear, but I couldn't stop myself from doing it.

He lowered his voice. "Let me take Gypsy. You're in no state to gallop up the road."

I shook my head. "I won't stay here alone, James, and there's no time to hitch up Goliath. You should search the fields." Our eyes met, and James saw the determination in my eyes. He let go of my arm and tugged the bridle over Gypsy's face while I swung into the saddle. I bent low, so I wouldn't hit my head on the overhead beams as I trotted out of the barn. I stopped and swiveled in the saddle. The tall cornstalks swayed in the moonlight. "Check the cornfield as well!"

Not waiting for a reply, I bumped the mare with my heels, and we were off. It had been several years since I had time to horseback ride. The children, garden, and house chores kept me too busy for the frivolous hobby that I had loved as a teenager. The moment was bittersweet. It was a shame that the exhilaration of having the wind in my face and the mare's muscles pounding between my legs was tempered with the gut-crushing, sickening feeling of knowing my babies were in dire straits, and I might not be able to save them.

31

SADIE

Russo straightened and removed his gloves. As he talked, he pulled out the camera from his leather tote and began taking pictures of the body and the inside of the shed. I had just returned from talking to David and Bran. The EMTs were ready to come in and retrieve the body when I gave them the word.

"Approximately when do you think the time of death was?" I asked.

Russo stopped snapping pictures and took a step back. "No more than six hours. This girl was murdered while the Amish were gathered on the hill."

"Wouldn't someone have heard her scream?" A hundred thoughts flew through my mind as I stared at Vivian's feet. She wore plain black tennis shoes, and her feet were small.

Russo took another picture before he spoke. "I'd say her attacker surprised her. The log is small enough to wield as a weapon but large enough to do a lot of damage on impact. The first strike probably prevented her from being able to speak, let alone shout." He pointed at her head, which I avoided looking at. "The attack was especially savage. I won't know for sure until she's on the table and cleaned up, but I'm safely guessing she was struck at least seven times." He frowned. "This was personal."

Russo hadn't heard the bishop's revelation. I took a step closer. Russo must have seen something in my eyes to make him lower the camera. "What?" he asked, drawing out the one word in a tentative fashion.

"The last person to see Vivian Hershberger alive is a teenager named Charlie."

"Fuck," was Russo's response.

"Charlie is an uncommon name for a girl, but not unheard of. It might be a crazy coincidence." I kept my voice level as I tried to convince him or myself—I wasn't sure.

"If we weren't standing over a body, I'd agree with you."

"Yeah, I know." I took out my cell phone and swiped the screen until I pulled up a map of the county. "Look." Russo bent over the screen. "Here's where the trailer is." I moved my finger. "And here is where we are. It's about eight miles as the crow flies."

"May I?" Russo took my phone, enlarged the map, and moved it around. "The forest behind the trailer stretches all the way to Burlap Road, which borders the Amish community. When she left the trailer through the back window, she could have easily traveled unseen in the trees the five miles or so to the farm settlements."

"It wouldn't have been easy. Those hills are steep and rugged in places. I consider it more of a miracle for her to cut through without getting lost." I listened to the sound of hooves striking pavement. The Amish seemed to finally be dispersing.

"I studied the map right after the initial shootings and again when Agent Makris informed me that Charlotte Baker hadn't died with her family and was still at large. In my gut, I knew she had been with Dillon even before the evidence proved it. My fear was that, if she had fled into the woods, she could have slipped off a cliff or with these high temperatures, died of dehydration by now. My next step was to organize a search of the woods, but the idea that she might really have made it out of there and ended up among the Amish seems unreal."

"Sometimes, the most fantastical stories are the real ones. I think we should go on the assumption that it's the same girl until we find out differently." Russo went back to taking pictures. "The crime scene is a forensic mess. With the dull lighting of the lamps, I still found several hair samples and at least four different foot imprints in the dirt. One of the Amish men told me before we stepped foot inside that the shed is frequented by community members regularly throughout the summer as volunteers chop wood and stack it here in preparation to heat the schoolhouse in the winter. All the samples are bagged and labeled. There will be clues here to help build a court case, but I'm afraid the scene is compromised by the high amount of traffic."

I liked his thoroughness, attention to detail, and complete focus on the job at hand. Russo had turned out to be a real asset to the department, and I liked his style. He wasn't pushy or arrogant but quietly confident. His parents did a good job raising him.

"What do you think about the bishop's reaction to all of this?" I made a sweeping gesture with my hand.

Russo paused with the camera still raised to his face. "Of course, I listened while you were inside the shed. The man feels guilty, although he'll never admit it out loud. Praying about it later is more his style."

"I think Vivian Hershberger was already dead when the other youth realized she was missing. The bishop holding off on contacting us didn't make a difference in this particular case, but it makes you wonder how many crimes happen in the quiet countryside that we never hear about." I spoke it out loud, but I was also musing.

"That's a keen observation, sheriff. The bishop strikes me as the type who likes to keep outsiders away at all costs. We're only here right now because a girl was bludgeoned to death, and her killer is on the loose. That's not something the Amish can handle on their own."

I agreed wholeheartedly with Russo. As I returned to the doorway and inhaled the fresh, middle-of-the-night air, I began to reconstruct what happened to Vivian in my mind. Why was she in the shed in the first place? The schoolhouse didn't need firewood during summertime, and she likely wouldn't be the one chopping it. Her killer invited her to the shed to talk about something. Since the attack was so violent, it was safe to assume their relationship wasn't the greatest to begin with. Her clothes were in place, and there wasn't any indication that a sexual assault occurred. We wouldn't know that for sure until Russo performed the autopsy. My gaze drifted to the wall of trees a short distance away and the darkness beyond their branches. Whoever killed Vivian slipped into the woods afterward; that, I was sure of. If memory served me correctly, there was a small creek that ran through the forest. It was a perfect place to clean up after the attack.

The bishop had mentioned that the girl—Charlie—had worked alongside the other girls cleaning the schoolhouse, and then was driven back to her cousin's home after all the chores were finished. It was difficult to imagine a young person being able to carry on as if nothing had happened for the rest of the evening if she'd been the one swinging the piece of wood at Vivian's head. Sure, murderers did it all the time, especially husbands or wives when they killed their spouses, but for an eighteen-year-old girl to show no signs of distress following something as horrible as what was done to Vivian was unusual. Callous.

"Don't you think whoever did this would be covered in blood themselves?" I tilted to look back at Russo.

"Depends. The injuries were blunt, not sharp. I'm sure fluids were transferred, but if Charlie Baker did commit the crime, her next stop was to clean out a dirty building. Anything on her dress could have escaped notice under the circumstances. Bloodstains turn brown quickly."

"You wanted to talk to me?"

The voice was as soft as the coo of a dove, but I still jumped. I stepped out of the shed and turned to the newcomer. She looked like a teenager, shorter than me, with round cheeks and a pear-shaped body. Her polyester dress was a brownish color and the hair that poked out from beneath her stiff-looking white cap was dark, too. "Are you Delilah?"

She nodded. I didn't bother to try to shake her hand as she had hers laced tightly over her chest. Vivian was her friend. They'd probably known each other since they were toddlers, and now Vivian had died in such a brutal way. I took that into account when I stepped up to her, making sure she stood back far enough that she couldn't see inside the shed. Several dark silhouettes stirred along the back wall of the schoolhouse. I recognized the bishop's form among them. I wasn't surprised that a small group would remain until the body was taken away, and I'd questioned Delilah.

"I'm sorry about your friend," I offered.

The girl sniffed, then loosened her arms enough to bring her hand to her face and dab at the tears with her fingers. Again, my own teenager invaded my thoughts. Chloe would be an absolute wreck if one of her friends had been murdered. At a glance, Amish kids seemed more mature and resilient during a crisis than regular kids.

"Do you think she suffered?" Delilah asked with a weak, trembling voice.

I hated lying to anybody, but this time, it was a necessity. If I told the Amish girl that her friend had experienced an agonizing death—one where she was well aware that her life was coming to an end—it would haunt her for the rest of her life. I had to live with the nightmares; this poor girl did not.

"I think it happened quickly. Vivian would have been unconscious."

A heavy tear ran down Delilah's cheek. "I still can't believe she's gone."

I placed my hand on her shoulder and squeezed, which only caused her tears to multiply. I deliberated with myself whether I should wait to talk to her in the morning. The empathetic and motherly part of me wanted to give the girl a little time to compose herself. My cop side reminded me that a murderer was walking free and others, including this girl, would be in danger until the killer was apprehended. Too much was at stake to give Delilah a break tonight.

"It's late, and I'm sure you're tired, but I'd like to ask you a few quick questions, if that's okay."

The girl nodded. "Anything to help Vivian."

Her state of mind was good. That definitely helped. "Your bishop mentioned that you had informed him that Charlie was the last person to see Vivian. How do you know that?" I didn't pull out my little notepad, careful not to spook her. It would be easier for Delilah if she felt like we were simply having a conversation about her friends. The more relaxed she was, the more likely she'd let her guard down and be completely honest.

She shifted her weight between her feet and folded her arms tighter around her chest. "I was right there when Charlie asked to speak to Vivian alone. Vivian agreed, and they left together after that."

"Where did they go?" I tried to keep my face neutral, but my insides were on fire as I held my breath.

She pointed up the hill. "We were standing behind the schoolhouse when they left. They came down the hill. At the time, there were about five or six buggies parked in between there and here. When they disappeared behind the first buggy they came to, I turned around and went to work inside the schoolhouse."

So, Delilah didn't know if they came all the way to the shed together. Russo's shoe print pictures and measurements might be able to prove that Charlie was in the shed with Vivian.

"Do you have any idea what Charlie wanted to talk to Vivian about?"

Delilah exhaled, and even in the moonlight, I saw her cheeks darken a shade. She didn't hesitate. "Marvin Miller. Vivian's been sweet on him since third grade, and she believed they were going to begin courting this summer. Then Charlie showed up and ruined everything for her." Delilah's voice had gained momentum and volume as she talked. Her willingness to talk about a boy and her friends' gossip made me reconsider how similar Amish kids were in some ways to other young people. The fact that a boy was involved sent a shiver up my spine. Everything became a hell of a lot clearer, too.

"I take it the girls weren't friendly?"

"Vivian didn't like Charlie at all. She accused her of being fake."

"Fake?" My heart rate sped up. "What do you mean?"

"Charlie comes from an Ohio community where they do everything differently than we do. She told us that she gets a lot more freedom and stuff." Delilah shrugged. "I thought Vivian was kind of picking on Charlie, 'cause she was jealous, but there *were* things that were odd about Charlie."

"Like what?" The rush of blood through my veins bordered on uncomfortable. I worked to keep my voice and body steady as excitement and dread built inside me.

"She talked funny—used strange words—like an Englisher. Nothing seemed to rile her either, and she stood awfully close to Marvin without hardly knowing him. We all thought her shameless."

"How long had she been visiting?"

"Only a few days. She was supposed to go home next week." The girl cocked her head, scrunching her face. "Why do you ask so much about Charlie?"

I answered quickly. "It's important for me to understand what was going on in Vivian's life right before she died. That's why, if you can remember anything else that might be important—about Vivian or Charlie—it might help me find out who hurt Vivian."

Delilah's lips puckered like she was thinking hard. "There

is something else. When Charlie walked back into the schoolhouse, the front of her dress was wet. Charlie's cap was never neat, but some of her hair fell out of it, and the ends were damp too."

It was like pieces of a puzzle falling into place. "Did she give you a reason for her appearance?"

"She said she was hot and splashed water on herself from the horses' trough." Delilah's voice faded. "Me and the other girls laughed about it at the time, but it was something none of us would ever do."

Something else flashed in my mind. "Miller—isn't that your bishop's last name?"

"Yes, Marvin is Zeke and Susan's son."

Whoa, now *that's* interesting. "So, how did Marvin feel about Vivian and Charlie vying for his attention?"

"I don't know anything about that, but he did sit next to Charlie at the ballgame. Then he offered to drive her home tonight." Delilah glanced at her watch and corrected herself. "Well, guess it's last night now."

Delilah's eyes widened when Russo appeared at my side. He bent over and spoke close to my ear. "The EMTs can take her into town anytime now."

I glanced at the ambulance and saw heads poking out the windows of the cab. Raising my hand over my head, I flicked my wrist. Immediately the doors popped open. They quickly unloaded the gurney with the body bag on top of it and rolled it past us, following Russo into the shed.

Delilah had inched further away, and I saw the discomfort written all over her wide-eyed face. She wanted out of there before her friend came out. I didn't blame her.

"Is Marvin here?"

She shook her head. "The Miller farm is just up the road on the right side. There's a silo right next to the road where the driveway is."

Delilah had risen a notch in my books. The girl understood that the next person I had to talk to was Marvin Miller, and she was being proactive.

She took several steps backward and began to turn around when I stopped her. "One more thing and then you can go. What does Charlie look like?"

Her eyes raised up as she thought, telling me she was picturing Charlie in her head. "She's really skinny and pale. Her eyes are kind of greenish-brown, and they're huge. She's pretty." Delilah's head dropped. "Can I leave?"

"I might need to follow up with some more questions later on, but yes, you may go."

Delilah spun around and jogged back up the hill without a backward glance. The timing was perfect. At that same moment, the EMTs and Russo emerged from the shed. I watched as Vivian's concealed body passed by and was carefully loaded into the back of the ambulance. Russo stood beside me. When the engine roared to life, it caused a horse to whinny, and the headlights illuminated the dew-covered field. As it made a U-turn, the lights shined on the schoolhouse. Dozens of people stood in a long line, waiting outside the building.

It was hard enough to grasp that we had another murder on our hands; but throw in the Amish community as a backdrop, and the night had turned into the *Twilight Zone*.

"Did the girl have any useful information?" Russo asked. We were alone except for the trilling sound of frogs in the bushes along the hedgerow behind the shed.

"She described the Amish Charlie, and guess what?"

"They look the same," Russo replied smartly.

"Yep. Delilah's description of the Charlie she knew was the same as the big-eyed girl in the file folder that Makris gave me. They are one and the same. I'm sure of it."

The frantic sound of pounding hooves turned both our heads in the direction of the roadway. A lone horse approached the schoolhouse at high speed. I actually thought I saw sparks fly between the hooves and the pavement. The rider turned into the driveway that led to the schoolhouse, but instead of slowing there, they kept on coming straight down the hill at a full gallop.

Russo stepped back, but I held my ground as the rider pulled the horse to a stop only a couple feet from where I stood. A splotch of saliva struck my cheek when the horse threw its head sideways. Steam rose off the animal's body, and I caught a whiff of its wet fur. At first, I thought the rider was a teenager. I didn't realize she was actually a woman until she dismounted and was close enough that I could see the lines at the corners of her eyes and her mature face. Her cap was askew, and the bottom of her blue dress was splattered with mud.

"My children are gone! You must help me find them!" She looked straight at me, ignoring Russo and breathing rapidly.

More than one child missing? "You have to calm down and explain what's going on."

The woman blew out a shuddering breath, then began talking quickly. "James and I arrived home a little while ago. Josh, Sarah, and the baby—Phoebe—are not there. Neither is the girl who was watching them. I think she took them somewhere, and I don't trust her."

I froze in place. "What is the girl's name?"

"Charlie—Charlie Baker."

32

LUCINDA

A muscle in the sheriff's jaw twitched, and her blue eyes went round. She'd recognized the English girl's name. The concerned look that flashed across her face made it difficult to breathe. I'd never met this woman before. The thin creases at the corners of her eyes and her thick brown hair made me guess she wasn't much older than me. Her direct and steady manner signaled she was professional, and her steady gaze gave me the impression she was trustworthy. The sheriff wore a felt hat, a tan shirt, and a gun was holstered at her hip. All these observations whipped around in my head in a jumble that made the cool, dark night feel even more nightmarish.

"You know Charlie?" I dared to ask.

The sheriff glanced at the dark-haired man standing beside her. He rubbed the top of his head but didn't say anything.

"I do. You're right to not trust her. The girl has problems and can be considered dangerous." She motioned me to follow, and I did. "Can you leave your horse here? We'll make better time in my car."

"Of course. Just a minute." I tugged Gypsy away from the officers, straight to the hitching rail where one of the Yoder boys was standing. "Please take my horse home with you, Levi. I must go with the sheriff. James will come for her tomorrow."

"I sure will, Lucinda. I'll pray for you all."

More tears threatened to fall, so I murmured a quick thank you and hurried back to the police car. The officers were already waiting inside, and the woman motioned for me to get into the back seat. Never in a million years did I imagine I would be inside one of these. The vehicle began moving as soon as I shut the door. I pressed up against the partition.

"Where do you live?" the sheriff asked.

"Turn left. It's three miles away." My heart danced inside my chest as we passed the bishop and Susan standing in front of the schoolhouse with a crowd of others. I didn't think anyone could see me. I'd noticed the tinted windows when I climbed in.

The man in the front passenger seat made a low humming sound. "That's a long way to ride a horse in the middle of the night, isn't it?"

His question seemed silly to me, but I responded anyway. "No longer than in the daytime."

The sheriff snorted. "She's got you there."

The car moved with smooth speed over the road. I lifted my chin to the narrow stream of fresh air blowing in through an open slit in the driver's side window, still finding it difficult to catch a proper breath. Being with the officers as they made their way closer to the farm calmed my nerves a little bit. The Englishers would know what to do.

"What's your full name?" the sheriff asked.

"Lucinda Coblentz. My husband is James."

I saw her head dip with a curt nod. "How is it that Charlie Baker came to be babysitting your children?"

There wasn't time to explain. "It's a long story." Seeing the driveway ahead, I pointed. "There it is!"

The car made the turn and stopped beside the house. The place was the same as I'd left it twenty minutes ago. Lights still flickered in the windows, but James was nowhere to be seen.

I grabbed the door handle, and the sheriff stopped me. "Wait a minute," she told me. Then she picked up what I assumed was a radio device and talked into it. "Darcy, we need backup out here in the Amish community. Contact Harlow county and see if they will assist. We have three missing children on top of the dead girl. I'm currently at a white farmhouse on Willow Springs Road, a few miles west of the primitive schoolhouse. Yes, please hurry. Time is of the essence." She set the radio down and swiveled in her seat to look directly at me. "We're going to do our best to find your kids, but you have to answer the question, Lucinda. How do you know Charlie?"

I looked away, searching out the windows for James and the children. "She appeared almost a week ago. The girl was half-starved and stealing eggs out of the coop to eat. She'd slept in the barn the night before I discovered her." I swallowed a gulp of air as I remembered that first night. I'd felt so sorry for her. "You see, I'd seen the girl once before at the community market. She came up to our horse and began petting it. I could tell by the tattered clothes she wore and the hollowness of her face that she was poor and hungry. I gave her a couple of fried pies, taking pity on her. An angry man suddenly appeared. He dragged her away and shoved her into a small, old-looking car." I chewed the bottom of my lip and tapped the car door with my finger. "I never thought of it until now, but I think when she escaped that evil man, she must have looked for our horse in the field. That's how she found me. Goliath is unusually large. He'd stick out if someone searched for him. That's the only way she could have come here. We hadn't exchanged names or anything so familiar."

"You think you were targeted by her?" the sheriff asked.

I lifted my gaze. When our eyes met, I saw bright eagerness there, but she didn't move a muscle. Her stillness in the seat caused me to slump in mine. "It is hard to believe it to be random coincidence. Because I desired to help the girl, I asked my husband if she could stay for a short time—long enough to fill up on good food and get her bearings. James didn't like the idea but relented. We decided that pretending she was a visiting cousin was the best way to handle the situation." I saw her brows lift, and on top of the fear burning inside of me, I felt incredible regret. Regret for not listening to James and for trusting the strange girl.

"Let me get this straight. Charlie Baker has been with your family for a week, and during that time, she pretended to be Amish?"

I nodded, wiping my eyes and nose with the back of my hand. The sheriff saw the gesture and quickly snatched up a few tissues from a box and pushed them in between the bars.

"Lucinda, this is important." She waited until I looked up from a tissue. "Was Charlie spending time with Marvin Miller?"

My heartbeat surged into my throat. "Yes, she was. It's odd. Marvin took an instant liking to her. After one meeting, he talked to his parents about a possible courtship."

The man in the passenger seat looked back. "That's quick."

When the sheriff ignored him, I shifted my gaze to her again. "What does this have to do with my children?"

The sheriff's face clouded over as if she was deliberating what to say. She gave a shake to her head and took a deep breath. "Charlie Baker disappeared from her home in Cincinnati two years ago. Her family had been murdered, and at the time, it was thought that she too had been a victim. Now, after more evidence has come in, we fear that she's the one who killed her parents and younger sister. It's imperative we find them as soon as possible. We have to be smart about it, though." She flung open the door and stepped out of the car. I followed her actions and was soon standing in front of her. The sheriff looked around, her attention settling on the barn. "That's a large building. Are you sure you checked it thoroughly?"

"My husband did."

"How about the smaller outbuildings?"

I shook my head vigorously. "They aren't on the property. He checked them all."

"Where's your husband?" the man asked. I had almost forgotten him. He had also exited the vehicle and was scanning the yard.

"He said he would check the cornfield." I looked past her shoulder, and she turned to follow my gaze. "I don't know why he isn't back yet." Pressing my hand to my mouth, I stifled a gasp. My entire family was missing, and Charlie might be a murderer.

The sheriff touched my shoulder. She looked back at me with calm determination. "Where did you see him go in?"

I pointed to the place where I thought he went, and the sheriff took off at a jog. The man and I followed her through the damp grass, in and out of the long shadows stretching from the barn and coop. We stopped behind the sheriff.

The sheriff spread the plants carefully with her hands. "Someone on horseback came through here." She motioned at the hoofprints in the mud and stared at me. "Do you or your husband ride back here?"

My mind went straight to earlier that same day when I'd found Charlie's bed made up to look like she was in it, but she wasn't. "No, it damages the corn." I took a trembling breath. "Charlie was missing for several hours"—I glanced at my watch—"yesterday. I suspect Marvin took her horseback riding."

"Where does this lead?" Her sharp voice snapped me to attention.

"I don't know. The field goes on a long way. There's some woods in that direction." My legs suddenly felt like jelly, and I wobbled. The man's hand thrust forward to keep me from falling. Pressure inside my head made me feel woozy. My limbs were weak. I still managed to shrug off the man's assistance and reach for the fence railing instead to brace myself.

Hoofbeats on pavement turned all our heads. It was a lone rider. When he galloped onto the driveway, I raised my hand and waved at him. He saw and aimed his horse toward us.

"Who's that?" the sheriff asked.

"Marvin Miller."

33

SADIE

The young man barreling towards us was a good rider. He pulled on the reins, and his horse skidded to a stop in front of us. The black horse stomped its hoof and snorted.

Marvin leaned forward to catch his breath. "Miss Lucinda, Father told me about your children. I think I might know where Charlie took them."

Lucinda ran to the horse's head and grasped the reins. "Where, Marvin? Please, tell us now!"

I tilted my head to look up at Marvin. Stubble covered his chin, and I remembered that I'd heard sometime ago that Amish men didn't grow their beards until they were married. The lad's eyes flashed with dread.

"There's an old hunting cabin in the woods beyond the cornfields." He dropped his gaze, fiddling with the strings on the saddle with his fingers. "I took Charlie there yesterday, so she knows the way."

"Can we drive there?" I approached the horse. Steam rose

off its sweating body. Marvin must have galloped the entire way.

He shook his head, taking a raspy breath. "There's no access roads nearby. The only way in or out is hiking or riding a horse."

I glanced at Russo. He raised his hands. "Count me out."

Russo getting on a horse hadn't even crossed my mind. The three Amish kids were in grave danger. Charlie Baker had likely killed Vivian Hershberger, and if she could shoot her ten-year-old sister in the face, she was capable of anything. I returned my attention to Marvin. "By horseback, how long to reach the cabin?"

"At a fast clip, maybe fifteen minutes. Walking will get you there in forty-five minutes."

Minutes mattered. "I need a horse," I told Lucinda.

"You know how to ride?" The Amish woman's jaw dropped.

"I had a horse growing up," I said as I started walking towards the barn.

"Is that really a good idea, sheriff? We should wait for backup to arrive." Russo followed on my heels.

"We don't have time for that." I kept going. "You'll wait here for the rest of the crew, and in the off chance that Charlie returns with the kids. She isn't armed, as far as we know." I stopped in my tracks and looked over my shoulder at Lucinda. "Do you have guns in the house?" The Amish might be pacifists, but they loved to hunt.

She nodded. "Several rifles."

"Do you keep them locked up?"

"No," she said quietly.

Out of the corner of my eye, I saw Russo's head drop forward. Damnit. "Check them right now. I need to know if she's armed." Lucinda ran off. I spun around to address Marvin, who was right behind us, still mounted. "You'll have to be my guide. At night like this, I'd be blind as a bat in a maze of fields, crops, and trees." He gave a firm nod. "Get one of those other horses saddled for me and be quick about it. I'll hold your horse."

Marvin jumped off and departed as quickly as Lucinda had left.

"This is highly irregular—" Russo began, but I cut him off.

"Welcome to small-town hill country. You should have already gotten a taste of it in our dealings with the Dovers. We have to think out of the box and act quickly." I took a step closer. "That crazy girl is a murderer. She's desperate, and those kids are at her mercy. I'll never forgive myself if anyone dies, and I didn't do everything in my power to save them."

"I get it. I do." Russo looked around to see if we were still alone. "After seeing what Charlie did to the Amish girl, I'm afraid the children might be dead already."

My stomach clenched. He was right. "Either way, I have to make the arrest." I turned my head. "I grew up not far from here." I blew out a soft breath through dry lips. "It's a shame that wicked girl came to our town."

"Don't forget, Dillon has been pimping her out for two years. She's damaged, not necessarily evil," Russo said.

"I never took you for the forgiving type, Russo." I touched the horse's warm nose. The action slowed my racing heart. Ever since we'd been out to the Dovers, I'd been operating in dreamlike territory. Possum Gap had its troubles, no doubt, but shootouts, murders, missing kids, and a teenaged killer were far from normal in our small, hill town. To say I was beginning to feel a bit overwhelmed would be accurate.

He frowned. "If someone does me dirty, I'm not."

By his humorless expression, I believed him. Lucinda rushing towards us caught my eye.

She was still a good distance away when she shouted out, "The .22 is missing!"

"It keeps getting better and better," Russo mumbled under his breath.

Marvin led a giant black horse out of the barn. This must be Goliath. I'd need a ladder to reach the stirrup. I traded reins with Marvin.

"I'm coming, too!" Lucinda nearly bumped into my back when she stopped running.

I shook my head, but before I had a chance to speak, she grabbed my arm and pleaded. "Please, those are my babies. When you find them, they'll need their mother." Tears welled in her eyes, and she pressed her lips tightly together. "It's my fault they're in danger."

Being a mom myself, I got where she was coming from. She didn't want to sit still while someone else saved her kids. Since she blamed herself, it was even worse. "Being generous and nice isn't something you ever have to apologize for. The only person in the wrong here is the girl who has taken your kids."

The corners of her eyes crinkled, and she cocked her head. "Please let me come," she whispered.

I didn't look at Russo. The lack of protocol already ruffled his feathers. From a practical standpoint, handling the three kids—if they were still alive—might be difficult. I thought of Chloe and how there was no way in hell I'd leave her fate up to a stranger. I would demand to go. "We only have two horses—"

"We can ride double." Before I could stop her, Lucinda lifted her foot high into the stirrup and pulled herself into the saddle. Marvin's mouth dropped open, but he remained silent.

Arguing with her would waste precious time. "All right, but I'm in front, and you had better listen to instructions. Getting emotional could ruin everything."

Lucinda nodded firmly and scooted behind the saddle, so she sat on the part of Goliath's back where the saddle blanket poked out from beneath the saddle. With more agility than I thought I still had, I managed to get my boot into the stirrup and pull myself up without any help. Sitting down and taking up the reins in my hands, I tried to remember when the last time I'd ridden had been. Twenty years maybe?

I bumped the horse's sides to catch up to Marvin, who cantered right into the spot in the cornfield where the leaves were folded back. Who knew what we were riding into? Lucinda's kids could be dead already, and Charlie might be in position to shoot us right off the horses. As Lucinda grasped my waist, I urged Goliath faster, saying a silent prayer in my head that we weren't too late.

34

CHARLIE

A bird chirped loudly in the branches above my head, but I didn't look up to find it. It was strange that one would be awake in the middle of the night, but the thought was fleeting. I stood frozen in place, holding my breath and squinting into the darkness. There was movement in the bushes. I thought I heard breathing, but it might have been the wind. My heart felt like it would explode out of my chest. When the leaves parted and a shadowy form emerged, I brought the butt of the rifle down hard.

The person stumbled forward. It was James. He grunted, reaching for a tree trunk to catch his fall, but I was faster. I struck him again. This time, the blow brought him to the ground. He wasn't moving. I couldn't shoot the rifle for fear anyone looking for the kids would hear the sound and find us. I had to make sure James didn't get back up. I raised the rifle over my head to bring it down again but stopped when I heard crying.

I swiveled my head to find Josh standing between two

slender tree trunks at the bottom of the steps that led into the cabin. The boy's red face and his sniffling breaths made me cringe. I advanced on him, aiming the gun at his chest.

"Don't cry like a baby. Now get back in there like I told you," I said through gritted teeth.

"You hurt Da—why would you do that?" Josh's voice shook. He held his ground when the point of the rifle pressed against his skinny chest.

"You're not that dumb, are you?" The fire inside my gut flamed up into my throat. My head hurt, and my legs ached from the long hike through the woods carrying the fat baby. I needed to think, but my thoughts were rattled, and the kids wouldn't shut up. I didn't lower the weapon. Seeing the stubborn lift to Josh's chin made me seethe. "Get back in there," I hissed.

"Why are you being so mean?" A blonde head poked around the doorframe. It was Sarah. I could see Phoebe crawling on the floor behind her. At least the baby had finally stopped crying.

I tipped my head to the girl. "Because I'm a bad person." I swallowed down the hard knot that stuck in my throat. "I've been this way for a long time. If you don't get your ass back in that cabin, I'm going to shoot your brother." The girl's eyes, which were already wide open, managed to grow larger. She didn't move fast enough. "I don't need all three of you," I growled the words out, cocking the rifle for more affect.

She grabbed her sister under the arms and tugged her out of view. I returned my attention to the boy. "I'll say it one more time. Get back in there!" I said forcefully, yet quietly.

Josh still didn't move. "What are you going to do with us?"

Black dots blurred my vision. "You're just like Lucy—pestering me until I do something terrible to you."

FREE FROM SIN

"Your sister?" Josh's voice lost its edge. His curious nature erased some of his fear, although his eyes kept darting to where his dad lay crumpled on the forest floor.

I lowered the gun a tad. It was beginning to hurt my arms. My idea to escape with the kids to the cabin was rash. Now, I regretted it. I would have gotten further away if I hadn't dragged the kids along. But then what? I couldn't hide in the woods forever. At least this way, I had some leverage. That's what I thought, anyway. Now, I wasn't so sure. I could still leave, make a run for it, but the kids would tell everyone that I was the one who took them. My brow knitted as I stared at Josh. If Lucinda's kids couldn't talk, then no one would know that I'd kidnapped them—or killed Vivian. Stupid Vivian. She couldn't just leave me alone. No, she had to taunt me. It was her own fault—just like Lucy. I blinked. The pain on the side of my head grew worse. I took one hand off the rifle to press it into the throbbing spot. "She wouldn't do what she was told either."

"What happened to her?" Josh asked in a small voice.

He shivered, and I noticed the drop in temperature and the scent of rain in the air. A shadow passed over us when clouds covered the full moon. Shifting my gaze to the side, I stared at the bent tree trunks. They looked like creepy, old, deformed men staring back at me. Then I looked past them and saw only blackness.

A prickling sensation raised goosebumps on my arms. I shook the eerie feeling off. Tomorrow would be sunny and warm again. I'd finally find the place where I belonged— where I would be safe. Gross men wouldn't touch me with their filthy hands, and there would be lots of good food, like Lucinda's pies. I would get my driver's license, then buy my own car. My chest tightened when it occurred to me that I was eighteen and I'd never driven before. It couldn't be too hard, right? I'd get a job at a veterinarian office or maybe a zoo. I liked animals. They didn't ask dumb questions, and they wouldn't judge me for what I had done. And I would buy my own horse, one just like Goliath—a gentle giant.

My head cleared, and the sweet thoughts vanished as the wind picked up and the tall trees swayed. Their branches made scratching noises above my head. I rested the rifle against my shoulder and rubbed my arm with my free hand. These stupid dresses might be okay in the heat of day, but on a damp, cool night, they weren't thick enough. I would be happy to wear blue jeans again. It had been silly to think I'd make it pretending to be Amish. Most of the people were friendly enough, and the food was great, but all the rules were infuriating. I was a loner. Joining a group—or cult—wasn't my thing. Being with Marvin had been nice. I'd probably never find such a kind man again. Having sex with him had been different than the other guys. There was something almost innocent about it, which was strange. He really liked me and might even miss me when I'm gone.

"Lucy's dead." I ignored Josh's sharp intake of breath. "It wasn't my fault. I tried to help her, and she wouldn't listen. It was just a matter of time before our stepdad would have started visiting her in the middle of the night, just like he'd done to me. Those nights weren't any fun. It hurt, and he'd be all sweaty." I took a few steps away from Josh, glancing down at his dad. I could see the shallow rise and fall of his chest. He was still alive. "My mom wasn't like yours. She denied it, but deep down, she knew what was going on. She didn't protect me, and she wouldn't have protected Lucy." I rounded on

Josh. "What kind of mother lets something like that happen to her daughters?" I blew out a long, hard breath. "They deserved what they got, and now I'm free of them. I didn't plan for Lucy to go with them. If she had listened to me, she'd be alive right now."

"What did you do to her?" Josh's voice spurted the words out like water trickling from a sink.

I raised the gun and charged him. The boy fell backward onto the steps, then pivoted and lurched up them. He ran straight into the cabin without looking back or saying another word. I stood in the doorway, my chest heaving. The blankets on the bed where Marvin and I had sex the day before were still disheveled, and the dry, dusty smell in the air reminded me of the quick yet pleasant time I'd spent in here with him. My gaze skipped to the corner where the kids were backed flat against the wall. Josh took up a position in front of Sarah, who struggled to hold onto Phoebe. The baby started to fuss. At first, the sounds coming out of her mouth were like a soft mewing before they ramped up to choppy crying.

I filled my lungs with air and looked over my shoulder at the woods. Light rain began to fall, and then there was a punch of colder air through the open doorway. Streaks of water trailed down the window, obscuring the view and the tapping of raindrops on the tin roof almost smothered Phoebe's cries. Almost. I advanced on the kids. "Shut her up! I can't think!"

Sarah dropped to the floor, hugging Phoebe while Josh spread his arms wide. "I won't let you hurt them," he shouted.

"Da's getting wet," Sarah chirped from behind her brother.

It would be so easy to end it right here. This was as good a place as any to die. Eventually, we all stop breathing. What difference does it make when it happens? I raised the gun, but my hands shook. I hesitated. Josh's eyes widened. Sarah closed hers as Phoebe continued to wail.

"Shut her up!" I demanded.

Their faces blurred as tears burned my eyes. *Maybe I could still get away and buy that giant horse.* The downpour grew louder. *No one would hear gunshots now. Those noisy kids will not keep my secrets. They will tell everyone what I've done.* Thoughts darted around my head as I tried to hold the gun steady. I kept blinking to clear my eyes. *They're just little kids. They never did anything to you. Lucy never hurt you either.* Their small, round, trembling faces were abruptly replaced by my stepdad, Mom, Dillon, and a hundred strangers. I shook my head, trying to get rid of the unwelcome faces, but they wouldn't go.

"Go away!" I screamed. "Leave me alone!"

"I will pray for you, Charlie," Josh said in a quiet voice that I could barely hear over Phoebe's crying and the raging rainstorm striking the cabin.

But somehow, I did hear him. I opened my eyes to find tears running down the boy's cheeks.

"I'm sorry you're so sad," he said. Then he sniffed, rubbing his eyes with the back of his hand.

I dropped the gun an inch as my throat tightened. "Don't feel sorry for me," I whispered.

"Put the weapon down!" an unfamiliar voice shouted out from behind me.

I stood frozen in place. Phoebe's wails increased in volume. A cold draft whipped at my back. I inhaled the fresh scent of the rain and remembered how much I liked the smell. It was familiar and made me feel sleepy. I took a deeper breath. My heartbeat slowed. I could breathe easier. They came sooner than I thought they would. I should have left the kids in their house—just like I wished I'd walked out of the garage that day without firing at Lucy. I closed my eyes. It would be good to go to sleep, and not worry about what I'd done anymore. My life was over, anyway. I was the worst kind of sinner. Lucy was innocent, and I had killed her. Even Vivian didn't deserve to die.

"Please, Charlie. It doesn't have to be this way. I know you don't want to hurt the children. You're a good girl. You wouldn't do that."

It was a voice I knew well. I took a step sideways and turned my head, looking back. Lucinda's eyes were full of tears. Her breaths were choppy and wet. But it was her eyes that held me captive. There was fear in their shiny depths but also sympathy. Even though I'd knocked out her husband, taken her precious kids away at gunpoint, and beat a girl in her community to death, she somehow found compassion for me. This is how a mother is supposed to act. Lucinda took me in, not just from pity, but because she wanted to mother me, save me from the world—myself—whatever I needed saving from.

She couldn't save me. I wasn't religious like her, but I knew if there was a hell, I'd go there for the things I'd done. The woman at her side was a police officer. The gun she gripped in her hand was pointed at me, and it didn't waver. My rifle was still raised, but it was so heavy.

The cop's head dipped a little. "Drop it, Charlie. You can start to fix things by putting the gun down and leaving those kids alone. I will get you the help you need. It's going to be all right."

Beyond the door, in the falling rain, I heard a horse whinny. The fog in my head cleared a little. I looked between the cop's and Lucinda's shoulders. Goliath stood in the pouring rain;

his reins were gathered in one of Marvin's hands. Marvin's other hand gripped onto James, who leaned against the horse's slick, black body.

Our eyes met. Marvin was too far away to speak to me, and in the deluge, I wouldn't have heard him. He raised his hand. The gesture caused my limbs to loosen. I was so tired, and every part of me hurt. Lucinda was wrong. I wasn't good. I was evil.

"Mamma," Sarah's little voice cried, and I heard Lucinda's sob in response. I couldn't see her, though. The cop wasn't there anymore either.

The sound of a million taps on the roof disappeared, replaced by birds chirping happily. I glanced down, and I was riding Goliath in thick, knee-high grass. My heart lightened as I lifted my legs away from his side. I had always wanted to gallop across a field. Now was my chance. I bumped the horse with my heels, and his muscles gathered beneath me. Then we were off. Warm wind pummeled my face, and I didn't need to grab the saddle horn to balance myself. Somehow, I knew how to ride, and I was good at it.

There was a shout, "Stop!" But it was far, far away.

The meadow faded to blackness, and the sensation of flying vanished.

It was quiet. It was peaceful. It was home.

35

SADIE

I saw the glazed look in Charlie's eyes right before she spun around, raised the gun higher, and turned it on the kids who cowered in the corner. Damnit. *Why?*

I had no choice. I fired three times at the girl. Once in the back of the head and twice in her upper back. She never got a shot off. When she fell, Lucinda rushed to her kids, and I went to Charlie's side. My peripheral vision caught Lucinda hugging the boy and girl before she picked up the crying baby. Their tearful reunion was in the back of my mind as I carefully turned Charlie over. The exit wound from the bullet that struck the back of her head was larger than its entry and had broken through her forehead. She'd died instantly. My heart rate had accelerated after I had shot her, and now, I took shallow breaths, willing my vitals to return to normal. The kids were safe. James needed medical attention, but he'd survive. It had ended better than expected.

I'd seen too many dead people to count, so the only jolt to my senses was how young the girl looked in death. There was something else. I pursed my lips and leaned forward. Charlie's hazel eyes were vacant, but her mouth curved upwards. She was smiling.

I swayed back. I'd never seen anything like it. I heard Lucinda shuffle the kids across the room. She told them to stand there.

Lucinda's husband stumbled into the cabin with Marvin's help. "Thank the Lord, you're all right." He was speaking to Lucinda. She met him at the door and put her arm under his to help him over to where she'd left the kids. He knelt on the floor, and the boy was the first one to throw his arms around him. The girl came next.

With the baby propped up on Lucinda's hip, she spoke to Marvin in a soft voice. "Ride out and tell everyone we have the children and they're fine. I believe the bishop can bring his Bobcat back here, and that's how we'll get James out. He'll need to go to the hospital. Alert the Englisher who came with the sheriff to call an ambulance."

Lucinda's concise and smart instructions impressed me, but in her relief to be reunited with her family, she failed to see the horror on Marvin's gaping face. I rose quickly and reached for the blanket off the bed. With a flapping motion, I covered Charlie, hiding her body, and subsequently bracing the young man with my hand.

"Are you okay?"

Water dripped off the rim of his hat. We were all drenched straight through to the bone, but looking at his pale, wet face and large pupils, I knew he was in shock.

"Why did she do that?" He looked at me with wild eyes. "She wouldn't have shot those children. She wanted you to think she was going to."

He had hit the nail right on the head. I thought the same. It was suicide by cop but not in the usual way. From the glassy, faraway look on her face right before she turned with the gun, it was almost as if she wasn't aware of what she was doing. I sighed, rubbing my forehead. The mind was a funny thing. Maybe the self-preservation mechanism could be as strong as its self-destructive side.

"We'll never know for sure what she was thinking." I swallowed hard and licked my dry lips. "Charlie was a very troubled girl. She'd suffered through unimaginable things, and those experiences corrupted her heart and soul. It's best to try and remember the good in her." I squeezed his shoulder. "You'll never forget this day, but it doesn't have to affect you negatively the way those bad memories did Charlie. She's at peace, and you should be too."

Marvin gave a curt nod. His gaze dropped to the wooden floor, and his jaw loosened. As if his mind was made up to take my advice, he muttered, "I'll ride fast," and then he was gone.

Lucinda stepped away from her family and came to my side. Glancing out the doorway, I saw that the rain had dwindled to a drizzly mist. The sky lightened from darkness to gray, and the sun broke through the trees in a blaze of golden beams. Morning had finally arrived.

"You're right about Charlie. From the small talks we'd shared, I learned that she had been abused most of her life. I think she was searching for things that were elusive to her—security, freedom, and love. By the look on her face, I believe she found them. Her troubled soul is at peace now."

Lucinda must have seen her strange smile too.

36

SADIE

Russo covered Charlie's face back up, straightened, and stepped back. While waiting for news from me, he'd studied a map he'd pulled up on his phone and made a few phone calls. About one hundred feet from the cabin was an old ATV trail. Buddy had a friend haul a couple to the nearest roadside so Buddy and Russo could drive to the cabin. One of the ATV's pulled a cart behind it, and that was how we would take Charlie's body out of the hills. The Coblentz family had already left on the Bobcat and were probably back to their farm by now.

Lucinda was a strong woman, but in the days to come, Charlie would weigh heavily on her mind. The entire family would probably benefit from therapy. In a couple of days, I'd check in on them to finish up the paperwork and see what they needed. In the short and stressful time that I'd known Lucinda, I knew I liked her very much. Perhaps we could be friends. Only time would tell.

I motioned for Buddy to come over. He'd been standing

in the doorway, watching the sun rise higher in the sky. Death made my first deputy uncomfortable. I got it. When you became too used to it, you might as well retire. "She's ready to go. Just take it slow and easy."

He nodded. "Right." He knelt to pick up Charlie's body, hesitated, then looked back. "Don't feel bad, sheriff. You had to do it." He grasped the body and easily hoisted it with his large frame as he stood.

Emotions sprang to life in my gut, and tears threatened to break from my eyes. "Thanks, Buddy. I hope I don't have to kill a teenager ever again."

Buddy nodded once. His frown said it all. The way things were going, there were no guarantees that I wouldn't have to, and that realization filled me with deep sadness. Charlie's story had come to an end in the most brutal way, along with several cases at once. The trailer shootings would be tied up in the courts for a while, and exactly how that fiasco went down might never be fully known. Christen's testimony would put Dillon behind bars for a long time. The Hershberger family—and the entire Amish community—might never fully recover Vivian's horrific murder, but at least we had her killer. After a death like that, all we could do is make sure justice was served, and in this case, it was. The Dover clan would continue to be a thorn in my backside and, I feared their take-matters-into-their-own-hands ways would pull me back into their holler sooner than I wanted. Whether any of them were arrested for the deaths of Billy Becker and Randall Birdie was anyone's guess. Dillon's testimony wouldn't be taken seriously after his track record. Even if he shot Jax Dover in self-defense, he'd held girls hostage and forced them into sex slavery using violence and drugs. He was a shit of a man who deserved whatever he got behind bars. Everyone in the trailer that fateful day was dead, except Christen, and she wouldn't incriminate her kin. My guess was the Dovers would get away with murder.

Today was a bad day, but it could have been so much worse. I'd be grateful, and at the same time, be ready for what came next.

"What do you think will become of her body?" I asked Russo as he packed up his camera and the evidence he'd collected from the scene.

"There's probably a great aunt or a cousin who will take responsibility for it. I doubt she'll be buried alongside her family, though. That rarely happens in murder cases like hers." He didn't look up and continued to work quickly. The remote location and dingy appearance of the cabin made the city slicker uneasy, or so he'd already said. "Cremation and an unmarked grave might be her fate, if truth be told."

Yeah, I was thinking that. Even in death, the girl doesn't have anyone to take care of her.

"If she survived, I believed she would have been institutionalized and not imprisoned. In this line of work, we see all kinds of criminals," I said. "It's been my experience that rarely are any of them are truly insane, but I think Charlie Baker was. Whether it was because of the sexual abuse she suffered at the hands of her stepfather, Dillon, and God knows how many Johns, or if it was something genetic or physiological that made her capable of brutally killing four people, including a child, that girl wasn't thinking straight."

Russo zipped up his bag. I followed him out of the stuffy dimness of the cabin and into the bright sunshine. The trees swayed in the breeze, still dripping the rainwater from the night before off their branches. There was one ATV left. We were the last ones to go. As I straddled the machine, I stared down at the muddy tracks in front of the cabin. An hour ago, the place had been swarmed with people, and now it was empty. A rabbit nibbled grass at the edge of the woods, and the air was filled with birdsong. I inhaled the tangy pine scent, along with the decaying leaves and mud. After we left, the trampled area would be taken back by nature. I wondered if Charlie's ghost would linger in this wild place, but I didn't dare say it out loud. Russo had a scientific mind. He'd think I was nuts.

He eyed me. "Don't trust me to drive, eh?"

"Not particularly." I didn't crack a smile, being sure his trip up the mountain had been his first time. He'd probably gotten lucky when he'd survived it.

He secured his bag in the back and faced me. The pensive look on his face caused me to release the key in the ignition. "What?"

"I have to go back east for a week or two. I'm sorry it's such short notice." He wore his usual dress suit, but I noticed the top buttons of the shirt were unbuttoned, and the hair across his brow was sweaty.

"Do you mind elaborating on the reason?" A dusting of leaves fell out of the nearest tree, scurrying madly around us. Summer was softly coming to an end, and autumn was right around the corner. It was a cheerful time of the year in Possum Gap. The Apple Festival would kick off festivities next month, and then my favorite holiday, Halloween, would arrive. It used to be more fun when I could dress Chloe up in cute costumes and go trick-or-treating, but those days were gone. Melancholy squeezed my gut. Funny how a few fluttering leaves could affect a person's mood in such a profound way. Where I was sad before, now I was downright depressed.

"It's just something I have to take care of." Russo cocked his head as he looked back at me. His jaw was firmly set. No amount of badgering would get him to open up about his abrupt trip back to New Jersey.

"You're a mysterious guy, Russo. If I had a wild imagination, I might view your evasiveness as meaning you were up to no good." He continued to watch me with a stony stillness that I wasn't used to. "Once you finalize the Amish girl's and Charlie's autopsies, you're free to take your vacation time," I grunted without thinking. "After the past week, fingers crossed, things should remain quiet in Possum Gap while you're gone."

"I appreciate it, sheriff." He climbed on behind me. "Perhaps someday I'll explain the reason for my trip home."

I made a humming noise. My curiosity spiked. "The fact that you're still referring to it as your home worries me." I drew in a quick breath. "I usually wait until evaluation time to discuss job performance, but I want you to know you're doing an excellent job. We're lucky to have you on the team."

"Thank you." He chuckled. "You've impressed me as well."

I leaned sideways and turned my head to look him in the eye. He returned my gaze, and I knew he wasn't kidding.

He went on. "These cases were hardcore, like the stuff you see in the big cities. With your small-town budget and skeleton workforce, you did just fine."

I picked up on the long, almost southern inflection of his voice when he said the word *fine*. Either he was making fun of me, or he was finally starting to fit in. I'd reserve judgment for later.

"It doesn't feel like it. I wish I could have saved Charlie Baker. She was a tragic figure in an awful world."

"You can't save everyone; you can only do your best." His words sounded cold, but they were so very true.

I turned the ignition key and the engine roared to life. The rabbit jetted into the bush, and I couldn't hear woodland sounds anymore.

"How fast did you get this thing going?" I shouted over my shoulder.

"Ahh, not very—"

I hit the gas pedal, and Russo had to grab onto my sides to keep from falling off. Hearing his shriek lifted my mood a little. I would give the city slicker a ride he'd remember when he was doing whatever he had to do back east. Hopefully, it didn't scare him away from coming back. Somehow, I reckoned it was just the type of thing that would encourage him to return.

I didn't get the chance to knock on the door before it flew open. Chloe was in sweatpants and a t-shirt. Her hair was damp like she'd just showered. I wasn't expecting her to rush up to me and throw her arms around my shoulders, but that's exactly what she did. It had been a while since the moody teen had embraced me with so much vigor. I hugged her back, breathing in the smell of her shampooed hair and the laundry detergent scent that clung to her clothes. She was my exact same height. When did that happen?

"I saw you on the TV," she said when she pulled back. "You're lucky you weren't killed." I heard her father's voice when she said it and knew she was mimicking his words.

"It was a little dicey," I admitted.

"And you rode a horse?" Her mouth dropped open in awe.

"You know I used to have a horse. What's the big deal?" Her sudden friendliness put me off balance.

"Maybe we can get a horse. I've always wanted one." She reached around the corner and pulled out her duffle bag and pillow.

I watched her march by and jog down the steps right into my car. "Since when?" I muttered to myself.

When I opened the driver's side door, Chloe asked, "Can we eat Mexican and go to the movies tonight?"

"Ah, sure. Sounds like fun." I had my girl back. The giddiness might not last long, but I'd take any amount of it.

"Goodbye!" Ted stepped onto the porch. Chloe threw her hand into the air to wave without looking at her dad. She slammed the door shut.

I turned to my ex. "What the hell happened to her?"

Ted avoided looking directly at me. Instead, he gripped the porch railing, leaning over it. The sun was close to setting. It had been a long day with a lot of meetings and paperwork. I had planned to go home, have a long, hot shower, followed by a large glass of wine. Chloe's change of heart had fully revived me. Mexican dinner and a movie had never sounded better. I wouldn't let Ted ruin the moment.

I didn't wait for his reply. "Well, thanks for having her," I said, turning to get into the car.

"Wait." He jogged down the steps and grasped my arm. When I looked down at it, he quickly let go. Seeing the nervous look on his face, I shut the door and fully faced him.

"Chloe and Sandra got into an argument. Sandra said something that upset Chloe, and she had a meltdown. Nothing serious, but she might not want to come over for a little while."

I tried not to judge. After all, I had fought with Chloe a week ago. My brows still rose, and I crossed my arms.

"What did Sandra say?"

Ted shifted between his feet and dragged his fingers through his hair. "Something snarky about you. You should be happy. Chloe is your biggest advocate, even though you don't know it." When he raised his head, his eyes glistened. "I know you've had a rough week. I'm glad you're home safe and sound. You do a nice job balancing work and motherhood. You're a good mom."

Did my ex just pay me a compliment? I wished I had it recorded because I knew that in a week or two, Ted would be back to his usual obnoxious self. For now, I'd take it with a smile on my face and a deep sigh.

I didn't know what to say, so I gave a nod and left as quickly as possible.

"I'll be in touch on Monday to discuss these cases," Ted called after me.

Yeah, it sucked having to work with my ex, but it was a price I had to pay for living in a small town.

When I closed the door and looked over at Chloe, I said, "I missed you, kid."

She smiled. "I missed you too, Mom."

The curve of her lips reminded me of Charlie's mouth. I really hoped that poor girl was in a better place.

Sadie & Russo's next case/adventure will be available during the second half of 2022!

Thank you for reading!

While you're waiting, you might enjoy checking out SERENITY'S PLAIN SECRETS, the TEMPTATION series, the WINGS OF WAR series, WILLOW CREEK, or THE FORTUNA COIN by Karen Ann Hopkins.

You can visit Karen Ann Hopkins and see all her books at https://www.karenannhopkinsfiction.com & Karen Ann Hopkins, Serenity Series, at Amazon

Facebook: Karen Ann Hopkins Amish Fiction @ temptationbook

Twitter: Karen Ann Hopkins @KarenAnnHopkins Instagram: karenannhopkins

Made in United States
Orlando, FL
31 January 2024